W9-AJO-489

ERH 100

1st Edn

9/14

GARY - 1

Other books by Samuel Hazo

POETRY
Discovery
The Quiet Wars
Listen with the Eye
My Sons in God
Blood Rights
Twelve Poems
Once for the Last Bandit
Quartered
To Paris

TRANSLATIONS
The Blood of Adonis *(poems of Ali Ahmed Said)*
The Growl of Deeper Waters *(essays by Denis de Rougemont)*

CRITICISM
Smithereened Apart: A Critique of Hart Crane

FICTION
Inscripts
The Very Fall of the Sun

The Wanton

NORTH POINT PRESS
SAN FRANCISCO 1982

Summer Air —————————

Samuel Hazo

Copyright © 1982 by Samuel Hazo
Printed in the United States of America
Library of Congress Catalogue Card Number: 82-081479
ISBN: 0-86547-085-5

To My Wife Anne

Gagnon's Mediterranean

From the porch of his apartment he looks out at the meadowgreen Mediterranean and keeps exhaling through his slightly parted lips the smoke from his meerschaum. Dissipating almost immediately in the sea winds, the smoke seems to him a perfect symbol of his past, his present—his life. He holds the thought in his mind the way a man might hold a sip of burgundy in his mouth before swallowing it. Then he removes the meerschaum from between his teeth and grips it in the habitual, comfortable interlock of fingers of his left hand. He keeps looking dreamily at the green meadow. Directly in front of him scurry sailboats and butterfly craft on their way to their marinas. Beyond them two illuminated yachts are sailing to opposite wings of the horizon. They move so slowly that they hardly seem to be moving at all. Without blinking he lets his gaze sweep from the distant promontories of Antibes on his right to the high, compact silhouette of Eze on his left. Between them splays his district. Again he clamps the meerschaum between his teeth and sucks in the flavor of perique and burley blended with the summer air. From inside his apartment drifts the final movement of a sarabande for harpsichord. Yes, this is a moment to savor. This is how he wants to pass the evening, pass all his evenings. He forgets the routine that will be his tomorrow: verifying or rejecting dubious promissory notes from the casinos in his district, inquiring into his daily quota of petty thefts, exposing an occasional fraud, clamping down on the inevitable smugglers from Tunisia or Morocco. He even forgets his right arm which a bullet from a German sniper immobilized during a battle beyond Nice. He does remember how he would have lost the arm had it not been for . . .

The ring of the telephone disrupts his musing. He waits until the third ring before he rises from his chair and enters the apartment. Without making a move to pick up the receiver, he stands over the telephone and watches it. The phone keeps ringing, and his stare

3

congeals as he watches, as if intensity alone might make the telephone go silent. By the time it rings for the tenth time, he lifts the receiver to his ear with his left hand. He continues to smoke his meerschaum and speaks with his teeth tight on the bit, "Inspector Gagnon here. Yes. This is Inspector Gagnon. Who is calling?" Cradling the receiver between his ear and his shoulder, he removes the meerschaum from his mouth and balances it bowl-up on the telephone stand. An undulating snake of smoke keeps twisting up from the bowl. "Yes, Monsieur de Savigny. This is Gagnon. Yes. To what do I owe the pleasure of this call?" He bumps the telephone stand so that the pipe tips and a few sparks spill out of the bowl. Ignored, they turn almost immediately into white ash. "What makes you think she came to Nice? No. We have no report of anything. Have you checked the manifests of all the aircraft that came into Nice from Paris today?" He holds the receiver in his left hand again and sways the corkscrew cord above the stand like a rope bridge over a canyon. "But I thought you told me that your daughter did not care for the American. Why would she come here to see him?" He keeps swinging the cord. "Yes, I understand. But this would put a completely new light on what happened in Eze. You *do* understand that?" He stops the cord from swinging and steps toward the porch so that the cord accordions tautly to its full length. "Yes, I see." He faces the Mediterranean. The sailboats and butterfly craft are gone now in the invading dusk and the two yachts are at the very corners of the horizon. "Just one moment, Monsieur de Savigny. Let me see if I've understood you correctly. Your daughter may be on her way here by motorcycle and you think that she may be heading for the hospital in Cimiez to see this Dennis Holt. And you want me to intercept and detain her until you arrive. Yes. Are you at Orly now? Yes, I know the flight. You should be here in less than an hour." He turns his back to the sea. "I will do what I can for you, of course, but when I have located you daughter—if I locate her at all—then I want to sit down with all the parties concerned—your son particularly—and find out what really happened in Eze. And if there is any wrongdoing involved here I will have to prefer charges against your son. I want you to understand that now, Monsieur. I hope I make myself clear. This was not just a minor affair. Holt could have died, and, as it is, he has been seriously injured." Still stretched taut, the corkscrewing telephone cord quivers as Gagnon speaks. "Yes, I will phone the hospital now. I don't think this business of finding your daughter will pose any problems. She should be easy to locate, particularly if she is riding a motorcycle. Yes. Yes. I will take every precaution. Yes. When you arrive in Nice, you can reach me at this number or at my headquarters. Someone is always on duty there. Yes. Good night." He places the receiver on its cradle hard. After lifting his meerschaum and clamping it in his mouth again, he rubs the back of his neck with his left hand and frowns. Then he sidles to the stereo and turns off the sarabande. Moments later he is again on the telephone. "Hello, Etienne. This is Gagnon. Tell me, are you in the middle of something now? No? Good. Do you remember that incident in Eze a month or so back? It involved the American and de Savigny's son. Yes. We could prove nothing, do you recall? Well, I think now that our suspicions may have been correct. I'll explain when I see you. In any case, I just received a call from de Savigny himself. He's at Orly. He's flying here tonight. He's probably on his way now. It seems his daughter not only knew this American, but she must still think enough of him to travel all the way from Paris by motorcycle to see him. Does that say anything to you? Does that sound like the action of a woman who had no interest in him at all? Yes. I agree, of course. De Savigny is convinced that she's on her way to Cimiez to see this Dennis Holt and he may be right. I want you to call the hospital or go there if necessary to make sure that the daughter is detained until we see her. No, I don't think you will have a problem. It sounds like nothing more than some kind of romance to me, that's all. But I've told de Savigny that we will reopen the case with his son and get to the bottom of this business. If the son was responsible for pushing the American and we can prove it, then we will have to prefer charges against him. Of course. But right now see to it that Mademoiselle de Savigny is detained if you locate her at Cimiez. Yes. I'll be here the rest of the night. Call me when you have some news." By the time Gagnon returns to his seat on the porch, it is already dark. The Mediterranean now seems to him much more a force and presence than it was by daylight. It seems almost forbidding. The yachts are gone. Gagnon looks again from Eze to Antibes and finds himself remembering the same geography as it appeared to him when he and the other members of the Maquis joined the Americans as they pushed the retreating Germans farther and farther into Italy. He recalls his last battle when, while leaning over to tie his bootlace, he was suddenly knocked forward by the impact of a bullet that struck him just above his right elbow. He lay on the road until the shock passed and then he started to pull himself toward the berm. Dragging his arm askew as he went and realizing that he had to stanch the flow of blood from the wound, he removed a handkerchief from his pocket and tried one-handed to knot it into a tourniquet around his bicep. He found it impossible to make a knot. At last all he could do was wad the handkerchief over the wound directly and try to hike back to Nice. Trucks loaded with soldiers passed him at high speeds. Despite his calls, no one stopped. He was on the verge of fainting when a woman rushed toward him and helped him to a doorway. Examining his wound hurriedly, she made a tourniquet from her scarf and told him not to move until she returned. When he saw her again less than a half an hour later, she was with a nurse. Together they helped him into a small ambulance and sped off. The woman who had applied the tourniquet sat beside him. She asked him his name, and he told her. She responded that she was Clothilde de Savigny and that she was taking him to the hospital at Cimiez. He smiled weakly at her and immediately lost consciousness. Several days afterward one of the doctors at Cimiez told him that he would have lost the arm and possibly his life if the tourniquet had not been applied. All during his convalescence, Gagnon kept reminding himself of that, and after the war he made a point of tracking down Clothilde de Savigny so that he could thank her. She told him that thanks were unnecessary, that it was merely her duty, that she appreciated seeing him again. It made no basic difference to him that the arm was almost useless. At least he was alive, and he was alive because of her. That he could not forget. After he became the ranking inspector in his Mediterranean district, the investigations developed regarding those who had collaborated with the Germans during the occupation. The husband of Clothilde de Savigny was one of those under investigation. Gagnon pursued the inquiry with divided attention. When it became apparent that many of the charges were impossible to corroborate, he deliberately did not pursue the matter further.

For years he heard nothing more of the de Savigny family until the incident involving the American at Eze. But even then he tended to give de Savigny and his son the benefit of the doubt. After all, there were enough doubts to justify leniency, or so he told himself. Was the hospitalized American making any charges? No. Was there any reason to doubt de Savigny's statement that his daughter had barely known the American, had regarded him as a nuisance and that the girl's brother, Seth, had simply tracked the American to Eze in order to discourage him from seeing his sister again? No. Of course, there were some unanswered questions. What was the American doing in Eze in the first place and how was he found there? Who was the woman who had arrived with the American, as the waitress in the Eze restaurant testified, but who had vanished without a trace?

Trapped in the crossfire of his own memories, Gagnon weighs the old evidence and his old conclusions against the call that he has just received from Sanche de Savigny. Why would the man say that his daughter was traveling by motorcycle to visit a hospitalized man who, according to the father, was nothing but a nuisance to her? Why did de Savigny call him and alert him to the girl's coming? Surely he must have known that his call would undermine his previous story about the incident in Eze and his son's part in it. Why the phone call then? Desperation? Guilt? Or did he want to stop the girl regardless of the consequences?

Gagnon is still acting as questioner and defendant when the phone rings again. He walks hurriedly from the porch into the apartment and seizes the receiver, "Gagnon here. Yes, Etienne. No, I have heard nothing at all. What do you mean *he's not there*? How could he have walked out of the hospital? The last report I saw said that he had lost the sight of one eye completely and had only a small chance of partial vision in the other. Of course, someone must have led him out. What did the nurse say? Yes. Very well. Let me think for a moment. Don't leave the phone." Keeping the receiver to his ear, Gagnon turns and faces the porch and the sparkling mass of the sea beyond. "Let's assume, Etienne, that the de Savigny girl somehow took him out of the hospital. How long did the nurse say he's been missing? The last time

7

she saw him was before supper? Well, that's little help. He could have been gone for hours or he could have left ten minutes before you went there. Well, no matter when he left, I doubt if the two are in the area. At least, I doubt if they will remain in the area. Have you called the border guards? Very good. And the guards have seen nothing? You are sure of that? Then perhaps they *are* still in the area. Perhaps they are just waiting for dark. Here's what you must do, Etienne. Immediately. Station several patrols on each of the corniches heading west in case the girl and the American decide to head for Marseilles. Post those patrols as soon as you finish talking to me. Make sure they have descriptions. Remember the motorcycle. I'll leave for Eze myself right now and station some men at the three corniches in that area. We'll find the two of them one way or the other. If de Savigny arrives from Paris on schedule, he should be calling you in less than forty minutes. Bring him with you and join me in Eze. Any questions, Etienne? Very well. Goodbye."

The Clown Who Walks the Wind

Staring against but never through the layered gauze, forgetting for just seconds the itch and burning in his eyes, the smarting of the ointment on his eyelids, the scent that is more than pure alcohol but not quite witch hazel, forcing his eyes to focus even on darkness, straining until he thinks he can make out a light, yes, a light like a nearing planet behind and beyond the gauze, touching with the back of his right hand the mound of bandaging over his eyes and across the bridge of his nose, resisting, resisting the separate will in his fingers to reach up and strip the tacky gauze from his face so that he can see, see, see anything, see whatever he can, whatever is there, see perhaps nothing else or more than the ceiling, see as if through a scope the steadily approaching moon of a face, see at last and again after so long her face, the face of Denise, the face that even now he sees without actually being able to see it but which is there in the darkness like a portrait lit by moonrays, he lies on his back awake from what was not quite or else is not yet sleep. Wondering if his dream has abandoned him or he the dream, trying to make his eyes do what eyes are supposed to do, he changes slowly into himself again. Alcohol and witch hazel are all he can smell. He touches the eye bandages with his right hand, softly, fearfully, inquisitively, like a surgeon probing an open wound. Then he returns his hand to his side. Against his shoulder blades and buttocks and calves the cool, taut territory of the bedsheets is both the hospital's and the combined memory of all the bedsheets in all the institutions that were home to him in Maryland, in Illinois, in Louisiana, in the west of Texas. Whenever his mother moved from one nightclub to another, he moved. But everywhere, no matter what or where the institution, he would sleep and wake in what became more and more the same ward, and he would come to memorize the same sheetlike, showertype curtains that could be jerked on a pulley rack into a square around the bed to create the illusion of a room, and he would hear the same whimpers in the night from other cubicles in the wards, and there would be the same voice in the night with its

11

warning to him or the other boys, "Sleep with your hands on top of the covers, boy, always on top of the covers, never under." Even now, more than two decades later, he realizes that his hands are by his sides over the covers drawn tightly to and over the impediment of his body and tucked under the length of the mattress. It reminds him again of institution after institution where his mother enrolled him. Whenever she would leave him, she would say the same words, "They will be good to you here, Dennis. This is one of the best schools for boys in this part of the country." And then she would leave, and leaving, she would kiss him in the presence of which or how many officials he has long forgotten. What he does remember across the hopscotch of years and the miles of state after state and even the separation of continent and continent is the scent of her dead kiss on his eyebrows or forehead (never on his lips) and the skimming touch of her hair-ends on his cheek just as she was leaving, as she was leaving, as she was always leaving.

Even though he flinches to keep it from happening, he is drawn back to be again the boy he was but hated being, taking his place and picking up his tray in the refectory line, finding the play area with groups of other boys similarly left by their parents to the same institutional custody while they, the parents, worked, traveled, entertained themselves or simply acted as if their children, though undeniably theirs, had no real need of them and less claim. And at night there would inevitably be the feel of the cold, tight sheets in the dormitory wards and the sweatery weight of the counted blankets, each marked with the name of the institution and numbered, and the living darkness of the ward like a night without moon or stars. Surviving those years, he learned to rely on himself. To escape from his surroundings he often took to impersonating others or clowning so that he could see the impression he was making by reading the faces of those watching him. Later, when he actually decided to become a clown, how could he explain his decision to anyone else except to say that it was something he had always been. The wirewalking came later; he tried it, found that he was good at it, did it as part of his repertoire. But about clowning, no one who asked him why he did it ever was satisfied with his answer, and he, rather than clarifying what he had said, was content to leave the implications to mystery and the questioner. But if someone were really concerned about his reasons, he would have said that it was the impersonality of clowning that intrigued him and lured him from the start. As a clown he could be both himself and not himself. Once he put on his costume and his paints he was a character without a memory, a name, a destiny. The only identity he sought and needed was to create himself anew with every performance. Wirewalking was another matter entirely. In a way he could not hope to explain even to himself, he both hated and prized his ability to keep his balance on the wire with or without a pole. From performance to performance he even dared himself to fall by attempting tricks that became more and more spectacular, but he never fell, never came close to falling. The cable on which he performed might as well have been a paved road, and he came to regard it with the professional scorn that the best matadors have for bulls. On the other hand, in a deeper and more transforming way, clowning made him seem more plural (there was no other word) while wirewalking forced him to be more skillfully himself with every performance. In his clown's costume, he felt that he was participating in an institution just as a soldier in uniform becomes all at once every soldier in uniform, the way a nurse becomes all nurses, a priest every priest, and so on. But the real advantage of the garb and greasepaint was the permission it gave him to observe others as they actually were while they were looking at him, not as he really was but as he was pretending to be. That to him was the real satisfaction of clowning, to be able to watch individuals in an audience as individuals while they willingly watched him in his clown's role. He remained the same while the audiences kept changing, and consequently every audience became a new chance for him to renew his curiosity in what he saw in their faces, their eyes, their gestures. More and more he came to understand why he had always admired the taxi drivers, maids, and elevator operators of the world as beacons of certainty in the midst of swirls of population. Like the choruses in ancient drama, they commented on the passing scene simply by remaining in permanent contrast with it. Yet, in the end, he came to admit that this was really an illusion, that no one enjoyed the luxury of anonymous observation indefinitely, that he, like taxi drivers, maids, and elevator operators, was as

13

involved in the ongoing changes of life as were the seemingly impersonal choruses in the dramas of the Greeks.

It was while he was thinking in these terms that he noticed her for the first time as she sat in the midst of a watching crowd a few rows back from the barrier of the main ring where he was performing. He kept turning his sloppy cartwheels, falling like Chaplin when he tried to stand, looking with his fixed expression of bemused helplessness at the laughing crowd. Only she was not laughing, not even smiling. While everyone around her was responding to his antics and the slice-of-watermelon smile painted on his face, she seemed to be looking at the face behind his mask, the face behind even his own face, a face she herself created simply by seeing it there. When she turned her eyes away from him, he felt something inside of him cease to exist. After he traipsed out of the ring in a caravan of other clowns, he returned to see if she had remained, but her seat in the crowd was empty, and he just glimpsed her leaving through the tentflap exit.

For days and weeks afterward he could not forget her, could not forget her eyes, the searing steadiness and justice of them. Straddling the familiar horsepower of his black Anubis, he motorcycled on weekend after weekend through the entire Esterel, as if the cycling, by forcing him to concentrate only on the road ahead of him, would distract him from his almost reflexive habit of having to remember her and would impress him that she was after all nothing more than one girl in a crowd, one face among thousands. But her gaze stayed with him like a brand. He kept seeing her face before him on the roads to Cagnes, to Menton, to Vallauris, to Monte Carlo, even to the wedged cobbles of Eze, where he parked Anubis in a lower lot and hiked the hill to the cannon-guarded village portal and walked through and around the levels of Eze like a man discovering it for the first time or seeing it for the last time. When he was in Eze, he was always oblivious of the tourists with their cameras and Michelin maps and guides. For him a walk in Eze was always like a walk in the environment of someone he might have loved. It had been that way from his first sight of it, and later, when he read book after book about the place, he came to see what Friedrich Nietzsche must have seen in it.

14

He tried to reinvoke his old interest, but the girl's face kept interrupting his communion with the quiet, rocky charm of Eze, and he returned to Anubis more troubled than he was when he arrived. Remounting and cycling on, he steered for the Franco-Italian border, crossed it, then sped and braked through the straight or looping roads of the Italian north, arrowing from the outskirts and then through the Alp-cupped, uncomplicated geometry of Cuneo before he turned southward to Savona and finally lost himself in the spooling curves and dips of the lesser alpine roads. Her face traveled with him in Italy and kept on traveling without distortion or diminution as he sped back to his cottage through hillscapes of lemon orchards and fields of carnation and jasmine, stayed with him even when he reached his cottage and, after he housed Anubis in the midnight cool of the wisteria arbor that served as its garage, changed into his dreams after he flung himself facedown on his bed and slept. And his dreams of her gradually transformed themselves and blended with his old dreams so that it seemed to him as if he had been dreaming of her all his life . . .

The gauze suddenly seems to be tight over his eyes. He adjusts it with his fingers. Then, still thinking of his first trip through the Esterel, he slips awake into the real dream of the telegram that meant his father's life had ended by bullet in the south of France. Across the years he listens to the sobs of his mother as she holds the telegram in her lap. He hears her cursing the army, the war, cursing the day his father enlisted in the first place, crunching the telegram in her palm and screaming, "He would still be here, Dennis. He just left us, deserted us. And for what? For a piece of paper and some words. What are we going to do now? What in the name of God are we going to do?" Again he becomes the boy at the side of his keening, screaming mother, wondering why the father he scarcely remembered would never return. In the years that followed he learned, word by grudged word and episode by episode, how the Americans invaded France near Cannes and how the invaders, his father among them, pursued the fleeing Germans as they retreated stubbornly but steadily into the Italian north through Ventimiglia, Ospedaletti, San Remo, Savona, and Mondovi, leaving as they went a havoc of dynamited bridges, roads, and villages, and how his father, "Staff Sergeant Louis Holt, against innumerable odds and without regard for his personal safety, diverted a company of German infantry and panzer units from the town of St. Paul du Vence until, out of ammunition but still unwilling to take cover, he was felled by a sniper." And this story, refusing to end, became another story of how the citizens of the town bequeathed to the "child or children of Staff Sergeant Louis Holt a cottage adjacent to St. Paul du Vence free of all rentals, liens, or encumbrances in perpetuity," adding, with the proper touch of Gallic mystery, that, in the event that the inheritors were in fact twins, the property, in accordance with French law, would be registered in the name of the twin born last as the older of the two.

Still bothered by the tightness of the bandages, Dennis touches the gauze at the bridge of his nose and the new and old dreams drift away like teasteam. He blinks several times at the blinding gauze and wonders how or if he will ever walk a wire again. Then he remembers with a pang that Dr. Russi has given him little if any hope for the right eye and only moderate hope for the left. With his hands hardening into fists at his sides, he tries to keep back the tears that are already seeping into the ointment and the gauze, but the tears come anyway and keep coming and, with them, a series of sobs that shudder like a fever through his body. To distract himself he tries to invoke the memory of that incident in Nice that made everything else not only possible but real. He constructs it in his mind until *it* and not the immediacy of the bandages and the hospital bed becomes the present. As if it is actually happening, he imagines that he is slicing fresh Gruyère at a sidewalk table in a cafe in Nice. He looks over the cup and candle on his table, over the handlebars of his parked Anubis, over the shoulders of three Spanish sailors at the curb, and there she is. His knife stops in midslice as he watches her stride past Anubis and wait at the corner for the stoplight to change. Her face has the same serious but relaxed cast that he remembers having seen in it when the girl was just one of thousands in the circus crowd. Dropping the cheese and knife on the table, he reaches for some loose francs in his trouser pocket, splays them on the table and leaves. For an instant he thinks he has lost her again. But he glimpses her halfway down the block. Leaving

Anubis where he parked it, he hurries after her. With less than ten feet between them he matches her stride for stride. By the time she comes to the next crossing, he is almost abreast of her. Then he moves beside her. She looks at him casually before she shifts her gaze to the stoplight and waits for it to change. He touches her shoulder. Frowning, she edges away from him while he says to her in French, "Do you remember? Last Monday in Monte Carlo? The circus? I haven't been able to forget you." The light changes and the girl rushes across the street, moving not in a straight line but diagonally so that she places other pedestrians between herself and him. Shouldering his way after her, he manages to keep pace. When they reach the opposite curb together, he touches her arm again and says, "Why are you running away from me? Don't you remember? At the circus last Monday night? You were the only one who was not laughing. I can't forget that. You've been on my mind for a whole week now." Frowning, the girl turns and confronts him face to face. As she scrutinizes him, her frown fades, first from the eyes, then from the forehead, then from the whole face. She steps back, brings her hand to her lips, and gasps slightly. When she removes her hand, she smiles and says, "You! You are the comedian, the clown!" He nods, smiles back, and bows, as if introducing himself to a lady of the court . . .

Recalling Denise at that moment, he smiles into the darkness of the swaddles of gauze and reassembles the relaxed seriousness of Denise's face in a triple vision until the three faces synchronize into one. "Denise, Denise," he whispers into the darkness. The sound of her name on his lips consoles him for a moment before the solitude of the room returns and engulfs him like a warm sea. It makes him think of the solitude of his last night in Eze—the warmth, the closeness. The memory of Denise submerges in the solitude and he is alone again on the height of Eze. He is leaning against the wall below the old and only church, *La Chapelle des Pénitents Blancs*. When he hears footsteps, he turns to see Seth de Savigny and another man whom he does not recognize. In seconds they are on him. He mounts the wall and walks it like a tightrope, but they follow him and suddenly he is falling, falling over and down the wall. A branch and a thorny vine slash across his eyes, and the end of a heavier branch jabs against the front of his throat like the butt end of a vaulting pole. He tries to shout. His throat seems clogged. Then he sucks down the taste of the coin of blood on his tongue. He blinks into a different darkness than the darkness of the gradually deepening dusk over Eze, and that is the last thing he remembers before the weeks of cool, hospital sheets and the gauze mesh over his eyes and the loose scarf of cotton and gauze around his throat . . .

He still cannot believe that it has been more than a month that he has been in the same hospital bed, that it is his body on these sheets, that it was really he, who had no idea that it would lead to this when he left Anubis parked in its rack while he followed one girl in millions to a streetcorner in Nice, and how that one meeting made possible another on the following day near the esplanade above the beach. He sees himself with her again on the esplanade. He is saying to her in French, "You see, we have the same first name." "Yes." she answers, "but mine is feminine." "That gives you a final *e*. It's academic, like one more rib. Apart from that, we're twins." She smiles and they walk without talking until she asks, "And your last name? What is the origin?" "Who knows? Just American." "My father says that de Savigny, our family name, goes back to the thirteenth century. It is a long history, yes? There was a de Savigny in the army of Charles Martel. And there was another with Charlemagne." Dennis smiles with just the hint of a dismissive, American smirk. "When I saw you, I didn't see your history. Just you. I don't know why everyone keeps reaching back for something, for credentials. When you really get down to it, the best credential is breath, isn't it?" "Breath?" "Yes, a time of breath. Life." She is silent for a moment. She smiles, as if this is the first time she's been asked to think of herself apart from her history, and she nods approvingly. He starts to make another point, but she interrupts him gently and says, "Dennis, I think we should speak in your English. My English is not so good yet, but it is quicker than your French." He takes her hand, and they walk farther along the esplanade. As he always does, he notices the remains of concrete pyramids the size of Renaults every fifty yards or so along the beach, but he says nothing. When he looks at her next, he sees her take a handkerchief from her blouse and wipe her forehead. He hears him-

18

self ask her in literal French, "Are you hot?" The girl blushes. He
stops and smiles, "Did I say it wrong?" "Very wrong. You were speaking
of something else." She replaces her handkerchief and they leave the
esplanade for the beach. Shuffling through the pebbly sand, she asks,
"Where did you learn Franch?" "From my mother's daughters."
"You have sisters who speak French?" "No, just some circus girls.
Yvette, Solange, Michelle. They're part of a trapeze team." "But why
do you call them your sisters?" "I didn't." "You said they are the
daughters of your mother." "Only in spirit. They remind me of her."
He spits into the pebbles. She sees it and asks, "Did you mean that for
your mother?" "Maybe." "You should be ashamed for that." "I don't
feel shame for anything. There's too much talk about shame. It just
makes life harder, and life's hard enough the way it is." "Do you feel
this way about your father also?" "No." "But your father and your
mother are the same. You come from them." He looks into her eyes
and confronts a blend of sincerity, certainty, and innocence that makes
him turn his eyes away. "Denise, you're unbelievable, do you know
that?" "No, I am believable. I just think that you should not say such
things about your mother and father. You diminish yourself when
you speak that way. Even if you feel that way and keep it to yourself,
you diminish yourself, but not as much." "Then I've been diminishing myself for a long time. But that doesn't apply to my father. He
did what he had to do." "And what was that?" "He didn't diminish
himself. He died in the war. He fought for one of your villages near
here. He's buried somewhere in France. I've tried to find the grave,
but I never could." Again he looks at her with a hint of a smirk. "He
didn't fight with Charles Martel or Charlemagne, but he earned his
own place in your country. That's not a bad credential." He sees the
girl's eyes suddenly dim with hurt, and he regrets what he has just
said. She stops and says, "I must go now, Dennis. I have to meet Seth."
"Seth?" "My brother." "Okay." As they return to the esplanade through
the same pebbly trail, she looks occasionally at him as if she expects
him to say something more, but he just walks slowly on beside her.
Gesturing at the clustered pyramids on the shore, he says as much to
himself as to her, "The Germans put those things there. And then
they strung barbed wire between them. They thought the invasion
would come here at Nice, and they wanted to make it as hard as

possible for the infantry to get off the beach and move inland. But the invasion never happened here. The Americans came ashore west of here near Cannes." "How do you know about such things?" "I did a lot of reading. I wanted to learn everything about the war that I could, especially the war here in the south. I read everything I could get my hands on." "I must go now, Dennis. Seth is waiting for me." "Are you free tomorrow?" She pauses and asks, "Are you making a rendez-vous with me?" "Nothing that complicated or romantic. Just another chance to see you." She keeps walking on while he pauses. When she is a short distance away, he asks, "Okay?" "As you like," she answers and waits for him to reach her. "I'll take you for a ride on my horse," says Dennis as he takes her hand again. "Do you have a horse?" "An iron one. His name's Anubis." "Until tomorrow, Dennis." "Noon. Right here." She nods and walks on. When she reaches the esplanade, she turns and waves. Waving back, he keeps watching her until there is nothing more to watch, but he watches anyway, postponing as long as possible the moment when he will be absolutely alone on the beach. He then feels the same loneliness he felt for the first time when he was ten and was permitted to spend Christmas with his mother. He received the bus ticket and directions in the mail from his mother, and the school's director made sure that he was placed on the correct bus. The long, lonely bus ride from the east to the west of Texas where his mother was performing and living took almost the entire day. He had never felt as alone before in his life. Everyone else on the bus was Mexican. It was not reassuring at all for him to look at the set and solemn faces of the Mexicans, so he looked out of the window at the baked flatlands, at cactus after cactus, at spools of tumbleweed ca-reening or ballooning at the whim of the winds. While the other passengers slept, he remained awake, studying the scenery until it blurred. At last it finally changed into a city, and the bus found its port, and, after rereading the typed directions in his mother's letter, Dennis headed for the hotel where she was staying. He was deter-mined to find the hotel without assistance. And he did. He presented himself at the desk in the lobby and asked for the room of Mrs. Holt. The clerk wiped his mouth with a blue polka-dot handkerchief and looked down at him with a smile that was not quite a smile. "You must be Violet's kid," said the clerk. "She's in 410." Dennis entered a drop of several thousand feet on the other. She screams and backs away while he smiles and continues to walk until he has crossed almost one-fourth of the bridge. "Dennis!" she shouts. "Please! Please, come down." Again he smiles, pretends to lose his balance, regains it, and keeps on walking. When he reaches the halfway point, he jumps lightly from the railing to the walkway and saunters back to her. "Dennis," she asks, "why did you have to do that? I was almost away from my mind." "*Out* of your mind." "You frightened me, really. You might have fallen. Why did you have to do that? For what reason?" "Just to do it, " he says, shrugging, and adds after a pause. "It's what I do." "But the danger . . ." "There's no danger when you know what you're doing." "But it's so easy to have an accident, to slip. You have to think of what might happen." "Maybe, but sometimes I have to do things like that just to let death know that he can't go to sleep. I don't want him to take me for granted." Denise turns and heads back to the motorcycle in the parking lot, and he follows her. By the time he reaches her, he sees something in her eyes that he has never seen before, never even suspected. It seems to tell him that it is not she who is affronted but life itself. As he tries to confront her, she keeps avoiding him, not moving away, just turning with the slightest lift of her shoulder as he circles her. "Denise, how long are we going to play this game? "It's not a game, not to me." "What's your name for it then?" "You put yourself in danger on the railing. It's like life is nothing to you, cheap . . . nothing. Why? Do you have to take risks just to know you are really alive?" "I told you. It's what I do. I'm not bad at it. In fact, I know what I'm doing every minute." "But *why* do you do it? Why is it necessary? It's the same on the motorcycle. You speed everywhere. Why do you dare death all the time? What is there about it?" "It's not for cowards, if that's what you mean." "Do you think you are brave because you try to look death in his face? Is that it? Well, you are not. There is no bravery in it, just foolishness." "It's not foolishness to me, Denise." "But death is nothing. What courage does it take to look at nothing?" "Who says it's nothing? It's more than nothing to me, believe me." "How do you know? Why *can't* it be nothing? It could be the easiest thing in the world. Who's come back to tell us what it is? Who knows?" She takes several steps away from him and then turns before adding, "You waste your courage on a

the elevator while the desk clerk, who was also the elevator operator, took him to the fourth floor. Dennis watched the sweating shoulders of the elevator operator as the car rocked and steadied at the fourth floor. After he stepped out, he walked in the direction indicated by the desk clerk until he reached 410. The door was an inch open, and Dennis waited. His mother's voice was the first sound he heard—or overheard—and he moved back a step and turned back to the elevator as the words reached him, "Leon, for the love of Christ, give me something to wipe myself with. I have you all over my leg." Dennis stopped, faced the door again and knocked hard so that the door edged open even farther, revealing only the darkening darkness of a shaded hotel room. "Who's there?" he heard his mother ask. He did not move, and he heard her again, "Leon, see who's there. Jesus Christ, you left the door open, Leon. You left the door wide open, you dumb bastard, and there's someone out . . ." Suddenly Dennis saw her in the darkness just as she saw him. "Dennis!" she said. "My God, Dennis. When did you get here, honey? How long have you been standing out there?" Belting herself in a bathrobe, she hurried toward him and shepherded him into the room and closed the door. Then she seated him in the room's only chair while she began straightening the bedclothes and shouting in the direction of the bathroom, "Leon, why don't you come back and fix the sink tomorrow some time when I'm not here? Do you hear me, Leon? My baby's out here. My baby came to visit me and we have to use the bathroom. Come back tomorrow." Dennis heard the bathroom door being unlocked and pushed open. A man stepped out. He was wearing only an undershirt and socks. He stood there for a moment, sizing up the scene in front of him, before he hurriedly pulled on his trousers, gathered his shirt, tie, shoes, and other effects in a bundle and, after going to the door and peeping quickly up and down the hall, slunk away. Meanwhile, Dennis sat in the chair while his mother busied herself with the bed and asked, "Well, honey, how was your trip? You're a big boy now to be able to make a trip like that all by yourself. I would have met you, Dennis, but I was busy here. Mother was working, Dennis. You understand that, honey. I know you understand that. Say something to me, honey. You didn't come all this way in a hot bus just to sit there and look at me, did you? Talk to me,

Dennis. Say something. Damn it, Dennis, say something and stop looking at me that way. Stop looking at me that way, I said. Oh, please, honey . . ." She knelt in front of him, reached for him, embraced him, pulled him toward her so that he could feel her wet cheeks against his forehead. She kept saying, over and over, "Oh, my baby, my baby, I'll make it all up to you. I'll make up every minute, Dennis. From now on, it'll just be the two of us. I swear to God, Dennis." He let himself be held and talked to, and he kept listening later all through the dinner which his mother ordered for him in the room. Still later, when he slept in the same bed that his mother had been using when he came into the room, he listened to her in his dreams. And he dreamed himself awake and wondered when she would finish singing in the hotel's lounge and come back to the room. But he slept long before that, and, when he woke the next morning, she was sleeping beside him, her makeup and her evening clothes still on, and there was the scent of cigarettes and beer on her breath, and he could tell from the tears that were still wet on her cheeks that she must have been crying during the night . . .

It is not beer but witch hazel that shatters his memory of Texas. He shakes his head slowly, dislodging what he has been thinking like a pattern in a kaleidoscope, but it reassembles almost instantly, and he sees himself steering Anubis along the Grand Corniche between Monte Carlo and Nice, and Denise is seated sidesaddle behind him with her arms around his chest and her cheek against his shoulder, saying, "It frightens me, Dennis. Do you have to drive so fast? I'm frightened, really." He says over his shoulder, "Relax. This isn't half as fast as I usually go." "Please, Dennis. Please stop." Slowly he brings Anubis to a halt in the parking lot just below Eze and says to her, "You can open your eyes now. The roller coaster's stopped." She eases her arms from around his chest and dismounts. "I'm sorry to be so afraid, Dennis. But I fear speed. I fear what might happen." You should trust me more, Denise. When you swim in deep water, you don't think of all the water under your body, do you? You just think of staying on the surface, staying on top. It's the same with speed. You don't think about how fast you are going or what might happen. You just think of how you are balancing on your tires and what's ahead of you."

"But I *do* think of all the water under my body when I swim in deep water. I can't help it." "Then why do you go swimming? You're always afraid if you think that way. It spoils everything." "That's why I don't swim in deep water very much." "Then I'm going to have to work with you. You just can't let yourself be a victim of your fears, Denise. You can't let yourself be trapped that way. Live a little. Forget the risk. Everything's a risk. Getting up in the morning's a risk." He sees that his words are biting at her like the tips of whips, and he stops and says, "Do you like lemon pie, Denise?" "Lemon pie?" "They have very good lemon pie here." And they walk together toward the restaurant at the foot of the short, steep road leading to Eze. When they seat themselves, Dennis orders two slices of lemon pie and two cups of capuccino. Later, with the pie slices eaten and the cups of capuccino standing like two empty, stained gourds between them, Denise says, "Why did you talk before about your mother as if you hated her?" "Why do you remember that?" "I don't know, but it stayed with me. I'm just sensitive to words like that. I'm sorry I brought it . . ." "Never mind, Denise. My mother's been dead for years now. What I feel about her doesn't really matter any more." "It matters to you. And it matters to me. We've been together now four times. And each time I learn more about you. Don't you know that about women, Dennis? They want to know everything about a man. I want to know everything about you." "Don't bother. There's really not that much to know." He looks up to see her looking at him exactly as she was looking at him the first time he saw her in the crowd at the circus. It is as if she is looking right through his shield of words and expressions into a part of himself that has no defenses. He shifts and says, "Where did you learn to look at people that way?" She averts her eyes immediately, "I'm sorry. It is rude to look, I know." Dennis stands up and smiles at her, "Come on. I'll show you the view from the bridge." When they reach the bridge, he points down to the second Eze by the sea and then outward to the Mediterranean itself, afloat with yachts and small craft. She asks, "Do you ever wonder why the water makes us stare at it? It is like fire. It draws us. We have to watch and watch and watch." When she turns toward him, she sees that he is standing on the railing of the bridge. Then he starts to wirewalk the bridge railing, balancing between the safety of the walkway on one side and

question without an answer, Dennis. It is foolish." "Why are you so
upset about it then? What did I do?" "I can't stand to see life under
the microscope. Do you know how many nerves are in your eye?
Well, there are thousands. Thousands. And if I damaged just one of
them—the right one—you would never be able to see again. Never.
When you think of life, think of that. And when the baby is forming
here inside the mother, do you know how all the nerves, the muscles,
the bones have to be perfect? It takes so little to be wrong for everything to be wrong." She seems so dominated by her passion of the
moment that she cannot stop herself. "That's what I know. Death
and the rest, they are nothing to me. Only life is something. Life is
what we need courage to face, Dennis. It can be terrifying when you
think about what can go wrong. But it's all we have now. All we
know." "If I knew you'd feel that way about what I did on the bridge,
I never would have done it, believe me." "I just don't want everything
to be wasted between us. I want it to be beautiful. When life is beautiful, it is more generous than anything. It can make you forget what
can be wrong. That's what I use my courage to face, Dennis. Not
death." She makes a gesture back to the bridge, adding, "Not that
death." For a moment he can think of nothing to say to her, but he
knows that he really has no more to say on that subject. He reaches
for her hand and says, "Come on. Let's take a walk through Eze. I'll
give you my private tour." "But I've been there, Dennis. I know Eze."
"All of it? All about it? Come on. I've read everything there is to read.
How can you refuse me? You're going to have your own private
guide."

As he recollects their first walk through Eze, he forgets the bandages
across his eyes, forgets the burr in his throat that still makes it occasionally difficult for him to swallow his own saliva, forgets the hospital bed that has been like a home to him for more than forty-five days.
All that is real is his memory of Denise's hand in his as they stroll over
the cobbled walks and stairwells of Eze, and he sees her stop as one of
the villagers leads his small, sleepy horse toward and past them. Denise pats the animal on the jowl so that he stops and looks at her while
she smiles and pats him again, whispering "Sweet, he is so sweet, so
gentle, *très gentil, doux.*" Watching her makes him realize that life,

any life, any hint of it is enough to draw a like response from her, and he knows in the honesty not only of his mind but also of his blood that such a response is beyond him. The realization makes him back off as if the very possibility of trying to respond to life as she does will change him, make him change even against his will and then live on as a stranger even to himself. Thinking about it makes him want to return to Anubis. He wants to rev the motor until his eardrums ache with its mounting horsepower, wants to push off and race on roads and off roads, wants to feel the power of the machine through his calves and thighs and into the vortex of his loins. Instead he thinks of walking the wire again in an empty circus tent at night with only a tent-high beam to show him where the wire is, so that he can step off into shadow over the deserted bleachers and the empty ring, smelling even at wire height the rising musk of sawdust and soil. Reaching for another distraction, he slips into a memory of his first night with Yvette, the youngest of the trapeze sisters. He sees her disappear into the bathroom and then emerge naked and walking on her hands until she is in front of him upside down so that he embraces her knees and runs his hands up and down her inverted body before she tells him to step back, to give her room. Then, still balancing on her hands, she lowers her legs to the floor but not in the way that he expects so that she forms a bridge with her palms and the soles of her feet flat on the floor and her body arched breasts-up, belly-up, pubis-up like a bow. Then, slowly opening her legs without changing her position, she dares him to take her that way while she talks to him all the while, saying that no other woman on earth could or would let a man enter her in such a manner . . . He watches Denise pat the horse's jowl and shank, watches her smile as if she is touching a child. It is only then that he realizes, yes, realizes all of a sudden what she reminds him of, and the similarity strikes him with such force that he pauses and steps back, and Denise has to come up to him and ask if there is something wrong, "Dennis, what's on your mind? You are thinking of some- thing. I can tell." "I was just thinking of Isis." "Isis?" "Yes, this village is named after Isis. In all the books I read about Isis, there was always the statement that she brought life to everything she touched. She even brought her husband back from the dead. That's how strong her love of life was. For a minute there, I thought of you and Isis in the same way. It just came to me all of a sudden. Maybe it's because of what you said on the bridge or the way you just touched that horse. I don't know. But there it is. You and Isis. Sisters." Denise again regards him with the penetrating look he can neither fathom nor deny nor even return. He says nothing more as they walk hand in hand past the small Eglise Paroissiale and stop in the rocky plaza in front of the entrance. "They call this *La Frache*," he says, but she nods in a way that indicates she already knows that. They move on toward the rock shrine of the war dead of Eze and read the bronze names of those killed in World War I. Just below that list are two separate plaques for François Granton and Rudolphe Warschavsky, each identified with a single phrase . . . "*Victime des Nazis*." Denise diverts her gaze and walks back to the wall opposite the shrine and peers down at the empty parking lot. When he joins her there, he waits for her to speak, but she is silent for so long a time that he begins to think that she must be looking at something in the lot that has distracted or mesmerized her. At last she says, "I am so tired of being reminded of the war. My father talks about it all the time, as if it happened yesterday. Or as if it's still happening. He won't let it die. It's gotten so that I ask to be excused from the table or the room every time it's mentioned. My brother loves to hear about it, but I hate it. I hate it." He sees from the set of her face that she is going to say nothing more, bequeathing to war and the very thought of war her special scorn of silence. After a pause Dennis asks her, "Did he fight with the Maquis, your father?" "I don't know. I don't ask. I leave all that to Seth." He puts his hands on her shoulders and squares her around until she is facing him. Then he says, "Do you know that if it weren't for the war I wouldn't be here. I don't know where I'd be, but I wouldn't be here. I wouldn't be what I am." He proceeds to tell her of his father's death in France and how he as his father's only son inherited the small cottage near Vence. She interrupts him, "You are French then. You are one of us." "No," he responds with a grin, "just American." "But your father fought for us. We were always taught that you earned the right to a country if you fought for her, if you contributed something. In Paris there are many statues and streets in memory of people who are not French, but they are French by adoption. Your father is like that." Again he faces that direct but fey look in her eyes. He tries to accomodate it but fails. At a loss he takes her by the hand and walks with her toward the tiny cemetery at the end of *La Frache.* Standing over the neat graves, he looks down at the fresh flowers and feels no urge to return to Anubis, no wish to walk the wire, no desire for Yvette, no desire for anything but to remain standing with Denise's hand in his. He feels suddenly emptied, as if there is nothing left to his being but what the moment is willing to give him. Denise tightens her hand in his and says, "I want to go now, Dennis. Please." "Just give me a minute. I just want to stay for a little longer. I don't want the mood to go away just yet. I don't have many moods like it." Later, as they descend to the parked motorcycle, he no longer feels any impulse to tell her about how the Phoenicians came to this coast and founded and named the village after Isis, how the Romans once occupied it, and how they were followed by Saracens, Guelphs, Ghibellines, the sway of the House of Savoy, decades of rule and counter-rule by French or Italian families, how Dante was supposed to have visited it, how Nietzsche really did climb the seaward hill to visit Eze, and in the process conceived of Zarathustra, and then how the tourists came and came and came. All of these bits of history seem suddenly secondary to the mood of the moment, a mood induced by the village itself. When they reach the parked motorcycle, Dennis straddles it while Denise mounts the bumperseat behind him. As he eases the helmet over his ears, he says, "I was going to tell you all about the history of this place, but it just doesn't seem important any more. I don't really give a damn about the past. All I know is that it gives me a kind of peace to come here, to see that the life of a small place like this doesn't end, no matter what." He points upward at the silhouette of the village against the darkening Mediterranean sky. "For all these centuries it's been Eze. And it's still Eze. Isn't that something? It keeps on living." "Maybe." He kicks over the motor and lets the bike coast slowly to the main road. "Dennis?" she asks apprehensively. "Yes." "You will not speed, will you?" He answers by driving no faster than thirty kilometers per hour down the corniche toward Nice . . .

Under his blindfold bandaging, Dennis remembers that first visit to Eze and the slow trip afterward. He sits up in bed and eases his legs over the side of the bed like a swimmer testing the water from the side of a pool. His feet slowly nose their way into his slippers. He grips the edge of the mattress with both hands and stands erect. Once he is on his feet, he pushes the bed away from him on its rollers so that he cannot touch it even if he stretches. He takes one step and then another before he hears the door being opened. Almost instantly the nurse is beside him, holding him by the arm and guiding him gently back to the bed. "Mr. Holt," she says to him scoldingly in French, "it is not prudent for you to walk alone like this. Dr. Russi has been quite insistent on that. You can injure yourself. It is fortunate that I was passing your room and heard the sound of the rollers. Otherwise I would not have come in. But, please, you must be careful." As they approach the bed together, the nurse's grip becomes less and less hers with every step until it changes for him into Denise's. He is walking with her in Cannes where they have just finished a small lunch. "You're not still afraid of Anubis?" he asks her. "No, not now," she answers, "not since you taught me to ride him. He's just like a little horse." "Not that little. There's a lot of horsepower there." He remembers how difficult it was for him to persuade her to mount the motorcycle and drive it, how she cowered and shivered on the seat at first and then how, little by little, she gained confidence until she was able to drive it alone for several blocks and then return to him. Now, with her arm pretzeled around his, she strides beside him with a new certainty about her. "My father wants to meet you, Dennis," she says as they walk. "He hears me talking about you. It's only natural that he wants to see the man I'm talking about." "No thanks, Denise." "But why? Don't you want to know him? I want you to meet my family. This is the way it's done in France." "Your father won't give a damn about me, Denise, believe me." "But how do you know?" "I just know." He does not tell her that various friends of his in the circus have told him about Sanche de Savigny and his extensive family holdings in jasmine and his equally extensive distributorship of perfumes made from his own flowers. Yvette has even made a special point of telling that de Savigny is one of the oldest names in the south of France and that the de Savigny chateau in the district near Grasse has been in the family for centuries, adding that such families have a kind of private code that keeps strangers at a distance when it comes to important matters. The exclusivity of the family was never spelled out further for him, but it never had to be. The sarcasm in Yvette's voice said it all. And the point stuck. Even though he resented it, he found himself accepting it almost as an absolute. "But my father will like you, Dennis," Denise is saying, "I know it." "When does he want to meet me?" "Tomorrow for dinner. Can you come?" "I have a matinee tomorrow. I'll come after the matinee." Denise touches his arm, but all at once it is no longer her touch but the nurse's again, and he is not in Cannes but in Cimiez, and the nurse is saying to him, "You may sit on the edge of the bed, Mr. Holt. Dr. Russi would have no objection to that. Would you like to sit on the edge of the bed?" He seats himself on the edge of the bed without the assistance of the nurse. He lets his legs swing free. After a moment he hears the nurse wish him a good night, hears her not quite silent footfalls as she opens the door and closes it, hears at last the silence of the room as it reassembles and rises like a sea around him and again assumes command of his life. He takes up his memory where he left it, and he sees himself driving toward the de Savigny chateau near Grasse, trying to imagine what to expect. He tells himself to be prepared for something like the opulent castles and chateaus of the Loire, but the Chateau de Savigny, when he finally does see it, is almost a perfect rectangular two-story home with its second-floor windows shuttered, its first-floor windows curtained with lace, and the stucco on its windward and seaward sides peeling and scabbing near the roof. Dennis coasts Anubis up the elm-lined driveway toward the fountain-centered circular turnaround directly in front of the house. When he parks and cuts the motor, he detects the scent of carnations surging in the crosswinds. He removes his helmet and crams it into its rack behind the seat of the motorcycle. It will be four hours before he will don the helmet again and mount Anubis for the short ride back to his cottage and all the way back he will remember how nothing was quite as he expected, not the dinner where he sat between Denise and her brother and observed how Denise's father presided like a patriarch at the head of the table while her mother sat demurely at the foot, not the very appearances of the father and brother and mother themselves. Speeding through the moist darkness on Anubis back to his cottage, he compares the picture of the Sanche de Savigny he expected to see and the man himself, not a short, balding merchant in a vested business suit but a man of more than six feet with a full head of gray hair and a deftly barbered goatee and mustache. In his dinner jacket he seemed even leaner than he was. Dennis remembers the habit he had of letting his mouth shape a slight smile before he said anything at all, light or serious. His wife, on the other hand, said very little. She had the look of a woman who spent too much time indoors. Her hair was graying evenly and the lines that rayed from her mouth became obvious when she pursed her lips as if they were being tightened by a drawstring. The son resembled the father to the point of facsimile. He combed his hair in the same way and, although he had neither goatee nor mustache, he could easily have passed for a younger version of the father. Dennis could not help being struck by the fact that Denise resembled neither of her parents. Her face was fuller, her hair auburn and more luxurious than her mother's, her cheekbones higher, her gait more casual. Above all he noted how no one else in the family had her eyes, which were brown, full, and enhanced by long lashes and eyebrows that arched slightly downward before they disappeared just above the bridge of her nose. After dinner, Sanche de Savigny invited Dennis for a walk around the premises of the chateau before they were to meet Denise, her mother, and her brother at the gazebo for demitasses. At the beginning of the walk, de Savigny said little, allowing Dennis to survey the sweep of his holdings from the hothouses on the south hills to the whitewashed perfume factory in the north. "This area was once a great center for making leather goods, Mr. Holt," said de Savigny finally. "Saddles, belts, shoes, boots, they were all made from leather that was cured here. But one of the Medici women—it may have been Catherine herself—was overwhelmed by the stench of the leather as it was being cured, so overwhelmed that she suggested that the people should become involved in a less oppressive form of industry. And that was the start of flower-growing and perfume-making in the south of France, and the leather makers went north to Lyons and Grenoble where they still are. But I'm sure I'm telling you something you already know, Mr. Holt. Denise tells me that you are always reading something and that you know a great deal about the history of our country." "I know a few things, Mr. de Savigny, but I didn't know what you just told me."

"I'm surprised that you have so much time for reading in your profession. Denise tells me that you work with the circus." Dennis sensed something behind de Savigny's statement, but he was unable to tell whether it was patronization or sarcasm. Either way he was uncomfortable and did not respond. As they approached the gazebo, de Savigny began speaking to him about jasmine. "The jasmine buds are extremely delicate, but jasmine remains the basis for the best perfumes. You cannot imagine the delicacy. The gardeners who water the jasmine must do so only at night and they cannot have eaten onion or garlic before they visit the jasmine beds. The flower is so delicate that it will inhale the smell of the garlic or onion, and then its real scent will be ruined. It is like a pedigree, Mr. Holt. The strain must be kept as pure as possible. One outside influence and the strain is corrupted forever." Again Dennis sensed that a different meaning was intended than the one he took at first hearing. But by then they had reached the gazebo where Denise, her mother, and her brother were already seated. Opposite them was a clergyman who was introduced to Dennis as Monsignor Lascaux. Dennis noticed that Denise's mother treated the monsignor with deference, serving him the first demitasse, refilling his cup immediately when it was empty, asking him quietly but repeatedly if there was anything else he wanted, if he was comfortable, if he needed more sugar. At one point the monsignor turned to Dennis and asked, "Are you of the Roman Catholic faith, Mr. Holt?" "No, Monsignor, I'm not." "What is your confession then, Mr. Holt? Where do you worship?" "In my work, Monsignor." The monsignor smiled in the direction of Sanche de Savigny before he turned to Dennis again. "And what is your work, Mr. Holt?" "I'm a clown." Just then Madame de Savigny intervened and took the monsignor's empty cup. The monsignor paused before he asked his next question. "Do you mean a clown in a circus?" "Yes, Monsignor," answered Dennis, looking directly at him. "That's what I mean exactly." There was a disquieting silence before Denise said, "He loves his work, Monsignor. It takes special training. Dennis studied at a university in the United States, but it was not what he wanted." Dennis looked at her and frowned, "You don't have to explain me to him, Denise. He asked me a question, and I answered it, and that's all that had to be said." Detecting Dennis's testiness, Sanche de Savigny said, "There's no reason to be sensitive, Mr. Holt. It's not every day that Monsignor Lascaux or any of us has a chance to meet a clown." Almost an hour later, after the monsignor had left and after everyone but Dennis and Denise had returned to the chateau, Denise walked with Dennis to Anubis. Finally, she broke the silence by asking, "You did not care for the monsignor, did you?" "No." "Why?" "I'm always uneasy when I'm in the presence of someone in a uniform. I just don't like people whose first allegiance is to some outfit or other and not to what's right in front of them." "Is that why you were rude to him?" "I could have been ruder." "And my family? How do you feel about my father and my mother and my brother?" Dennis reached for his helmet and put it on. Then he mounted the motorcycle and said, "If it weren't for you, Denise, I never would have come here. You know that. I knew what your family's attitude toward me would be before I set eyes on them." "But were you fair? Sometimes I think that you don't give people a chance." He slipped the goggles over his eyes and said quietly, "Tell your father that I won't breathe on his jasmine. It might make him happy to hear that." "What jasmine?" "He'll know what you mean." "Dennis, what are you saying?" Her question was drowned by the crescendo of the started motor. She backed away and then shouted, "Dennis, when will I see you?" "Who knows? In another life. Maybe." Dennis zoomed Anubis around the circular turnabout and down the elm-lined aisle toward the main road . . .

Every minute of his visit returns to him as he continues to steer Anubis away from the chateau. He lets the warm wind bathe his eyes when he lifts his goggles. He sees the faces of the de Savigny family rotate before him like targets on a rifle range. He shakes his head in a fierce no, revs the motor, and careens past the turnoff to his cottage. When he reaches the circus grounds, he stops in front of the trailer where Yvette and her sisters live. After he taps the horn of Anubis, he waits until Yvette appears in the doorway. He waves her toward him and points to the passenger's seat behind him. Smiling, she skips toward Anubis and mounts it. Still without saying a word, he turns a complete semicircle and heads back to his cottage. Once there, he stomps into the kitchen and sits in reverse on one of the kitchen chairs while Yvette sits opposite him across the table. Yvette keeps smiling and waiting, her arms crossed under her breasts. Dennis removes his helmet and rolls it like a bowling ball into a corner. "The whole family was there, Yvette. And the good monsignor was there to ask to see my credentials. The whole scene was like an examination. And the worst of it was that she was watching the whole show. It was as if this was something that had to be done. And when she did speak, she made it sound as if my whole life needed a defense." "*Merde*," says Yvette. "They are all *merde*, Dennis. I warned you this would happen. I know how these people treat foreigners." "Well, it's the last time I put myself in that position, believe me." "Wait. You will see her again. You will find some reason." "Not on your life, Yvette." "But you *will*, no matter what you say. Wait." "Shut up! Who in the hell are you to make prophecies about me? Get out of here! Get the hell out of here!" "Why did you bring me here? Just to listen?" "I don't know, and I don't give a damn." "Why didn't you leave me at home then?" "Shut up." "You have to take me back. I can't walk all the way back by myself." "Well, I'm not taking you back. You can slide back on your ass for all I care." "Then I'm staying." She walks around the table until she is standing beside him. He watches her all the way, watches the curls of her short, red hair, the small, high breasts and the short, athletic set of her frame. He puts his arms around her and pulls her down on his lap. She resists but only halfheartedly. For a time she keeps her face turned away from him. Finally, she faces him and laughs. In minutes they are both laughing. The chair tips, and they fall to the floor in one another's arms and keep on laughing so hard that they have to release their grips and lie supine until the laughter stops. He sits up while Yvette looks up at the ceiling and keeps on smiling. Dennis's laughter is now gone completely and he is frowning, "Shit on her! Shit on that family! Shit on their church! Shit on their perfume! Shit on their history!" Yvette begins laughing again and says, "But you still want to see her again, don't you?" He turns to her, "And shit on you, my little frog." "But this little frog has everything you want, Dennis. And I know what to do with it, don't I?" She snaps into a standing position and removes her smock by zipping it down the front. She does it quickly like an actress slipping out of costume between scenes. When she is finally naked, she stands at his feet and lets him study her from floor level. She strikes a pose and says, "Is she as flat as I am here?" She pats her firm stomach with her right hand. "Is she full? Does she have anything here?" She puts her hands under her breasts and lifts them as high as they will go. Ignoring her, Dennis says, "Do you know what I should have told the good monsignor? I should have told him how one of the princes of his church stayed on the friendly side of the Nazis when they were in Paris. Did you know that? I should have asked him why de Gaulle ignored the holy cardinal when he finally came back to Paris. That would have made him squirm a little. Or I should have reminded him about the holy men of Spain and how they pulled for St. Franco to win. Why in the hell didn't I say those things to him?" Yvette is still trying to capture his attention, "Does she know how to shake herself like this? Or do a split like this? What can she do?" "And the great Count Sanche de Savigny and his prince of a son. You should have seen them. And the mother. If you put white wigs on the three of them, you'd think they just stepped out of the eighteenth century." "Can she bend over backwards all the way like this?" Dennis stands, walks past Yvette and takes a carafe of wine from the shelf above the table. Yvette flips over into a standing position, picks up her clothes, puts them on hurriedly and leaves the cottage, slamming the door behind her hard. Dennis watches her go, tips the carafe to his lips and gulps down several swallows of wine . . . The next day he is in the middle of his wirewalking matinee routine when he spots Denise in the audience. She is waving at him, waving her right hand from side to side until he cannot help but notice her. For a moment it makes him break his concentration on the wire, but he never wavers. She keeps on waving, but he looks away from her, drops his balancing pole into the net below him and continues to walk the wire without it. An unorchestrated chorus of gasps rises from the audience, and all the other performers in the ring beside the net stop in midroutine and look up nervously before resuming their acts. Even as they resume, they look up apprehensively at Dennis on the wire. Dennis smiles down at them as he walks. He darts a quick glance at Denise and notices that she has stopped waving and is sitting forward in her seat with her hands to her lips. When he looks down at the wire again, he pretends to lose his balance, and the gasps from the audience instantly become screams. Then there is utter quiet. The ring performers stop their acts as if on cue, and the eyes of everyone in the tent are cocked upward to the wire. With his arms outstretched for balance, Dennis takes two more steps until he is in the exact center of the wire so that the wire is stretched into an angled dip at the point where he is standing. Then he flexes several times before he leaps and reverses direction. Again there rises a crescendo of screams, but this gives way to a hush as Dennis wavers back and forth on the wavering wire. Dennis looks quickly at Denise just in time to see her leave her seat, stumble, and rush up the aisle to the exit. He smiles again, waits until the wire steadies and flatwalks quickly to the small platform where one end of the wire quivers at anchor. The audience hush evolves into sounds of clapping here and there, but it is only clapping, not applause, as if the clappers are not sure how to react to what they have seen or even if they should react at all. Still smiling to himself, Dennis climbs quickly down the platform ladder to sawdust while the performers in the adjacent ring begin to move about again. The entire ambience in the tent resembles a film that has been stopped in midscene and then started again. Dennis retrieves his pole from the net where he dropped it and marches through the sawdust to the performers' exit. He does not acknowledge either the crowd or the dismayed expression on the face of the lion tamer as he strolls by him.

From the circus he drives on Anubis back to his cottage. He enters via the kitchen and finds Yvette seated beside the table. Pouting, she looks at him obliquely and says, "I had to come back. I forgot my shoes." "Did you find them?" "Yes." She points to a spot on the kitchen floor where the shoes are lying like discarded gloves. She stands and walks toward the shoes. While she is slipping them on her feet, she asks, "Why do you care about her? She is not for you. All she will bring you is sickness, here, in the head." "It's none of your business, Yvette. Stay out of it." "But I make you much happier. And there is no headache afterward." She sidles toward him and lets her dress begin to slip from her shoulder. In the semidarkness of the early dusk he makes out the glint of her shoulderskin and the familiar lines of her body. Without a word he reaches toward her, but she eludes him. He follows her into his front room and sits on the couch while she

stands beside him with an air of conscious nonchalance. Without
speaking, he reaches out and grabs her around the thigh and rubs his
hand up and down the length of her taut leg. She responds by seating
herself beside him on the couch, trapping his hand between her thighs.
She whispers to him, "She does not have what I have, Dennis. No one
has what I have." "Don't let it go to your head, Yvette. Every woman
has exactly what you have where you have it." Smiling, she stretches
out beside him and begins to kiss him abundantly on the cheek, the
forehead, the eyes while she whispers to him, "I will make you forget
her, Dennis. I will make you forget everything about her by tomorrow morning. Relax. Just lie back. You just have to lie back. I will do
everything." She rings his neck with her arms and draws him toward
her so that she pressures his cheek with her breasts . . .

The following day, after his performance for the matinee, he is leaving his costume wagon, his clown-smile still painted on his face, when
he sees Denise waiting for him. He pauses and then continues to walk
toward her. "Dennis," she says, "I had to see you." "About what?"
"About nothing. I just wanted to see you. Is it wrong?" "Not wrong,
just useless." He looks beyond her while she continues to study his
eyes. "Dennis, why are you being this way? One day you act as if we
are close and the next day we are like strangers with one another."
"Didn't that evening at the chateau tell you anthing?" "It told me
that you did not like my parents or the monsignor. But they are still
my parents, Dennis. In my country we do not deny our parents. We
don't spit on our parents." "The last thing I have in mind is coming
between you and your parents, and that's enough to kill our future
right there." "Please, Dennis, it's not that simple for me. I cannot put
away my feelings for you like that." "You'll learn how to do it. It's not
the hardest thing in the world." "Dennis, please, I don't understand
this mentality. I don't understand you." Dennis removes a soiled sec-
tion of torn towel from his hip pocket and proceeds to wipe the
clownpaint from his face. When he finishes, he walks toward Anubis,
parked behind the costume wagon. He dons his helmet and turns to
her, "I'm going home. I'm tired. If you like, I'll drive you to the
chateau on the way." Looking at the ground, she answers, "No, thank
you." "Okay. Have it your way." He mounts Anubis, starts the motor,

and looks at her again. Without returning his look or saying anything, she mounts the seat behind him sidesaddle and circles his chest
with her arms as he coasts Anubis to an exit behind the parked wa-
gons and, like a captain heading a speedboat for open water, opens
the throttle and roars down the highway. Instinctively, he waits for
her to tell him to go slower, but she says nothing. Her only reaction is
to tighten her grip slightly around his chest. He concentrates on the
road, which Anubis seems to him to be devouring. Ahead of him the
first hint of evening taints the sky—a touch of azure mounting into
the higher blue. The hillsides and trees seem rinsed by the changing
light so that their contours, their colors, and their short shadows impress him as having been underlined for emphasis. He finds himself
remembering what one of the artists from Vence told him about the
light in the south of France, how it was the purest light to see and
paint by because it seemed to come in at a slant and illuminated
everything indirectly. The artist added that the light of the tropics
was vertical, and its intensity invested all surfaces with the flatness of
torpor. Then he noted that the light in Scandinavia seemed to illu-
minate things horizontally, thus suffusing them with ochres and se-
pias that cast them in melancholy. But, continued the artist with a
wink, the Mediterranean light was the perfect balance between the
vertical and horizontal, and one could find this form of slant-lighting
all the way from Gibraltar to Greece, but especially in the south of
France. As if to confirm the point, the artist, who had known both
Renoir and Picasso but whose own work, though competent, had
never given him a comparable reputation, told Dennis that Don Quixote
had regained his sanity only when he returned to this part of the
Mediterranean. "And no wonder, Dennis," exclaimed the artist, "no
wonder at all, because in this part of the world he could see, he could
really see again!" Reliving his encounter with the artist, Dennis adjusts his goggles and steers on into the azure. He feels Denise tight-
ening her grip around him. Then she leans her cheeks against his
back, just above the right shoulder blade, and he responds by going
ten kilometers faster, then fifteen, then twenty kilometers, until he is
taking the turns at more than forty kilometers an hour before he revs
up to sixty-five and even eighty kilometers on the straightaways. From
time to time he forgets entirely about Denise and gives himself totally

38

to Anubis and the road, letting the sense of his own speed overpower him like a drug until there is nothing else that exists but the very motion he is creating together with its concomitant sensations. Even the names of the towns he passes along the way become mere markers, mere signals, no longer individual places where people live and work and die but only part of the rhythm of the trip itself, and their names in a series seem to develop their own tempo: La Turbie, Cape d'Ail, Beaulieu, Villefranche, St. Laurant-du-Var, Cros-de-Cagnes, Villeneuve, Antibes, Juan-les-Pins, Cannes, Mougins. He steers on through the warm winds of the valleys like a horseman riding into the only country he knows. When he reaches the long driveway to the de Savigny chateau, he slows down momentarily before he roars up between the elms to the turnabout in front of the house. There is not a light anywhere in the chateau. He taxis to a halt at the front door and lets Anubis lean to the right as Denise relaxes her grip around him and eases off the seat. "Did it make you happy to drive that fast all the way, Dennis? Does it please you when you frighten me?" "Yes, it made me happy to drive that way. And no, I wasn't trying to frighten you. It's just the way I drive. If you come with me, you should expect that. Otherwise, you shouldn't come." She turns and walks toward the chateau. After a few steps she stops and faces him. "Can I make you something to eat before you leave?" "No, thanks. I'm not in a mood to face the jury again." "No one is home, Dennis. They are in Marseilles until tomorrow night." "It's still no. I have to get back and see a friend." He throttles the motor and coasts Anubis into a slow start. Just as he completes his circle of the turnabout and heads toward the main road through the aisle of elms, he sees something dart across the road in front of him and collide with his front wheel. He brakes quickly. When he looks back, he sees the body of a young hare on the gravel. The hare keeps trying to stand but without success. Denise runs across the turnabout to Dennis and asks, "What happened? Why did you stop like that?" Suddenly spotting the hare, she stoops down and lifts it in her palm. She begins petting it carefully with her forefinger just above its eyes. Turning to Dennis, she says, "It's broken, here, in the legs." "What do you expect me to do? It just ran in front of the bike." "It is shivering in my hand. I can feel the heartbeat like thunder." She continues to soothe the hare by petting it above the eyes. Dennis rethrottles the motor and says, "Give it to me. I'll get rid of it on the way home." Denise responds by holding the hare closer to her. Dennis repeats, "Give it to me. It can't survive the way it is. It'll just starve to death, or else a dog or a cat will get it. It's not as if you can put splints on the thing and just wait for it to heal." Still holding the hare close, Denise says, "I know." "Then give it to me. I have to go." "But . . . I can't. I just can't do that." "Okay. Have it your way. You get rid of it. It's all the same to me." When she answers him with a look, he again feels himself in the presence of whatever it is in her eyes that disarms him. He becomes annoyed with himself for feeling so completely at a loss, so childlike, so much the victim of emotions and thoughts that he believed were behind him. He asks, "What are you going to do? Hold it like that all night until it dies?" She faces him. He diverts his look from her eyes to the eyes of the hare and notices with a shock that the expression in her eyes and the look of muted alarm in the eyes of the dying hare are almost a perfect rhyme. Changing his tone, he says, "Come on, Denise. Be reasonable. Give it to me. You can't make a big thing out of this." With the hare cupped in the nest of her palms, she walks toward him. Instead of giving him the animal, she reseats herself behind Dennis on the motorcycle. "What are you doing, Denise?" "I'm afraid, Dennis. Just drive with me for a little while, please. I'll be all right in a little while. Then you can bring me back. I don't want to be alone in the house right now." "Are we going to take that rabbit with us?" "Yes." "Why, for God's sake?" "Because . . . it's alive. It's still alive." Dennis huffs audibly and steers Anubis back to the main road. Since Denise can hold on to him with only one hand now, he goes much slower. As they motor toward Cannes, he turns his head in her direction and half shouts, "When are you going back to Paris?" "In one month." "Then what?" "Then back to the Sorbonne. I will finish my studies." "And you'll forget all about clowns . . ." She does not answer him. After a pause Dennis adds, "It's good for you to get away from here, and the sooner the better. We'll just say we had an experience. You were dreaming. I was dreaming. Dreaming and living are two different things." She still does not answer him. Approaching a small bridge, he slows down and veers Anubis to the berm. "Why are you stopping, Dennis?" "There's a deep stream in the gorge under this bridge. I think the kindest thing to do for that rabbit is to drop it into the stream. The current is strong, and the whole matter will be over in a few seconds. You can't let it suffer like this." "But I can't . . ." "Well, you can't keep holding it, and you can't put it back in the woods. Here, give it to me. If you can't do it, I'll do it." "But I can still feel it breathing . . ." "Denise, I thought you were a student of biology. If the animal is dying, it's just a matter of time. And meanwhile it's in pain. What about an hour from now? A day from now? It's just going to suffer more if you keep it alive." "I know. I know that." "Then give it to me." "I can't, Dennis. I can't just yet. Give me a minute." After a pause he says, "I can't understand why life means so much to you. What's one rabbit? It's just a little thing that got in the way of my tire. There are zillions of rabbits like that." "I can't explain it, Dennis. I just can't *see* anything die." "Even when there's no hope? What's life without hope? You can't live out the string if there's nothing to live for." Slowly Denise dismounts from Anubis. While caressing the hare, she walks toward the bridge as she might walk up the aisle of a church. She stands at the railing and, holding the hare in her cupped hands reaches as far out as she can into space. Without looking down, like a priestess offering a sacrifice, she lets her hands separate, and the hare disappears instantly downward. Then she rushes back to Anubis, resumes her position behind Dennis and sits there, shivering. For Dennis the entire scene has been like a mirage. He never believed that Denise would be capable of doing what she has just done. It is as if another person suddenly took possession of her body, did what had to be done, and then permitted Denise to become Denise again. He turns to her and asks, "Where do you want to go now?" "Nowhere. Anywhere. Just drive with me." He guides Anubis back on the road, throttles out, and lets the machine devour mile after mile as he retraces his route from Cannes, Juan-les-Pins, Antibes, Villeneuve, Cros-de-Cagnes, St. Laurant-du-Var, Nice, and then sharply north toward Vence. All the way Denise says nothing. By the time they reach Dennis's cottage, it is almost evening. The sky has already purpled over the gables of his cottage. Dennis parks Anubis in its stall and helps Denise to her feet. "Come in for a minute. I'll fix you some coffee and then drive you home when you feel better." "I don't want coffee, Dennis. All I wanted from the very beginning was to see you." As

they walk toward the cottage, they notice simultaneously that someone is sitting in shadow on the doorway stoop. Denise stops, but
Dennis keeps walking forward and asks, "Yvette, what are you doing
here?" Yvette rises from shadow into light. Posing, she regards Dennis like an intruder, "I told you you would find some reason to see her
again, Dennis." "Why don't you just go home, Yvette ..." Yvette
walks past him and takes a good look at Denise. "She has nothing,
Dennis. She is not even that pretty." She swaggers toward Denise and
says to her in French, "Your father's perfume money will buy you the
right lover or the right husband. Why do you bother with Dennis?"
Dennis intervenes, "Shut up, Yvette." Yvette stands with her hands
on her hips like a pouting Carmen and responds calmly, "Why? Am
I supposed to talk only when you say so? Do you think you control
me?" Yvette turns again to Denise and continues speaking to her in
French, "He will throw you away when he finds another. He has no
feelings. He is like all the Americans, this one. And then he will come
back to me because there is no one else who understands him the way
I do." She swaggers past Denise to the gate. Just as she passes Dennis,
she gives her head a slight toss, opens the gate, and leaves. Letting her
gaze follow Yvette until she is out of sight, Denise asks, "Is she your
lover?" She does not ask the question like an interrogator but like
someone in need of clarification or direction. Dennis shrugs and says,
"She's Yvette. That's all there is to know." "But she talks as if she has
rights over you." "Look, do you want some coffee or not? Otherwise
I'll take you back to the chateau right now." "I don't want anything.
All I want to know is what happened to you." Dennis steps toward
her and says quietly, "First, you happened to me. Then your father
and your whole family happened to me, and that put a new light on
everything. That changed everything." "What light?" "To put it simply, Denise, I don't enjoy being tolerated. And I enjoy it even less
when I'm examined to see if I'll pass, to see if I can be admitted to the
club. After five minutes at your house, I knew I didn't pass and that I
would never pass. So, to hell with it. Why should I fight a battle that
I'm going to lose anyway? Your father will find the right qualifier
and you'll be set for life." "And do you think that I will just play my
part, that I have no choice, no feelings?" "Absolutely! You're no different than the rest. When it comes to the real choices, you'll climb

back into your family and your history and your life, and you'll stay there. The only difference between you and Yvette is that you've been born into a tradition and she hasn't. I'm sick of both of you, for God's sake. If you didn't have what you have below your navels, you'd turn into an endangered species overnight." "Dennis, why are you insulting me like this? Why do you want to degrade me? What did I do to you?" "It's nothing that you did. It's what you are. Can't you see that?" "I only see one thing, and that is that I feel only half myself when I'm not with you. I feel lost, Dennis." "You'll get over it. We met just by accident. We can part by accident. It happens all the time." "Yes, we met by accident. But what I felt afterward was no accident. What I feel *now* is no accident. I don't think of you as an accident." "You'll learn how to do it. It's easy. Just have another accident with someone else, and you'll be surprised how fast you'll learn." "Is that why you went to Yvette?" "That's part of it." "But then you are just using her. Doesn't that bother you?" "No, it doesn't bother me. She wants to be used. She enjoys it." "And you? Is that what you want?" "Why not?" "But is that what you want? You have to answer me, Dennis." "That's all the answer I can give you." He holds open the cottage door. After hesitating momentarily, Denise enters the cottage, walks to a chair in the front room and stands beside it with her right hand on the chair's back. "Sit down," says Dennis, "I'll give you a glass of wine or something and take you home." Degree by degree, Denise eases herself down into the chair. She keeps kneading one hand against the other in her lap. When Dennis returns from the kitchen with a glass of wine, he sees her dab the corners of her eyes with a handkerchief and then slide the handkerchief under the sleeve of her blouse. "Drink this," he says, handing her the wine, "and you'll feel better." She faces him and asks with a rising tinge of anger in her words, "Is that what you're really like? Is that the way you treat people? Do you just use everybody? Don't you respect anyone's feelings?" Dennis places the wine glass on the table beside the chair and says, "What's that supposed to mean?" "Why did you follow me that first time in Nice? Why didn't you leave me alone?" "Because I couldn't get you out of my mind. Why did you look at me in the circus the way you did? Why do you look at people that way if you don't want them to remember you?" "Dennis, stop it! Stop it, please!" She raises her hands to her face and tries to hide her expression from him. When she finally brings her hands down into her lap again, she tries twice to speak but says nothing. Instead she begins to bite her lower lip. "Look, Denise, no matter what you felt, we were going nowhere. There was nowhere to go. Everybody is entitled to a romance once in a while. They peak early and they usually end badly. That's why they're just romances. We both got something out of it. Nobody really got scarred. Let's leave it at that." "You make everything sound so painless, Dennis." "What else do you expect me to say? As soon as things got real, as soon as I saw you at the chateau, I knew it was hopeless, that it was just a dream." "For you, perhaps. But not for me." "Why not? You're no different. You just haven't admitted it to yourself." "I am not a child, Dennis. I know what romance is. And I know what love is. And I know the difference." "There's no such thing as love, girl. The sooner you learn that the better." "Why? Because you say so?" "No, not because I say so, but because it's true. Everybody thinks of himself first and last. We kid ourselves that we can love our way out of it, but it never works. That's one thing I learned from my mother. And it's true everywhere. It's the way we're made." "You have such a high opinion of people, Dennis." "Just realistic. It's the best defense I've found." "What is it when someone else's life means as much to you as your own, means more to you than yours?" "It means that you're confused." "Then why can't you look at me? You can't look at me when I tell you that because you know I'm telling you the truth." "It'll pass." "And what if it doesn't?" "It will. You can count on it." "You won't be satisfied until you kill everything between us, will you?" "There's not that much to kill, Denise. There never was. That's what makes it so easy." "Easy for you. Not for me." Dennis turns his back to her, takes one stomping step, and wheels around, "Listen, for Christ's sake. Do you know what love is, what it comes down to in the end? It means bumping bellies in a bed. And that's all it means. That's all. It hasn't changed since Eden. So forget love! And forget romance! And forget me!" "But I can't. I don't want to." "Well, it's not the same with me. Listen . . ." He grabs her by the shoulders, then adds, "I used to think that love was possible, Denise. But too many things in my life made me see how silly that was." Denise looks at him through her tears, and it is again the same look that he first saw in her eyes at the circus. For a moment he feels his voice fail him. He starts to wrestle with the impulse to put his arms around her, to put his pretenses behind him and face the consequences for both of them regardless, but he finds the act beyond him. Second by second he waits for his previous mood to return to him, but even this is gone. Coloring, he turns away from her. When he faces about again, he sees that she has not moved. She is standing like a statuette of an Egyptian queen, her hands fisted at her sides, her body almost at attention, her chin upturned. Her lower lip is quivering and tears are streaking her cheeks from both eyes. "Denise! Denise, what do you want from me? Forget this business about love, for Christ's sake. It's just making life hell for you. Ask Yvette what love means. She'll tell you it means that men get hard and women get moist." He waits for her to respond, but she continues to stand there. "Do you want that? Go ahead. Get undressed. Undress, and I'll show you what I mean. You'll feel differently afterward. Maybe we should have done this a long time ago." After a pause and without taking her eyes off of him, she begins to unbutton her dress from the neck down. When she undoes the last button, she lets the dress fall around her ankles like a robe. Then, still looking at him through her tears, she removes her underclothes and stands naked and almost at attention in front of him. Dennis finds that he cannot look at her. When he tries, he feels he has to look away, but something in him forces him to continue talking. "How do you feel now, Denise?" "Is this what you want?" "First, tell me how you feel." "I feel embarrassed. And I feel small. And I feel ashamed." "Well, don't." "I don't feel ashamed for myself. I feel ashamed for you." "Why?" "Because I don't believe what you've been telling me. I don't believe you were telling me the truth." She looks directly at him, and he cannot return the look. He looks down at her dress around her ankles. Then almost guiltily, he takes a step closer to her, lifts her dress from the floor as carefully as he might lift a grounded flag and hands it to her. For a moment she does not take it, and he has to offer it a second time. "I'm sorry, Denise." He turns away so that he will not have to face her eyes. "Put your dress on, please. I'll take you back home."

All the way back to the chateau, they do not exchange a word. When they reach the chateau, he helps her dismount and walks with his arm around her to the front door. At the door he kisses her lightly on the temple and she responds by standing close to him, then closer. Without speaking, she backs away, opens the door, and disappears. Dennis keeps looking at the closed door, trying to relive the evening with all its implications, trying to understand the stranger that he is already becoming to himself. By the time he remounts Anubis, he feels his body convulsing inexplicably in one sob after another. He grips the handlebars of Anubis as if his very sanity depends on it and the sobs continue to rack him. When they subside, he starts the engine and steers slowly back to Vence and, finally, to his cottage. Yvette is waiting for him in the kitchen. She is smoking a cigarette and the kitchen is stratified with layers of cigarette smoke. She looks at him and smiles. She continues to smoke and lets him watch her. Then she mashes her cigarette into a saucer and says, "I feel sorry for you, Dennis. Your love for her is all over your face, and I saw the same look in her face the first minute I set eyes on her." She stands and heads for the door. "You will both suffer for this, believe me. There is too much against you, more than you can see now, more than either of you can see. It would have been better for you if she had not come into your life. She will give you headaches. With me there were no headaches afterward. It was just like eating, like breathing." She pauses and adds, "You have to live with your choice, Dennis, but I see what's coming. And I feel sorry for you." She bumps open the door with her hip, edges through the doorway, and leaves. She is no sooner gone than he heads for his bedroom. Exhausted from the day's work and the trips to and from the chateau and his struggles with his own feelings, he lies on his back on the bed, folds his arms behind his neck, and waits for the new self within him to make its peace with the self that is already dying. In less than five minutes he is asleep, turning and grimacing as dream after dream buffets him. In the swirl of his first dream, Ramuz, the old clown, has removed his false teeth and, sprawled in his makeup chair, is telling Dennis, "Don't try to be funny in the beginning of your act if you intend to be serious later on. Be serious first, then funny. People can go from a frown to a smile easier than they can go from a smile to a frown, and the bonus is that they will be grateful to you for giving them a chance to smile at the end." To underscore his point he holds up his false teeth, clacks them in a mock grin, then laughs a full-mouthed, gum-rimmed guffaw at Dennis

that crescendos and glissandos and becomes in the dream the laugh
of an old woman in Vence as he, Dennis, goes through his first performance and realizes from the look on the woman's face that he can
clown, really clown, really do things to make people laugh. The two
laughters collide in separate dreams that become one dream, and they
echo and echo as he dreams himself suddenly on a tightrope strung
between the Matterhorn and Mont Blanc. He walks with a rush across
the whole of southern Switzerland, seeing everything below in a curving
perspective of the near and not so near from Annecy to the most
intricate details of the hanging bronze flowerpots of Yvoire and then
beyond to the casino at Evian and still farther to the perched houses
of Gruyère and Geneva's cusping shores. His walk on the wire leads
him westward over Spain, over Portugal, over the entire Atlantic to
the American coast and inland. And he is suddenly sixteen again, and
he has decided to surprise his mother by traveling unannounced to
spend his Easter vacation with her in Chicago. The train ride from
downstate Illinois to Chicago is monotonously long, reminding him
of the bus ride that he took years earlier to see his mother in Texas.
He arrives in time for the first show, and, entering from the stage
door, walks to the right wing of the stage and looks out through the
bunched curtains. His mother is seated at a piano, pooled in orange
light. He cannot quite hear the song, but at the end of each measure
he sees his mother tip the piano bench forward in rhythm so that her
upper lap bumps against the base of the keyboard as if she might be
tupping it. He continues staring for several minutes until he starts to
feel ashamed of himself for watching. Then he leaves through the
same stage door, hurries back to the train station and returns to his
school. He remembers looking out of the train window, not through
but *at* the glass, where his reflected face keeps wanting not to be seen.
Suddenly the dream swirls again, and it is not a train he is riding but
a jet, and the jet is about to land at the airport in Nice. Dennis feels
the touchdown of wheels as the jet races diminishingly to the run-
way's shunt, and two hours later he is standing in the front room of
the cottage that is his inheritance in Vence. But it is not Dennis Holt
who is standing there. He dreams he is someone else, someone who
resembles him. He thinks that he hears the firing of a machine gun
from a hill just below the cottage. As a reflex, he crouches below the

47

windowsill, loads his rifle with a full clip of cartridges and waits. When he peers above the windowsill, he sees nothing but trees and, beyond the trees, the road that twines its way to Nice. By the time he spots the first helmet, he is so surprised that he lets his rifle slip from his grasp, but catches it before it hits the floor. Peering again over the sill, he sees German infantrymen marching in single file along the shoulder of the road in parallel columns. Between the columns a camouflaged Tiger tank advances. It is followed by another identically camouflaged tank at a distance of twenty yards, and this tank is in turn followed by a third at the same interval. Dennis calculates that the entire column will pass less than forty meters from the front of the cottage. He raises his rifle and lets the base of the barrel rest on the windowsill. Then he presses his cheek against the warm stock and zeros in on the first soldier in the file nearest to him. He finds he cannot aim directly at the man's head so he lowers his sights until he settles for a spot just below the man's shoulder. Slowly he starts to squeeze the trigger toward him with his forefinger until a shot cranks off with a simultaneous kick and burst and the soldier in his sights suddenly lurches to his side, drops to one knee, and sprawls backward on the road. Dennis continues to fire round after round, and after every round another soldier falls until there is only one soldier left. By now Dennis's rifle is empty. When he reaches for another clip of cartridges, he finds nothing in his cartridge belt. Quickly he reaches to his side, lifts a pistol from the holster at his hip, assumes his position at the windowsill just in time to see the last soldier advancing in a zigzag run toward the cottage. Even as he watches, he sees the soldier stop and walk directly toward him, his rifle at the ready. The soldier seems to grow as he advances and he has the ability to walk through trees and fences. Dennis notices that the soldier is smiling. Dennis recognizes that the smile is the toothless smile of Ramuz, the old clown, but the face of the soldier is the face of Sanche de Savigny. He tries to raise his pistol into firing position, but the pistol is too heavy. Little by little he lifts it, but the soldier is drawing nearer all the time. Behind him he can hear Denise screaming his name again, again, again, telling him not to shoot. The soldier keeps advancing until he is directly in front of the window. He is still smiling as he reaches across the windowsill, seizes Dennis's weapon as if it were made of balsa, and throws it behind him. As soon as the pistol hits the ground it discharges. Dennis puts his hand to his right temple and pitches back, back, back. When he opens his eyes, he sees blood on his right hand. He recognizes that he is in a ward in the hospital in Cimiez. All around him are hospital beds with wounded, Oriental men in them. A doctor with the same toothless smile as the old clown is explaining to Dennis that these men are the wounded of the Nisei Division. He says that they have been brought to Cimiez from the Italian front, that they are recuperating well, that their casualties have been unusually high. When Dennis asks the doctor how long he has been here, the doctor smiles again and tells him that he, Louis Holt, was dead on arrival. Dennis tries to speak, to say that he is not Louis but Dennis Holt, that he is still alive, but the doctor and the quiet, wounded soldiers begin to fade, slowly at first, then all at once. The dreams collide and interweave like a fallout of sparks. They do not become clear again until he dreams himself alone in a bed in Texas, where his mother is leaning over him and saying, "They will be good to you here, Dennis. This is one of the best schools in the state of Texas. You believe me, don't you, dear? You believe your mother?" He turns his head away from her and turns back in time to see her walk away. As she walks, he sees her change into someone else, some- one Yvette once mentioned to him. It is no longer a hall in Texas but a road outside of Nice, and the female figure that is walking away from him is naked except for a pair of shoes. Dennis can see that the woman's hair has been cropped close to her scalp and that the job must have been done with dull scissors and no special skill. As the naked woman walks on, several other women in serge robes run up to her and spit on her and back away. A peasant approaches her and wipes what appears to be a handful of cow manure across her breasts. This harassment continues for some time until the woman is covered with spittle and filth. Dennis tries to reach out to stop what is happen- ing, but someone seizes his hand and slides quietly into bed beside him. He looks, and it is Yvette. She is speaking to him in French, "They want their justice here. They are like the Jews. They will not leave justice to God. How do they know what my mother was forced to do to keep us from starving when the Germans were here? When you are hungry, you will do anything. But they had to have their justice, these bastards. They took the clothes from my mother and cut off her hair with a shearing knife and made her walk that way until she was two miles outside of Nice. And all the way they kept spitting on her and throwing the shit of cows on her because they said she slept with the Boche commander. Well, why not? We were all starving. The commander at least gave her food for my sisters and me. We had nobody else to help us. My father was selected to be a laborer in Germany. And do you know who put his name on the list? The father of Mademoiselle de Savigny. He was the one who handpicked who would go to Germany and who would stay. No one ever proved it, but I don't need proof. I know he was the one. How did he keep his chateau and his factory when the Germans were here? Why did they leave him and his family alone? Why did they always have enough of everything? Answer me that. Why else were they so special? Answer me that. He is the one who deserved the spitting and the shit, not my mother." Dennis listens to her speak on through his dream, but the voice grows fainter and fainter until it is succeeded by another voice, a man's. Dennis keeps listening. He is one of a small audience in Beaulieu with Denise, and the man who is speaking is describing with scholastic care and precision just how the customs of Provence in the era of troubadours influenced the patterns of love throughout the West. When Dennis stands to leave, Denise insists that he stay a bit longer, that the speaker, even though a Swiss by birth, is the foremost authority in France on this subject, that he once gave a series of lectures at the Sorbonne that she audited. Frowning, Dennis reseats himself just as he hears the speaker state ". . . that the idea of marriage was not what captured the imagination of the writers and singers of Provence. For them romance was much preferable, and it is this concept that is the worm in the apple of love in the West, since romance is in essence passion disassociated from personality or rather passion at the expense of personality. Like jealousy or envy it feeds on itself. I do not mean to imply that there is not a healthy amount of romance in all love. There certainly is. What I am speaking of is romance as an end in itself. Its powers of seduction are limitless. In the beginning it creates an almost irresistible illusion of excitement and freedom. But it is the very enemy of true freedom since true freedom involves choice. Romance makes a mockery of choice. It is the enemy of any conscious choice. It is essentially passion without choice, without past, without future. It eventually enslaves by trying to create its own present despite time, even outside of time. And if the 'love' in question is either unobtainable or prohibited or both, it only intensifies the passion, which in turn intensifies the romance. It should come as no surprise, therefore, that romance as an end in itself stands as the antithesis of the passionate friendship that is marriage. Marriage is its enemy because true marriage is the enemy of all the illusions upon which romance feeds. While marriage can lead to true understanding and conjugal fulfillment, romance leads only to its undoing. Thus romance, however popular it has been made to appear in the literature and minstrelsy of Provence and in those currently popular songs and novels that are its offspring, is in fact the very stuff of which tragedy is made. And if you doubt me, I defy you to name one romance that had other than a tragic resolution either in literature or in the experience of your own lives." The speaker pauses and sips water from a half-filled glass on the rostrum. "Here in our native France the effect of romance has been corroding the springs of our life for decades, as it has throughout the Western world. And yet we have ourselves to blame for it since it is we who have created and fostered it. How? By our attitude toward marriage itself. For too long we have placed marriages based on mutual love secondary to marriages based on family standing, security, and mutual social advantage. The result is that husbands and wives soon begin to look outside of marriage for what they consider to be a happiness that is beyond realization within marriage. And the whole tradition of romance is ready and waiting to accomodate them. French husbands, for example, often have the seeming convenience of both a mistress and a wife, seeking in two women what one wife could easily give them—provided the wife was truly loved in the first and last place. For husbands less affluent, there is always the brothel, which is nothing but romanticism reduced to its dregs. In Paris alone it was recently estimated that onefourth of the male population occupies itself in this way as a matter of habit." Again he stops for water. "What is now happening . . . in fact, what has always happened and will continue to happen . . . is that the most flagrant indulgences associated with romance have created their own opposition from those who are usually called puritans. This is where we find ourselves today. There is the complete tradition and even the machinery of romance on the one side, and on the other there is the equally complete tradition and machinery of puritanism. But each tradition is equally devoid of the essential ingredient that makes any relation between man and woman truly human, and that is the realization that eros separated from or denied to personality is the very enemy of personality, while eros in the context of personality, that is, in the context of life, of blood, of breath, is the proper soil for its growth. Romance and counterromance or puritanism are actually inhuman conditions. They are unable to fulfill us as human beings since, as human beings, we need love for our inner life, and yet we can only find it in a culture which, because it has been weakened at its core by the worm of romance, makes it difficult to preserve and arrays strong forces against it." Dennis huffs and turns toward Denise, but it is no longer Denise who is beside him nor is he any longer in the audience. The speaker is gone. It is Yvette who confronts him. He sees that her hair has been jaggedly scissored like the hair of her punished mother, and she is saying, "I bite my thumb at these jackasses who say that love is a feeling. It is just a skill, and I have the skill, right here." She pats her pubis with her fingers before she stands face to face with him and continues, "Do you feel what happens to you when I stand face to face with you like this? You're all the same, you men. You are like horses. You will go after any woman who is close enough to make you stiff. It makes no difference. And then, after the first time, you want variety, you want technique. You want a woman who knows what she's doing. You want someone like me." "Is it as simple as that?" "As simple as that." "Yvette, you know a lot about sex, but you don't know a damn thing about love." "That's only what you think, Dennis. I know more about love than you will ever know. That's one thing every woman knows without even wanting to. Even the dumbest woman. We're all experts on the subject. We're authorities. That's our curse, you poor bastard. Haven't you learned that yet? We know about sex because that's all you see in us. That's all you want. We're experts at it because it's our defense." Yvette tilts her head back and laughs and laughs and laughs. Slowly her laughter

long I've been waiting for you to say that." Dennis stands, saunters away from the wall, and all of a sudden does a quick handstand and flipover before returning to Denise's side of the wall. "Why did you do that?" "No reason. Just to see if I could still do it, maybe. It's one of the tricks in my bag." He smiles at her and adds, "Let me tell you something you've probably never thought about. If I were a policeman and suddenly started blowing my whistle, you wouldn't say anything, would you? You wouldn't ask me why I was doing what I was doing, would you? But if I do a handstand, you have to ask me why. Why?" He smiles at her while she continues to look at him in her straight, disarming way before she says, "I'd rather see you do that walk on the railing of a bridge." She leans her head against his shoulder and they look out at the tilting sea. "My father wants me to go back to Paris next week, Dennis." "Because of me?" "I don't know. I'm not going." "Do you have a choice?" "I suppose I will have to go eventually. I must finish my studies." "And then?" "Then to America. I am accepted as a laboratory assistant in New York. It's part of an exchange program." "Are you going?" "I am obliged." "But are you going?" "If I go, will you go with me?" "You're not answering me, Denise." "I know. I don't know what to say." He helps her down off the wall and they walk slowly out of the garden and back to Anubis in the lower parking lot. "There's really too much against us, Denise. It's just as if there's no hope, no future." "Don't say that, please." "But it's true. Just look at the facts, and you'll see how true it is." She stops and faces him. "God is generous, Dennis. I believe in that. God does not want people to be unhappy." He smiles at her as they mount Anubis and begin to coast down to the corniche. He turns to her and says, "Haven't you heard? God is dead. When you go to your job in America, you'll see how dead He is." "I don't care about America. God is inside of me, inside of each of us. As long as you believe in God, He is not dead." "I hope God is listening." "God is generous, Dennis."

Now as he lies in his hospital bed and blinks hard against the loose gauze over his eyes, he hears Denise's words about God again and again and lets them swarm in his mind like a prayer. He wonders if it is day or night. He remembers a conversation he had with the doctor a week earlier. It was not the first conversation, but it might as well have been. The same questions. The same answers. Dennis reconstructs the series of scenes until they become one scene. The doctor is talking quietly to the nurse beside Dennis's bed. Then he says to Dennis, "How are you feeling today? You're not trying to move about yet, I hope." "It's very hard just to lie here, Dr. Russi." "It's dangerous if you don't. And it is simply unwise. The retina in you right eye is detached. Any kind of movement would be very bad for you. The damage might be irreversible." "You can be frank with me, doctor. The damage is already irreversible, isn't it?" "Not yet it isn't. Later this afternoon we'll take another test. I'm not pessimistic. You must have faith in me, you know. But you cannot take chances. You can tempt God once too often." "Somebody told me once that God is generous." "Not too often in medicine. You have damaged your eye severely. Remember that." "Why are you giving me all this attention? You've made me your special project for the past month. I asked the nurse about you and I've been told that you're the best not only in France but in all of Europe. Why all this special attention to me?" "It is simply my duty. You are a patient. I am a doctor. The relationship is not very complicated." "Who is paying you for all this?" "Why do you keep asking me that? What does it matter? The main thing is that you recover." "Is de Savigny paying for this? Is he the one who's picking up the bill?" The doctor again begins to converse quietly with the nurse before Dennis asks him again, "Am I right? Is de Savigny paying for this?" "That is not important now, Mr. Holt." "I'm right, aren't I?" "Maybe yes. Maybe no. The whole matter of payment is of no concern to me." "You keep a good secret, Dr. Russi, but your evasiveness gives you away." Dennis hears Dr. Russi turn to the nurse and tell her to leave the room. After she has left, he says to Dennis, "I sent the nurse away, Mr. Holt. I want the chance to speak to you in privacy." "I'm listening." "When you were brought to Cimiez from Eze a month ago, I was called into your case. I was told only that you were to receive primary attention and that money was not to be a consideration. I accepted your case on those terms, and I asked no questions." "But you know who's behind this, don't you?" "It is not my concern to inquire if everything is paid punctually, and every bill has been paid punctually." "But who does the paying?" "That's

my business, Mr. Holt. And I don't want any further inquiry into it.
What I do want to discuss with you is something that has nothing to
do with this. Suppose you were called into a case and told only that
your patient suffered a fall. Upon investigation you learned that your
patient was a circus performer and that he even had the ability to
walk on a high wire. And then suppose you visited the site of his fall
..." "What are you getting at, Dr. Russi?" "What I'm getting at is
that you did not fall from *La Frache* in Eze. The wall is too high. I
investigated it myself. You either jumped. Or you were pushed. And
if you were pushed, somebody pushed you. And that is a criminal
offense. You told the police that you fell, but I saw the look on Gagnon's face when you told him. He is no fool, Mr. Holt." "Who is
Gagnon?" "The inspector for this district. He knows that a man who
can balance on a wire does not fall from a wall that stands higher than
his chest. Why don't you tell him the truth? Why didn't you tell him
the truth a month ago?" "That's *my* business." "Is there someone *you*
are protecting?" "Let's just say that you have your little secret, Dr.
Russi, and I have mine. That should make us even." "Very well then."
The doctor opens the door and hesitates before he says, "I'll be back
later, and we'll remove the bandages. But in the meanwhile you must
remain in bed." Dennis hears the door being closed. Five minutes
later the door is reopened. Dennis listens to footsteps that he knows.
"Ramuz!" he says, and instantly the old clown is beside the bed,
holding his hand in his huge, sandpapery palms, and they are talking,
talking, talking as if they have to make up for the time they should
have been talking, and Ramuz asks in his plain, peasant way how it
happened, then adds with a nod, yes, a fall is possible, anybody can
fall, but not you, Dennis, not with what you know. "Who pushed
you, Dennis? Tell me, tell me right now. Don't keep it to yourself.
Why keep it a secret, for Christ's sake? If someone had it in for you,
you should let the police know who it is. Report it to Gagnon. Or just
tell me. I'll report the son of a bitch myself if I don't kill him first."
Then Dennis explains slowly and quietly to the old clown that he was
pushed and who pushed him and why. But he adds that reporting the
young de Savigny would only ruin everything between Denise and
himself, would just make a bad situation worse, and for what? After
all, he says, a brother is still a brother. Better to let the whole thing

seem an accident. Still, the old clown is unpersuaded. He asks Dennis
what is more important, his eyes or the feelings of a girl he will never
have anyway, and, besides, who cares about her or her brother, or the
whole damn family? "They made life hell for you already, Dennis.
This is your chance to get back at all of them." Dennis keeps talking
quietly and insistently to Ramuz. He makes him promise to say nothing of this to anyone, that he will handle it in his own way. Then
Ramuz is gone and the days go on repeating themselves, with the
routine visits of the doctor, the periodic emptying of bladder and
bowel, the cycle of breakfast, lunch, and dinner, the unavoidable time
of remembering his recent and remote life, until he has difficulty
separating memories from dreams, and dreams from facts. But the
fact of his second meeting with Sanche de Savigny remains as clear as
it was when it happened. As he thinks about it, the face of Sanche de
Savigny assumes a definition in his mind like a light that is blurred at
a distance but that is becoming clearer as it nears, and he, Dennis, is
again seated in de Savigny's study with Denise and her brother, Seth,
while the elder de Savigny relaxes behind his desk and regards Dennis the way a lawyer might regard a prospective, not quite desirable
but unavoidable, client. After a pause that only contributes to the
general discomfort, Sanche de Savigny asks Dennis how long he plans
to remain in the south of France. Dennis responds that he will stay
for the season, a matter of three more months, and then tour with the
circus through Italy and Germany. De Savigny smiles, relaxes in his
chair and then swivels around to face the bay windows behind him.
In a moment he swivels back and, still smiling, asks Dennis, "I can't
help but ask you why you do it, Mr. Holt, why a man with an education at an American university would choose to become a comedian
with a circus. It is strange, no?" "It's not really strange, sir. It's what I
do best. And I enjoy doing it. I've never felt like a man in a mold that
way. At the university I was told that I'd make a good lawyer, but it
wasn't for me." "But don't you think that you've deprived yourself of
opportunities to succeed? Just compare them—law and being a clown."
"But it wouldn't have been *my* kind of success. I mean I wouldn't
have been a success to myself." He pauses and glances at Denise before he faces de Savigny again. He feels that the mood of interrogation that he sensed during his first visit has now reestablished itself.

"It came down to a pair of choices for me, Mr. de Savigny. If I did what I really did not want to do—law or whatever—I might fail. I could survive but I wouldn't excel. But if I chose what I really wanted to do, I felt I couldn't fail, I certainly would survive and I might excel." De Savigny goes on swiveling in his chair. When Dennis stops speaking, de Savigny stops in midswivel and says, "That's very interesting, Mr. Holt. That's a very interesting personal philosophy, but when your personal philosophy starts to involve others, you should reexamine it, don't you think?" "I don't think that would change anything. The same things are at stake." "Come now, Mr. Holt," says de Savigny as he rises from the chair, "Let's be frank with one another. I'm not blind to the fact that my daughter has feelings for you. And I know that you've been seeing her. She's even discussed the matter with me." De Savigny looks at Denise and indicates with a nod of his head toward the door that he wants her to leave the room. Denise looks away as if she does not want to interpret his nod. Then her father speaks to her brusquely in French, and she stands and leaves. When she has been gone for several minutes, de Savigny walks from behind his desk and paces the length of the study several times like a general. Halting finally, he looks first at his son and then at Dennis. Seth de Savigny responds by straightening his chair. He resembles a lieutenant waiting for orders. At intervals he darts a look at Dennis without turning his head in Dennis's direction before he resumes looking at his father. Dennis is now convinced that the mood of interrogation is in complete command, and he toys briefly with the idea of following Denise. Instead, he watches Sanche de Savigny, who has now interlocked his hands behind his back and moved to the bay window where he posts himself like a king surveying his dominions or, in Dennis's view, like a general raping the countryside with his eyes. Dennis lets his gaze float around the room from shelf after shelf of books bound in red and black leather, from portrait after portrait of the male predecessors of the man standing at the bay window, from the various Persian rugs around and under the teak desk to the wall tapestry behind the desk—a tapestry of purple and gold. Dennis finally discerns the image of a girl in the fabric. He concentrates on the image until he sees that the girl is crowned like an ancient queen and standing within the furl of wings that seem to be her own and that gradually dissolve into a purple field. The voice of Sanche de Savigny breaks Dennis's concentration. "Mr. Holt, you will notice above my desk a tapestry of Isis. The myth of Isis is one of the oldest myths in history, but it is one of the truest. It even touches this part of France. If you know the village of Eze, you know that Eze was named after Isis." "Yes, I know the village." "According to the myth, Mr. Holt, there is a deep connection between Isis herself and the spirit of life. Where Isis reigns, there is life. It's even apparent in the tapestry. You can see that she is shrouded in wings, her own wings. But that is simply the artist's way of suggesting that Isis for the Egyptians was the spirit of life in the lungs, in the breath. This artist chose to let the lungs grow into wings." "I'm not sure that I understand what you're trying to tell me, Mr. de Savigny." "You will, Mr. Holt. Let me continue. As a matter of myth and a matter of fact, Isis gave life to whatever she touched. During her reign in the absence of her brother Osiris, she brought peace and plenty to Egypt. Later her devotion to life was so deep that she was able to restore Osiris to life, to gather the dismembered parts of his body and shield them with her wings until Osiris lived again." Dennis returns de Savigny's look but says nothing. De Savigny now moves to the tapestry and, standing in front of it, says, "There is a real similarity between Isis and my daughter, Mr. Holt. Denise has a deep concern for life. She was born with it. Her strength and her weakness, if I may say so, is that she is vulnerable to life. She cannot willfully cause pain to anyone. She cannot hurt anyone." "What are you trying to tell me, Mr. de Savigny?" "Well, I was hoping I wouldn't have to tell you directly, Mr. Holt. I thought the allegory would speak for itself. My son and my daughter are my whole life to me. Do you understand that? They need one another. Denise often mistakes sympathy for love. She lets her heart think for her more than she should. Seth is different. He is much more realistic. It means a great deal to me, and it means more to them, that the bond between them remain strong. My wife and I will not live forever and I am relying on my children to preserve what we have sustained for them." Dennis looks past de Savigny at the tapestry while de Savigny himself walks toward his son and stands beside him. "My son Seth knows very well what is expected of him. The de Savigny tradition is very deep within him. And it is important to him that he will have the support of his sister in the managing of our affairs. It is something that will require the two of them. This means, Mr. Holt, that his sister and, in God's good time, his sister's husband understand what is expected of them." "And what is that?" "In brief, it means that the man whom Denise marries must be unselfish enough to put her and her family's interests ahead of his own. This will, of course, require a man of extremely high character and unusual maturity, a man who knows something of the history of our family and its significance in this part of the country, a man who can work in association with my son in preserving what must be preserved." Dennis stands and smiles mirthlessly. "I think I understand the allegory, Mr. de Savigny. You want to keep Isis under your control. And I don't belong in the story." De Savigny pats his son's left shoulder with his right hand and again walks to the bay window and looks out. "As I said a moment ago, Mr. Holt, I am not blind to the fact that my daughter believes she has a real affection for you. She's told me as much. But I think we're both men enough to understand that this is not unusual in a girl of twenty years, and it is certainly not unusual with a girl of her vulnerabilities. But surely you must be sensitive to the fact that her role in life and what you seem determined to make your profession are not exactly compatible." "What does Denise think about this?" Seth de Savigny speaks for the first time, "What Denise thinks is not important." Sanche de Savigny waves his son into silence with the slightest lift of his hand and says, "Seth is correct, Mr. Holt. What Denise thinks is really not important in this matter. But I suspect that your reason for asking the question is that you want to know her feelings not for her sake but for yours. It's only natural that you want to know this, but frankly, Mr. Holt, that is equally unimportant to me. This is not a matter of what two people think. It's simply a question of history and of what is at stake for the future." Dennis crosses to the door and stops, "From what I've heard, Mr. de Savigny, you make quite a specialty out of interpreting history your way. I understand from several of my friends that your conduct during the war changed the history of quite a few men who wanted nothing more than to remain in France but ended up as laborers in Germany. It seems that some- one nominated them to the proper authorities." De Savigny turns abruptly from the window and approaches Dennis. For a moment they stand face to face like grudging duelers before de Savigny wheels, walks behind his desk, and sits down. He begins to drum quietly but steadily on the desktop with his fingers, then stops and indicates by the mere lifting of his index finger in the direction of his son that he wants him to leave the room. Seth de Savigny stands and strides like a lieutenant past Dennis, brushing him slightly but intentionally as he goes. When they are alone, de Savigny, his lips whitening and taut, says, "That remark was really unworthy of you, Mr. Holt, especially in the presence of my son. Those nominations, as you call them, were nominations I was ordered to give. I was given a quota and I selected only those stronger men who had the best chance of survival. If I did not do it, someone else would, someone who would not be that conscientious about it. The men I had to choose know why I did it, why I had to do it. They and their families understood the situation then. And some of them understand it still." "How many are left to understand it? That's the real story. The ones who were supposed to survive didn't. Only you survived." De Savigny slams the desk with the flat of his hand. "Mr. Holt, no one questions me, especially not a clown from a traveling circus!" "Well, I'd rather be a clown than a puppet, sir." De Savigny stands, strides to the bay window, stares for a long moment at his property, about-faces slowly, plants his legs slightly apart like a wrestler establishing a position, and speaks just above a whisper, "The name and reputation of Sanche Cassiano de Savigny are not things to trifle with, my friend. My family has been part of the history of France for generations. And I am not going to let someone insult that reputation. Do you understand me? I am not going to let a summer romance contaminate it. Who are you? You came here with no profession, no credentials, nothing but the nerve of a parasite. You have practically seduced my daughter. You can bring her nothing but misery, nothing but difficulties. She is too obsessed with you to see it, but *I* see it. I see it quite clearly." "I don't have any credentials but one, Mr. de Savigny. But it's the main one." "And what is that?" "I care for her. I never knew that I could care for anybody, but I care for Denise. No matter what you think, that's the truth." De Savigny laughs one short laugh and says, "Care? Care? And what do you think I should do about that? Congratulate you? In a mere two months, do you think that you can care more than I care, more than her family cares?" "Time has nothing to do with it." De Savigny's tone changes from anger to sarcasm. "Of course not. This is an affair of the heart with you. This is something that neither of you can resist or prevent. Come now, Mr. Holt, I was not born yesterday. I know what a man wants from a woman. I know what you want from my daughter. Do me the courtesy of not dignifying your motives for my benefit." "Well, what do you suggest I say? You've made yourself an authority on everything else. You might as well make yourself an authority on this." De Savigny seems ready to respond in kind before he thinks better of it, relaxes his stance, and says, "If you care for her as much as you say you do, really care for her and what is good for her, then I suggest that you end this romance immediately. I'm sure you know how to do that. If you don't know, then I'll become an authority on that subject as well." "And what if I'm not willing to end it?" "Then you give me no choice except to encourage her return to Paris imme- diately and then to inform several of my good friends in Paris that there is a certain clown in the south of France who should have his visa invalidated and revoked and be asked in no uncertain terms to leave the country within twenty-four hours." "You have a deep un- derstanding of your daughter's feelings, Mr. de Savigny, I must say." "Think what you like. But I'm not a monster, Mr. Holt. I realize that I am asking you to do something quite difficult. I also realize that you are not without some feelings for Denise. But I'm interfering for the good of both of you, believe me. If I did not interfere, the result would be a catastrophe. Some day you'll realize that what I'm doing is really in your best interest as well as hers." "It's very good to know that. It's always reassuring to know that you're so concerned for our good." "There's no need for sarcasm, Mr. Holt. I could easily have sent my daughter back to Paris and had you deported without any consulta- tion whatever. But I believe in civilized solutions. In fact, as a further incentive for what I am asking you to do, I have arranged for the delivery of 20,000 francs to your cottage in Vence. That comes to about $8,000 at the latest rate of exchange. I'm sure that will more than compensate you for this small sacrifice." "Thank you, Mr. de Savigny, thank you very much. Your generosity leaves me speech- less." "I'll continue to ignore the sarcasm, Mr. Holt. In addition to the 20,000 francs I've just mentioned, you will receive another 20,000 francs from me personally when you have brought me word that you have resolved this matter with Denise." De Savigny crosses the room to the door and holds it open for Dennis. "I suggest that you leave now without seeing Denise. You can be assured that I will keep—what shall I call it?—our arrangement secret. I'll expect to hear from you shortly, perhaps in a day or so. Have I made myself clear?" Dennis comes to the door and faces de Savigny. "You don't deserve to be her father, Mr. de Savigny. The amazing thing to me is how Denise is somehow free of any smell of you." "Thank you for your compliment, Mr. Holt. Good afternoon." Dennis walks down the hall as de Savigny closes the study door behind him. After looking to his left and right and seeing no sign of Denise, he walks toward the portico and out of the chateau. Heading for Anubis, he sees Seth de Savigny beside the motorcycle. "Are you here to see me off, Seth?" "Denise told me to say goodbye to you." "Goodbye?" "Permanently." "You're a liar." "I don't want you to see my sister again, Holt. I'm giving you fair warning." "You can go to hell." Dennis cranks down the starter on Anubis once, twice, three times before the motor kicks over. Then he wheels around and speeds down the long aisle of elms to the main road. All the way back to his cottage he feels a growing and thickening pulse in his solar plexus. By the time he passes through Vence he is as tense as a trapped man. At his cottage, he dismounts from Anubis and lets the machine fall with a heavy clatter on its side. Then he almost staggers toward the kitchen just as Ramuz opens the door and holds up a square, taped package. Approaching Dennis, Ramuz says, "Dennis, I was waiting for you. Look. This package came by messenger all the way from Nice. I had to sign for it. It's from the bank. What happened? Did someone die and leave you some money?" He laughs, but Dennis pushes by him, enters the kitchen, and sags into the first chair he reaches. Ramuz follows him, sets the package on the table, and tries to get Dennis to look him in the eyes. "*Mon Dieu*, Dennis, what happened to you? What the hell happened to you since this afternoon?" "Nothing. Everything." "Make sense, Dennis." "I met the enemy, Ramuz. The real enemy. And he means business." "What are you telling me? What enemy?" "Sanche Cassiano de Savigny himself. And he's some enemy, Ramuz. He has more guns than I do. More troops. More reserves. More everything." Ramuz straightens up and puts his hands on his hips. "Are you just discovering that? What did I tell you in the first place? What did I say to you? I told you that you were spading your own grave by going with that girl. I told you to pick someone else. Take Yvette, for God's sake. She's as free as drinking water." "This isn't a question of choosing one or the other, Ramuz. It's not a question of choice. In fact, I never really chose this for myself. It chose itself. You're French, for God's sake. You should be the first to understand that." Ramuz bends closer and studies Dennis's face as if he is about to paint his portrait. Then he looks directly into his eyes. Straightening up, he says, "I see." After a pause, he repeats, "I see now. You have that girl in your guts, boy. That's how it is, isn't it?" "That's how it is, Ramuz." "Then *we* have a problem." "*I* have a problem, Ramuz, not you." Ramuz tromps to the opposite side of the kitchen before he answers, "No, *we* do. Do you think I'm going to let you go through this by yourself? Do you think I don't know what you're going through? Believe me, I know." He pauses and tromps back to Dennis. "Listen, boy, did I ever tell you why I never got married?" Dennis looks up at Ramuz as if he is looking at him for the first time in his life before he answers, "No. No, never." "Well, let me tell you now. It might do you some good. It started when I fell for a girl from Avignon. Just like the one you found. Good education, religious, pretty, everything. Not just a hole between the legs, if you know what I mean." Dennis nods yes. Ramuz waits for a moment to let what he is about to say assemble itself in his memory before he resumes, "Well, I loved this girl so much that all other women looked like cows to me. I didn't have eyes for anyone but her, and she felt the same about me. I would have done anything for her. I would have left the circus. Anything, I swear. But, even though she loved me, she wouldn't take the risk with me. She wanted a sure thing. She told me that she would wait. She said that I could send for her when I was settled, when I was ready. She wanted everything to be safe." Ramuz looks away, thinking. When he does not resume, Dennis asks, "Well, did you ever send for her?" "Sure, I sent for her. But there was one problem. It was too late. She said she'd met someone else, someone from Avignon. They had known one another since they were kids. The families knew one another. You know how they are with families in France. That carries a lot of fucking weight.

So there I was. Stuck. I let myself love this girl, and I got screwed in the end. The problem was that she was in my guts. I couldn't forget about her. I couldn't get out from under. She made me so damn bitter that I never even opened up to any other woman after that. But she taught me about women, Dennis. They're all the same, boy. They all want this well-lined little nest. They won't risk shit without that, believe me. Well, I say if they don't want to take any chances, we can play the game the same way. They all have the same hole between their legs, don't they? Don't they? They know that that's what we want from them, don't they? So let's accommodate them. Tell them they can have a little nest. Tell them anything, what the hell. Make them feel comfortable. They'll come across sooner or later. But don't take the rest of the package. Don't even look them in the face, for Christ's sake. That's when the trouble starts—when you look them in the face, when you listen. Just take what they're giving and then tell them you had a change of heart. But tell them *after*, see. As long as you don't look at the faces, you're all right. Just look at them from here down, that's all." Ramuz walks to the cupboard, opens it, and selects a bottle of wine. After removing the cork, he pours the wine into a kitchen glass for Dennis and then swigs from the bottle himself. When he finishes, he wipes his lips with his sleeve and says, "Don't let her break you, boy. Go ahead. Drink your wine. Our evening's just beginning. Your whole life's just beginning." Dennis takes the glass of wine and drains it in three swallows. "There, Dennis. Don't you feel better? Let me fill your glass again. Let the wine work on you for a while." Dennis watches Ramuz refill his glass, watches the red wine rise in the glass like mercury in a thermometer, watches the thick, tattooed hand that grasps the bottle by its neck as if it might be a goose, watches Ramuz's smile broaden across his face that could easily be the face of a retired wrestler or of someone who's worked so hard and long at his trade that he is stamped by it, watches the sweat developing on Ramuz's scalp beneath the cropped and bristling hair. Ramuz himself keeps pacing back and forth in the kitchen, stopping intermittently to swig wine from the bottle. At last, picking up the package he left on the table, he offers it to Dennis and asks, "What the hell's in here? Did you win something? Are you holding out on me?" "It's de Savigny's money, Ramuz. That's his price." "What the hell do you mean by that?" "I mean that's what he's willing to pay me to leave his daughter alone, to take myself out of the picture. Forever. And there's more where that came from when I go through with what I have to do." Ramuz unwraps the package as if it might contain the sacrament. When he finally removes the thick gray paper, he looks with moon-round eyes at twin stacks of fresh francs. "*Mon Dieu*, Dennis. How much is here?" "20,000 francs." "And he's going to give you more?" "Yes, 20,000 more." Ramuz slaps his forehead with his palm in a gesture of disbelief. "Mother of God, Dennis, what the hell are you waiting for? If you don't break off with this girl for what's on this table right now, I'll do it for you. Count it, Dennis. 20,000 francs! And then 20,000 more francs! Think of what you can do with that. You can buy a hundred girls like her." "I don't want his money, Ramuz." Ramuz pushes the refilled glass of wine toward Dennis and says, "Drink some more of this. Keep on drinking until your head clears, boy. Right now you sound like a sick goat, do you know that? Just like a sick goat. But an hour from now if you drink some more wine, you'll be wiser, believe me." Ramuz pushes the glass of wine even closer to Dennis. "The wine won't make any difference, Ramuz. I don't want his money. Period." "Don't talk. Drink. Jesus, how much of a fool do you want to be for this girl?" "It's different for me, Ramuz. It's not that easy. Don't ask me to explain it to you. I couldn't do it." Dennis lifts the glass of wine and again drains it in three swallows. "Well, what are you going to do with these francs, boy? Give them back to that old son of a bitch?" "Yes." Ramuz pounds the kitchen table with his fist, "Good! Very good! Bravo! You deserve a real medal for that one, Dennis! Here the bastard is bribing you to do yourself a favor, and you show him how big you are by returning the bribe to him. Bravo!" "But I don't want his damn money. Can't you understand that?" "But *he* doesn't want it either! Take it, for God's sake! Use it! Enjoy yourself. You're going to have to give the girl up anyway. Why not get some pleasure out of it while you can?" "That's just the problem, Ramuz. I can't give her up." "You will, my boy. Sanche de Savigny isn't going to let you have his daughter, I promise you. What you feel and what his daughter might feel for you are nothing to him. Take my advice. Use the fucking money. At least make him lose something." "Shut up, Ramuz." "I'm telling you for your own good. I wish I had your choices when I was your age. I wouldn't be where I am now." He grabs Dennis by the elbow and tries to pull him to his feet. "Come on with me. I'll show you how to spend money and enjoy it, and tomorrow you'll be a different man, a new man. You just come with me. Leave everything to Ramuz, and we'll have a night, you and I. If you still want your little angel by tomorrow morning, you can have her. But until tomorrow let's put Mr. de Savigny's money to work. Let's give it back to the people who earned it for him in the first place—the poor people, the working people." Once on his feet, Dennis reels slightly from the effect of the hurried gulps of wine. He permits himself to be pulled ahead by Ramuz until they are out of the house and standing beside Anubis. Ramuz pulls Anubis upright from its sprawl, lets Dennis mount it, and then straddles the seat behind him. After he starts the motor, Dennis asks Ramuz, "Where are we going?" "Just go back down the road toward Nice. I'll tell you where to stop when we get there." Dennis steers Anubis through the warm darkness. He is hardly aware of the cars passing him from the opposite direction until he feels the side-rush thrum and suck of their passing. All that he notices from time to time are headlights in the distance that appear to be one headlight, which divides like a cell as the car comes nearer and nearer and then hurtles by him with a whoosh, leaving him alone again on the road to follow the single, spearing headlight of Anubis down the center of the right lane of the highway. After they have gone almost five miles, Ramuz pats Dennis on the shoulder and shouts over the motorsound, "Turn right at the next road and keep going until you see a bistro on your left." Dennis slows Anubis at the turn and revs on for several hundred meters before he stops at a lighted gate. "Park here, Dennis," says Ramuz, "we'll walk the rest of the way." "Where are we going?" "Trust me, my boy. We're going to eat and enjoy ourselves as you never have before." Ramuz walks ahead of Dennis through the gate toward what appears to be a converted barn. "The money!" says Dennis, stopping, "Did you bring the money or leave it back there?" Ramuz smiles and pats the package of francs under his shirt just as he knocks at the door of the barn. Dennis hears a bolt being pulled on the opposite side of the door just before it is swung open. Ramuz exchanges a few words with a man at the door and then enters, followed by Dennis. For several minutes Dennis sees nothing, but he smells the smoke of many cigarettes and a few cigars. When his eyes become accustomed to the lanternlike light, he sees that he is standing in the midst of a crowded circle of tables. Seated at each of the tables are men in working clothes, field clothes, shop clothes. Some of the men have tipped their chairs back against the barn walls. Some are holding mugs in their hands or drinking from them frothily. A few are forking lettuce and tomatoes into their mouths from large wooden bowls of salad set before them. The tables themselves are arranged in a kind of circle around an open, slightly elevated platform that is four or five meters in diameter. Rising from the center of the platform and running all the way up to the loft of the barn is a metal pole. The only light in the barn comes from squat candles housed in yellow glass chimneys centered on every table. After talking to one of the waiters, Ramuz tugs Dennis after him to the last empty table in the circle. "Sit down, Dennis, and leave everything else to me. We will start with some good ale or some wine, and then we will have snails and leek soup and then we shall see, we shall see . . ." He snaps his fingers for the waiter and says to Dennis, "First you must have some more to drink. You are still too sane." The waiter arrives with two mugs, bangs them down on the table, and leaves. Ramuz lifts his mug and touches it to Dennis's so hard that the liquids spill from both. "Pick it up, my boy. We will toast the future, your future." Together they drain the mugs, and Ramuz signals for the waiter to refill them. "Who are these people, Ramuz?" "Farmers. They are almost all farmers. They are my people. They all look like my father. They work like hell all week and come here on Friday to get away from everything, to forget, to relax, to eat, to enjoy themselves. Do you blame them? They work with their hands in the dirt all week. They step in the shit of cows and pigs. They want a change. Do you blame them?" "And you think that's what I need, a change?" "We all do." From an adjoining table comes the sound of scuffling. Two men are standing face to face, chest to chest, neither giving a centimeter, and they are shouting at one another simultaneously. A waiter tries to come between them, but the men remain in confrontation like roosters. A third man at the next table yells at them to sit down, that the show is about to start, that they should get the hell

outside if they want to fight. Even as the man is speaking, the loop of
blue lights around the rim of the circular platform in the midst of the
tables begins to brighten. From the loudspeaker comes the rattle of a
drum fanfare amplified from a record that has been used too often
for the same purpose. "What's coming, Ramuz? A bullfight?" "Watch.
Sit back and watch." Dennis relaxes in his chair. The wine has made
him almost lackadaisical. He concentrates on the metal pole that
soars upward like a mast from the center of the platform to the loft.
He follows the pole with his eyes up, up, up to the loft. When he
reaches the top, he sees a woman wearing nothing but a pair of high-
heeled silver shoes step out of the loft, seize the pole with both hands,
knot her legs around it like a firefighter summoned by an alarm, and
slide slowly down to the level of the platform. Once she is there,
Dennis notices that the woman is wearing a white turban with a
gleaming red jewel in its center just above her forehead. She looks to
be about thirty with heavy buttocks and thighs, but her breasts are
the nipple-high breasts of a much younger woman. She smiles at the
men seated directly in front of her around the platform, but she continues to embrace the pole with her legs. Gradually she lets her legs
release the pole. First she plants one foot on one side of the pole, then
the other foot on the other side so that she keeps the barrel of the pole
flush against her crotch. She grasps the pole with her right hand, leans
back, and makes a theatrical sweep of the crowd with her left hand
before she points at the pole imprisoned between her thighs. Then,
still holding the pole with her right hand, she brings her left hand up
to join it, interlocks the fingers of both hands, and begins to ease her
pubis up and down the pole like a doe in rut. The more she moves,
the more she lowers herself until she is almost touching the floor.
Letting her head fall back but still keeping her grip, she continues
rubbing her pelt slowly up and even more slowly down the pole.
Some of the men at the tables are standing. Suddenly the woman
stops what she is doing, smiles at the man nearest her, and whispers
something to him in French. The man laughs, reaches into his pocket,
removes several franc notes and throws them in a wad onto the platform. Seeing the money, the woman resumes her tupping but now
faster. More franc notes from another table splay themselves on the
platform. Then a quick shower of francs from various tables flutter

down like leaves around the woman before they settle like colored feathers. Ramuz reaches inside his shirt, emerges with a handful of notes and flings them on the platform. Noting the denomination of Ramuz's notes, the woman stops in midthrust, settles back and thumps so forcefully against the pole for several seconds that her buttocks shake and quiver in place like disturbed pools. "Why did you do that, Ramuz? I'm taking the money back. I told you that." "To hell with de Savigny. Why did we bring the money with us in the first place? Why did you ask me if I had it a minute ago? I'll spend it for you. His money's going to cure you, boy. That's all it's good for." Ramuz removes more francs from inside his tunic and scatters them across the platform. The woman stops thrusting against the pole, lifts herself to her feet and turns around to face them. Dennis notices a slight pinkness on her inner thighs from the pressure of flexing around and against the pole. She struts toward Ramuz's side of the platform and beckons to him to come forward. Ramuz laughs, remains seated, and points to Dennis. The woman faces Dennis, parts her legs slowly as if she might be about to do a split but stops when her feet are less than a meter apart. "Go ahead, Dennis. She's waiting for you." "To hell with you, Ramuz." "Go on up, Dennis. She's going to let you kiss it." Dennis stands shakily and turns toward the door. The other men in the barn are whistling and stomping with their boots on the plank floor. A farmer grabs Dennis by the hand and tries to pull him back, but Dennis shakes off his grip and edges through the tables to the exit. A waiter smiles at him as he passes. Ramuz is following Dennis and catches up with him at the door. "Dennis, why are you leaving, for God's sake?" "Let me go." "But we didn't even eat." Dennis looks past Ramuz at the farmer who grabbed his hand. He has left his chair and is waddling toward the platform where the woman in the white turban is still standing with her legs apart. The farmer plants himself in front of the woman, his eyes at the level of her navel. Almost all the men in the barn are standing and thumping on the planks with their boots. Shouts. Whistles. The woman arches her body toward the farmer until her belly is close to his face. The farmer waits a moment, then grabs the woman's hams with both hands and jams his mouth into the hair in her groin. The woman tries to keep her balance against the push and pressure of the man's head. As soon as the farmer releases

71

her to the hurrahs of the crowd, she steps back and wipes her crotch with her right hand. "See what you missed, Dennis." "Let me go, Ramuz. I have to get out of here." "Go ahead then. To hell with you. Walk out. Turn your back on what's good for you. Some son of a bitch gives you all the money you want so you can do what you should have done a long time ago, and what do you do? You grow a conscience. That's what you do." Dennis steps out of the barn into the darkness, letting the door close on the din behind him. He suddenly realizes that he can barely keep his balance. His head is still spinning from the ale, the shouts and whistles of the farmers, the bootstomping, the tobacco smoke. He heads in the direction of Anubis just as he hears the barn door opening and closing behind him. Turning, he sees Ramuz stagger toward him. "Wait, Dennis. Wait for me." Dennis wobbles ahead. When he finally reaches the motorcycle, he tries to mount it but ends by leaning against the seat to keep himself from falling. "How are you going to drive that thing, Dennis? You can't even walk straight." "I can drive it. Don't worry. I walked the wire when I was dizzier than this. I never fell there, did I?" "I don't know why you want to leave. We didn't eat what we ordered, and the show was just starting. We could have stayed there most of the night." "Last year that would have been interesting to me, Ramuz. Now it's like watching dogs." "You don't know what you're saying. It would have made you forget. They all fuck the same. From here down, they're all the same." "Shut up, Ramuz." "I'm telling you for your own good, you fool. Why do you think I go? Because it makes me forget. For thirty-seven years I've been forgetting." "How can you say you've forgotten if you have to keep going back? Why are you trying to fool yourself, you old bastard?" "Because I see the same thing ahead of you. If you keep chasing that girl, you're going to be disappointed. Really disappointed. Maybe more than disappointed. Believe me, I know what I'm talking about." "Why? Because you're still getting even with your old sweetheart who married someone else instead of you. Why didn't you look for somebody else, for God's sake? It's not the same for me, Ramuz. It's not one-sided with me. She's not going for somebody else. And neither am I." A silence develops between the two men. Dennis keeps leaning against the motorcycle. Ramuz shifts from foot to foot before he finally sits down on the ground.

When Ramuz breaks the silence, he speaks quietly and with absolute sobriety. "Dennis, I lied to you." He pauses and then continues. "The girl in Avignon didn't marry somebody else. She didn't marry anybody." "What's that supposed to mean?" "She died, Dennis." Again Ramuz pauses. "She died before anything could happen between us. Some disease of the spine. I don't know. It took only three days. I saw her the last day she was alive. My whole life happened on that day. Honest to God, my whole life happened on just one day. We hardly said a word to one another. We just looked. We just made love with our eyes. All day. Like it had to last forever." Dennis sees Ramuz change as he lapses into the grip of his memory. His hands go limp. His shoulders sag. He ages by decades in just a few seconds. "Why do you come to places like this, Ramuz?" Dennis asks quietly. "What's this supposed to do for you? What's the future in it?" "No future. Who gives a damn about the future? It keeps me from being alone in my mind. Do you know what that means? I can't *not* remember. What do you do if you can't *not* remember? You go out and drink. You drink yourself drunk. You swim in this shit. It makes you feel that nothing really matters anyway. And sometimes it works. It helps. It helps more than anything else." "Until you sober up." Dennis turns and swings his legs over Anubis and settles on the seat. He gestures to Ramuz that he should mount behind him. "Where are we going, Dennis?" "I don't know. I think better when I'm driving. But first I have to drive just to see if I can do it. How much of that money do you have left?" "More than half." "Half? Do you mean you threw half of de Savigny's francs on that platform in there?" "I don't know what I threw. I didn't count it." Dennis starts Anubis and steers shakily down the road toward the corniches. By the time he reaches the middle corniche, he feels sober enough to accelerate. Ramuz is holding him around the chest with both arms. Assured by the familiar feel of the handgrips in his palms, Dennis speeds by the few automobiles on the road. He passes Nice and a series of smaller towns en route to Monaco. Within minutes the lights of Monaco bloom below him and he hones in on them like a bee to a marigold garden. With the hills of France on his left and the Mediterranean on his right, he drives down to and by the old port, past the building where, according to Denise, Mata Hari was captured, past the yachts anchored in perfect rows like a queen's guard at attention in full regalia, past the lower concourse and up the winding road to the casino itself where he parks Anubis between a black Jaguar and a white Mercedes. "We're here, Ramuz." Dennis tries to look back at Ramuz over his shoulder, but Ramuz's tight grip keeps him from turning. "Ramuz, for God's sake, let me go. We're parked. We're here. Let go of me." Ramuz snorts and relaxes his hold. He looks around, burps and says, *"Mon Dieu,* where are we, Dennis?" "Come on. Get off. Let's have a cup of strong coffee over there and decide what we're going to do." Ramuz begins investigating his tunic with both hands. The packet of francs has slid to his side, and he sighs with relief when he finally relocates it. "I didn't lose the rest of the money, Dennis. It's still here." Ramuz dismounts and follows Dennis across the illuminated plaza to the Café de Paris where they sit at a table for two and order coffee, black. "Churchill," mutters Ramuz. "What?" "Churchill lived over there." Ramuz points at the Hotel de Paris across the square. "He used to come to visit here," continues Ramuz, "and then, after the war, he came to live." So what?" "So I'm telling you some history. Aren't you interested in history?" "We're both still too drunk to be interested in anything but coffee." After a waiter brings them two steaming cups of coffee, they drink in silence and wait for the coffee to have its effect. When he has finished, Dennis reorders for himself and quickly finishes off the second cup. "I have to go to the *pissoir,* Dennis," says Ramuz, standing. "Leave the money here. I want to count it." Ramuz removes the francs from inside his tunic and carefully mounds the disheveled stacks between the empty coffee cups. "There, Dennis. That's everything." Holding on to the backs of chairs as he goes, Ramuz staggers away while Dennis counts and restacks the notes. Of the original 20,000 francs he discovers with relief that almost 18,000 remain. When Ramuz returns, Dennis asks him, "How much money did you leave back there at the barn?" "I don't know. Half?" "You left 2,000 francs, Ramuz. Not half but enough. Now you owe me 2,000 francs, Ramuz. And do you know why? Because I'm going to give the whole amount back to de Savigny tomorrow morning and tell him what he can do with it." "I don't have 2,000 francs, Dennis. Do I look like a man who has 2,000 francs? Beside, why do you want to give the money back? What's the money to him? He won't even miss it." "I'm not thinking about him. I'm thinking about myself. I don't want anything from him." "And what about the girl?" "That's my business." "Well, she's her father's business too. Don't forget that." "I haven't forgotten it. But now I need 2,000 francs." Ramuz flops down in his chair and points toward the casino. "Go over to the casino and gamble for it. If you lose, you won't be much worse off than you are now. And if you win, you win. You might be lucky." Dennis glances toward the casino and then lifts his cup and sips what's left of his coffee. "Ramuz, that's a good idea." "Of course, you might lose. Most of the ones who go there lose." "I can't lose." "Bullshit. Anybody can lose, boy. Almost everybody loses." "But I have the best insurance against losing." "What's that?" "Because I don't really give a damn if I win or not. Even if I win, I'm not winning for myself." Dennis stands up and sandwiches the francs into his pocket. "You can't go like you are, Dennis," says Ramuz. "You need a coat." Dennis turns to the waiter and speaks to him briefly. The waiter leaves and returns almost immediately with a sport coat. After giving twenty-five francs to the waiter, Dennis dons the coat and heads for the entrance to the casino. "Dennis, do you want me to wait here for you?" "Yes. I have to return the sportcoat to the waiter." "Do you know what I'm going to do while you're in the casino, Dennis? I'm going to sit here and think about the wine cellar of the Hotel de Paris that runs all the way under the park out there." Dennis laughs, runs up the front stairs of the casino, and enters the foyer. From his left he hears a ringing chorus of slot machines like a battery of cash registers in full use. He walks into the central hall, turns left to the gambling wing, pays an entry fee, and steps into the main room. For several moments he just stands and surveys the games. On his far right, baccarat. In front of him, the U-shaped blackjack tables. Directly opposite the baccarat games, the scooped, canoelike tables for the dicers. Standing, Dennis cannot escape the feeling that he has been here before, listened to the ongoing gongs of the slot machines, watched the cat-and-mouse tactics at the blackjack tables, placed bets. But he knows that he has never before been here. That much is certain. Yes, he was in the casinos in Annecy and Evian. And in Menton. Suddenly he imagines that the casinos he remembers and the casino he actually sees are but one casino, as if all the outlying churches of chance have been consol-

75

idated into a universal church with the casino of Monte Carlo as its
Vatican. Dennis notes that each altar of this central cathedral has its
devoted parishioners—here a clutch huddled over baccarat, there a
pair of seated bettors at the blackjack horseshoes, and still farther away
a larger gang magnetized by the dicing tables like aficionados around
the pit of a cockfight. What impresses Dennis, what has always impressed him at every other casino, is the silence—very much like
church silence, a silence that says without qualification that *it* is the
rule, and speech and laughter the exceptions. As he enjoys the flow of
his thought on this subject and scene, Dennis pats the folded francs
in his pocket and walks through the hanging incense of cigar and
cigarette smoke toward a blackjack table where only one bettor is
seated in a quiet *mano-a-mano* with a young dealer. The dealer, his
sleeve held up and braceleted by garters around his biceps, has a look
of almost complete detachment. For a moment Dennis thinks the
man is bored until he notices that the dealer never for an instant takes
his eyes off the cards that are bracketed in a small, wooden slot on his
left. For each deal he slides out the necessary cards by pushing them
down the slot one at a time and sliding them farther along the green-
cushioned tabletop with his fingertips. At the end of each deal, the
dealer gathers the cards in quick sweeps and rebrackets them in the
dead-card bin at his right. Whenever the dealer wins a hand, he flicks
the lone bettor's francs with one finger toward a slot in the center of
the table and pushes the loser's francs down through the slot with a
wooden hoe. When he loses, he matches the bet of the winner, and
the game resumes. Dennis stands slightly to one side and watches for
a time before he goes to the exchange and converts a sum of francs
into a cylinder of chips. Then he returns to the table, sits down, places
the cylinder of chips on the table in front of him, divides the cylinder
into two equal stacks and indicates with a nod of his head to the
dealer that he wants to be included in the next game. Dennis bets
twenty-five francs, and the cards flash out under the dealer's fingers
and across the green felt—a card face-down to the first bettor, a card
to Dennis (the ten of hearts) and an ace of clubs to the dealer. On the
second deal-around, the first bettor draws a six of hearts and holds.
Dennis receives a king of diamonds. The dealer then slides his own
card from the bin—a king of hearts. He smiles quickly at Dennis and

his companion and hoes their chips into the slot at the center of the table. Without a word the other bettor at the table gathers his remaining chips in his hand and heads toward the baccarat games. The dealer looks at Dennis and asks him with his eyes if he wants to continue. Dennis returns the nod and counts out one thousand francs worth of chips and offers them as his bet for the next hand. "You want to bet one thousand francs, Monsieur?" "You're due to lose. I have a feeling that this is the hand." The dealer looks over his shoulder until he catches the eyes of a man in a blue tuxedo who is proceeding casually from table to table. The man in the blue tuxedo approaches the dealer, who whispers to him briefly. After listening without any change of expression, the man shrugs, says *yes* with several nods of his head, stands to one side, and waits for the game to begin. The dealer snakes one finger across the bracket on his left and slides a face-down card to Dennis and then a face-up nine of spades to himself. Dennis sees that his card is the ace of diamonds. Again the finger of the dealer shifts to the bracket and eases out the jack of clubs to Dennis. There is a pause. The dealer then asks, "Do you wish to double your bet, Monsieur?" Dennis counts out one thousand more in franc chips and places them beside his original bet. The dealer nods and gives himself the ace of clubs from the bracket. Dennis inverts his face-down card and shows his blackjack to the dealer. Again without any change of expression or comment, the man in the blue tuxedo removes two one-thousand franc certificates from his pocket and covers Dennis's bet, saying, "Congratulations, Monsieur. Do you wish to continue?" "No," answers Dennis, "I'm finished. All I needed was two thousand, and I have it. He pockets the franc certificates and, after exchanging the certificates and his remaining chips for francs, leaves the blackjack area. Rather than experiencing satisfaction, he feels that his winnings have come too easily, that he has not really known risk, not felt the drama of actually gambling. Now that he has won back what Ramuz threw away in the barn, he has the original amount that came in de Savigny's package. He tells himself that he should leave, that he has what he came for, that there is no further reason to stay. But the new wine of his luck is still tart on his tongue. He stops at the dicing tables, then turns around and walks back to the blackjack area. He sits on his same stool. In the interim the dealer has removed the cards from the bin on his left and fanned them in a neat, beckoning arc on the felt directly in front of him. There is no one else at the table. "Well, Monsieur, do you wish to play again?" "Do you have a limit? What is your limit here?" "The limit, Monsieur?" "The betting limit. What is it?" Dennis hears someone behind him say, "I'm sure we can cover whatever you wish to wager, Monsieur." When Dennis turns, he sees the man in the blue tuxedo standing like a *maître d'hotel*, waiting patiently for his decision. "I want to play one hand at ten thousand francs." "Just one hand, Monsieur?" "Yes. One hand at ten thousand francs." "Are you certain, Monsieur?" "Yes." The dealer has already made a solid rectangle of the fanned cards and is shuffling them from hand to hand before he separates the stack into equal halves and riffles them together into a single rectangle again. He slides a yellow marker down the side of the shuffled deck until Dennis tells him with a movement of his right hand to stop. At that point the dealer slides the yellow marker into the deck, cuts the cards at the marker and slips the newly shuffled and cut deck into the bracket on his left. Then, with five snapping sounds, he counts out five cards and places them face-up in the waste-bin on his right. "Are you ready, Monsieur? One hand for ten thousand francs." Out comes the first face-down card to Dennis before the dealer slides face-up to himself the eight of hearts. Tipping the edge of his card toward him, Dennis sees that it is the deuce of clubs. The dealer goes to the bracket and slides the three of hearts to Dennis. "Again," says Dennis. The dealer slides the five of diamonds to Dennis. "Again, please." Out comes the five of spades. Dennis sees that he now has four cards with an accumulated card count of fifteen. "One more, please." The dealer snaps a six of spades from the bracket and pushes it across the felt. Even before the card reaches him, Dennis has turned over his face-down cards to show that he has won automatically with a five-card total of twenty-one points. He faces the man in the blue tuxedo. Meanwhile, the dealer, just to finish the game, has dealt himself a three of clubs and a jack of hearts to go with his five of diamonds. Shrugging, he gathers all the cards and begins shuffling them all over again. The man in the blue tuxedo tells Dennis to gather his francs and follow him to the exchange. Once there the man converses in rapid French with the cashier, who immediately removes ten new one-thousand franc notes from the till, counts them out across the counter to Dennis and asks him to sign a blue receipt of the transaction. That signed, Dennis tucks the new francs around the sandwich of francs in his pocket and leaves. He almost runs across the square to the Café de Paris where Ramuz is slouched against the table, asleep. After returning the sportcoat he borrowed and tipping the waiter for the loan of it, Dennis sits at the table and shakes Ramuz by the shoulder until he awakens, not by degrees but with a start. Ramuz looks around, bewildered, "Dennis, where are we? Where am I?" "Just where I left you." Ramuz rubs his eyes. Little by little his bewilderment leaves him. After he stands, stretches, and belches, he looks down at Dennis and grins. "You have a good look in your face, Dennis," "I won." "How much?" "All that I need for de Savigny plus interest." "How much?" "The two thousand that you threw on the platform back there plus another 10,000." "*Mon Dieu*, I don't believe it!" "Why not?" "Because you could have lost. Most people lose." "I didn't." "What are you going to do now?" "We're going back to the cottage." They return to Anubis. The drive from Monte Carlo back to his cottage near Vence reminds Dennis of his old jaunts when he toured the highways and roads after midnight, using the drives only as an excuse to breathe the moist early morning air. Now with the francs bulging his pockets, he drives with a sense of debts squared, and he knows exactly what he is going to do. When he arrives at the cottage near Vence, he has to help Ramuz into the living room. Ramuz keeps talking in semisleep as he collapses on the sofa and begins snoring instantly. Dennis then removes the francs from his pocket and slams them on the kitchen table as if the violence of his swing will tame them forever. Then he begins to pace the kitchen, rubbing his hands together like a man attempting to keep warm. After five minutes, he stops, picks up the francs and flings them underhand up to the ceiling. The francs flutter down all over the kitchen like a paper storm. Standing in the midst of this snow of francs, Dennis feels the notes brush his face and ears as they fall. After standing among the fallen notes, he stalks into his bedroom, lies supine on the bed with his hands clasped behind his neck. He is determined not to sleep, but he soon feels himself slipping past the silence of the room into a deeper silence that eventually rafts him away. He is awakened at dawn by Ramuz, who is shouting at him that it's time to get up and drive to the circus, that there is a performance, that, *mon Dieu*, there are francs all over the kitchen. Dennis turns on his side and then slides into a sitting position on the edge of the bed as Ramuz enters the room and says, "What are you going to do with all this money?" "That's my business." "There's more than five hundred francs in the sink, for God's sake. I can't even get a glass of water." "Leave everything where it is." An hour later they arrive at the circus. Dennis hurries to his dressing wagon and slips into tights for the wirewalk. He tries to think only of what he must think of to give his usual performance, but his mind is filled with thoughts of Denise, of her father, of the francs strewn and left in the kitchen of his cottage. Even when he leaves the wagon and is finally standing at the base of the angled wire that leads upward to the performance wire itself, he struggles to concentrate on nothing else but what he must do. Up the wire he walks, balance-pole in hand, until he is standing on the small, circular pedestal that is his final resting spot before he steps off and balances in space. Below, the saving net sags and waits. The watchers in the stands go mute as the drumroll announces the start of the act. The drummer smacks the cymbal hard with a final flash of his sticks, and Dennis, as he has done hundreds of times before on the same wire, steps off the pedestal. He grips the wire with the sole of his left foot and his fisted toes before he takes a second step. He steadies himself with the pole as he proceeds step by step until he reaches midpoint on the wire. Again the drumroll mounts to an explosion of cymbals to herald that part of his act where he has to change direction by making a quick reverse jump, a jump so rapid that he is able to release the pole, reverse direction, and catch the pole before it is able to hit the wire. Now Dennis listens to the drums as if they are announcing a beheading. The soles of his feet seem cemented to the wire. He wills himself to jump, but he cannot. At last he returns to the pedestal with a caution that surprises him and waves to the audience as the confused drummer stops in midbeat. Slowly Dennis steps with the same caution down the angled wire to the hay-covered ground. He drops the pole, bows quickly to the mildly applauding audience and hurries to his dressing room. He enters, closes the door behind him, and leans against it as if for support. His hands are shaking, and his forehead gleams with its own sweat. After several moments he walks to his makeup table and sits down on a swivel stool just as Ramuz, without the warning of a knock or a call, enters the room. "*Mon Dieu*, Dennis what happened to you up there? I could have done better than that myself." "Close the damn door, Ramuz, and shut up." "Shut up? Wait until you hear the ringmaster. He should be here any minute. I want to see you tell him to shut up." Dennis is already shedding his tights and putting on his street clothes. "Tell him I had to throw up, Ramuz. Tell him I got sick up there. Tell him anything." "What the hell's wrong with you? Do you still have that girl on your mind? Are you going to let her take your guts, make a coward out of you?" "Not a coward, Ramuz. Not that kind of coward." He starts to buckle his belt and continues, "I just asked myself for the first time in my whole life why I was risking my neck up there, and I couldn't give myself an answer. I came up empty. And it paralyzed me. I couldn't go on." "You see? That girl is the problem. She's making you think. I warned you about this. She's going to turn you into *merde*. You'll see. You'll see." Dennis leaves the wagon, mounts Anubis, and drives with his newly acquired circumspection back to the cottage. Each car that passes him from the opposite direction seems suddenly to become the threat of a possible collision. He imagines himself failing to avert the swerving grill of car after car, smashing into headlights, ricocheting from bumpers, hurtling into a face-down sprawl on the shoulder of the road or over a precipice while Anubis careens past him and explodes. His clothes cling to his sweating body as if he has showered in them. When he reaches the cottage, he leaves the motor of his cycle idling softly. Then he enters the kitchen and collects all the strewn notes into a compact bundle. He places the bundled notes in a kitchen towel, slips the tight package under his shirt, returns to Anubis, and steers with unaccustomed slowness toward the de Savigny chateau. All the way there he wonders about his sudden preference for lesser speeds, as if his life suddenly matters to him, matters intensely, in a way that is beyond reason or avoidance. He breathes with a new sense of immediacy, as if every breath might be his last, as if the air that he has all his life taken for granted is as sacred as his own heartbeat, as the puff and easing of his lungs, as the song of his blood. The road before him is no longer a track that invites him to open the throttle on Anubis and go. It now seems like a danger that he must dare and somehow survive, not merely a distance that waits to be humbled by the scorn of his speed. Or rather it is a route where lives pass one another at high speeds, where the worst possibilities can become facts by something as minuscule as a pebble or a smear of sand or a spurt of grease. Riding on Anubis, he suddenly becomes aware of what being alone means. Past the rocky promontory near Boileau he steers—alone. Past the Negresco Hotel in Nice—alone. Still farther, past the new, S-shaped apartments on the road to Antibes—alone. The solitude of the ride introduces him to a different brand of fear, and it remains with him until he turns up the elm-lined driveway to the de Savigny estate. Elm by elm by elm he motors up the drive and then parks at the head of the key. Touching the stuffed towel inside his shirt to make sure it has not come undone, he heads for the main door of the chateau and knocks. While he waits for a response, he removes the package of francs from inside his shirt and holds it at his side like a book. Finally, the door is opened and Dennis is facing Seth de Savigny, who regards him as he might regard a peddler. The young de Savigny swings the door open all the way, stations himself in the doorway and asks in the tone of a demand, "What do you want?" "I am here to see your father. I think he is expecting me." Seth de Savigny studies Dennis suspiciously for a moment before he says, "Yes, follow me." He faces about and steps ahead of Dennis down the hall toward the study. Without even turning to make sure that Dennis is following him, he opens the study door and enters. By the time Dennis steps into the study, he sees Seth de Savigny standing at the right side of his father, who is seated at his desk. Without smiling or frowning, Sanche de Savigny watches Dennis approach the desk and stop a few feet in front of it. Then he says, "Good afternoon, Mr. Holt. I frankly did not expect to see you so soon." "I didn't think there was any reason to waste time. The alternatives were quite clear to me." "Very good, very good. I assume that my package was waiting for you yesterday." "Yes." "And I assume that it contained exactly what I said would be in it." "Yes." "I believe in accuracy, Mr. Holt, regardless of the situation. Don't you agree?" For the first time de Savigny permits himself a smile. Then, noticing the towel-wrapped package in Dennis's hand, he asks, "Did you bring your lunch, Mr. Holt? I doubt if our transaction will take that long."

He pauses and pushes his chair back from the desk. "Tell me, Mr. Holt. Would you rather that my daughter be present for this or not? I don't want to make this any more difficult for you—for both of you—than it has to be. But I think everything would be simplified once and for all if Denise were here even though it might be awkward." "Yes, sir, I agree. I would rather that she be here." Sanche de Savigny whispers to his son in French and sends him out of the study. When he sees that he is gone, Sanche de Savigny walks around the desk until he is facing Dennis. Then, with a gesture, he suggests that Dennis follow him to the bay window that offers a view of his estate. "I want to make sure you understand something, Mr. Holt. In your country there is really too much freedom when it comes to marriage. People marry for what they think is love and within a few years the marriage is over. But this is a Catholic country. Our values are different. In France we place much more emphasis on families, on the background of a person, on . . ." "On breeding?" "Yes, precisely. On breeding. It lasts much longer than love. It reaches from the past through the present into the future. It does not concern itself only with the moment, do you understand?" Dennis nods his head once before de Savigny continues. "This estate, Mr. Holt, has been in the hands of my family since the Middle Ages. It is part of the history of this part of France. We are older than the Grimaldis." He pauses again and gestures at the estate through the bay window. "My daughter, even after she marries, will always be thought of as my daughter, do you understand? And that imposes a kind of duty on her. So she must have a husband who will be able to help her fulfill that duty. Her future is really not a personal matter at all. It's involved with history, with background. What I'm saying is not directed to you as a person. In fact, if you were from the right family, you would be as eligible as anyone." "But I'm not from the right family, is that what you're trying to tell me?" "In so many words, Mr. Holt, yes." Hearing Denise enter the study, they both turn away from the window. Denise smiles and nods to Dennis and seats herself in a chair beside the desk. When Dennis looks at her and then at the Isis tapestry behind and above her, he is struck by the resemblance between Denise and the Byzantine features of the image in the tapestry. *"Bon jour, Papá,"* says Denise. "Did you want to see me?" Sanche de Savigny nods yes as he seats himself in his desk chair. Dennis returns to his initial position in front of the desk. At the same time Seth de Savigny reenters the study and stands like a soldier on post at the right hand of his father. For a minute or so no one speaks, and Denise looks apprehensively first at her father and then at Dennis. Finally, Sanche de Savigny, folding his hands on the desktop and pondering them like a presiding judge, says, "Denise, Mr. Holt and I had a conversation yesterday in which we discussed the feeling that has developed between the two of you over the past summer, and we spoke about the implications of this for the future . . ." Denise sits forward in her chair and says, "Yes, Papá." "This was all done at my suggestion. And I want you to know that it was done with your good in mind. I think that Mr. Holt now has a good grasp of the realities, and I am going to ask him to speak for himself at this point. He has something he wants to say to you." "What's happening, Dennis?" asks Denise. "What are you keeping from me?" Dennis looks first at Denise, then at her brother and finally at Sanche de Savigny himself. Just then he hears another person enter the room and stand by the door. Turning, he recognizes Denise's mother, Clothilde. He refaces de Savigny and says with an almost measured slowness, "Mr. de Savigny, I think what I have to say is really not going to be easy for me. I don't know if I can put it in the right words. It's true that my family tree doesn't go back to the Renaissance. And, to be perfectly frank about it, my work as a circus clown and wirewalker is not the best preparation for the kind of husband you want for your daughter. I'm not ashamed of my work. There's nothing else I'd rather do. I chose it. And I never thought much about family background until you made me conscious of it. And I certainly never thought about it in regard to Denise. She was just Denise to me, and that was enough." He looks at Denise for a moment and then resumes. "The only real distinction in my background is that my father was killed in France not very far from here, but that's my father's distinction, not mine. From your point of view I suspect that I have no credentials at all. And I would have to agree that I don't have what you're looking for. Not one credential. Except one." "And what is that, Mr. Holt? "I . . ." Dennis starts and pauses, "I love your daughter." Sanche de Savigny looks at his son, who begins to smile and then looks away in a kind of mock exasperation.

"This will be my wedding dinner—lemon pie and capuccino." They are both smiling when they enter the restaurant and seat themselves at a corner table. They are the only ones there. After Dennis places their order with the waitress, he rises from the table and says, "I'll be right back, Denise." She looks at him curiously, but he smiles reassuringly and says that he will be gone for only a few moments. With that, he leaves the restaurant and trots down the road for almost a hundred meters to a small, white perfume factory on the side of the mountain. He tries the main door. Locked. Then he tests each of the side doors. All locked. He is about to return to the restaurant when he hears one of the side doors being opened. A stout woman in a yellow uniform looks at him inquisitively while she shakes her dust mop in the air. He walks toward her and is about to speak when she says, "*Fermée, monsieur.*" She makes a motion with her hand—the act of locking a door with a key. Dennis then explains, partly in French and partly in English when his French fails him, that it is essential that he buy a small flask of the factory's best perfume. "Emergency," he says, using his hands for emphasis, "emergency." The woman shakes the mop again and repeats, "*Fermée, monsieur.*" Dennis implores her in French, "But, madame, it is for a new bride. It is a wedding present. The bride will be disappointed, very disappointed." He continues to speak beseechingly to the woman until finally she drops the mop, throws her hands in the air, mutters an oath, retrieves the mop, and withdraws into the factory, leaving the mop cross-angled in the doorway like a prohibitive pike. She returns in a few moments with a small, aluminum flask for Dennis, accepts the francs that he forces on her and then, with a gesture like a penguin flexing both wings, she goes back for her mop as Dennis trots back up the hill to the restaurant. Denise is still sitting like a waif at the corner table. The servings of lemon pie and the paired, filled cups are untouched in front of her. When she sees Dennis, she starts to stand but sits again as he reseats himself beside her. "Did you think I was going to disappear, Denise?" "I did not know what to think." "Close your eyes." "Close my eyes?" "Yes, close them. All the way." After she complies, he removes the flask from his pocket and stands it on the table in front of her. "You can open your eyes now." For a minute Denise does not seem to see it. Then she takes the flask in both hands

"Mr. Holt," says de Savigny, "why must we persist in this direction?" "It's not persistence, sir. It's how things are. I don't expect you to be impressed with this, but I'm saying it anyway. It's all I have to say. And the only way I can prove that I mean it is to do what I'm going to do now." Dennis places the package of francs on the desk and opens it. "You have all the aces, sir. You can make life hell for me just by snapping your fingers. And you can do the same for Denise. But I'm not going to give you the pretext to do it to her." "Dennis," interrupts Denise, "I can speak for myself." "Be quiet, Denise!" shouts de Savigny and slams the desk with the flat of his hand before he says, "That's enough of this! What are you driving at, Mr. Holt? Be quick about it!" "What I'm driving at, sir, is that I love Denise enough to walk out of this house and not make her life miserable. And that's more than you can do. You're not man enough to know when to let go or even how to let go. You talk like some duke out of the sixteenth century. How can you call yourself a father when you're nothing but someone who wants to pull the strings on people's lives?" "Mr. Holt, this is quite ..." "No, it's not enough. You're just a self-centered, small-minded, dictatorial little bastard, and you don't even see it. You don't even realize what you are." Seth de Savigny starts to move around the desk toward Dennis, but his father restrains him. Dennis continues talking, "Here's the money you sent to pay me off for not seeing Denise again ..." "Papá!" exclaims Denise and comes to her feet. "The money is all here, Mr. de Savigny," says Dennis, pushing the stacked francs across the desk. "Papá," screams Denise, "you gave him money!" Dennis takes his hands off the francs and stares at de Savigny, "There's 20,000 francs there, and there's another 10,000 francs in interest with it. You can use the extra money to try to buy back your daughter's respect for you." Dennis keeps looking at de Savigny to make sure that his words have hit home before he turns to Denise, who is not only in tears but has a look of bewilderment, almost terror in her eyes. Dennis then walks to the door, passing Clothilde de Savigny before he retraces his steps down the hall to the front door and out. He is about to start his motorcycle when he sees Denise dash from the chateau and run toward him. The motor starts with the first twist of the ignition, and he turns the motorcycle around toward the aisle of elms. Just then he feels Denise grab at his shirt and almost tug him from the seat as she screams, "Dennis, please, for God's sake, stop! Stop, Dennis!" She releases his shirt and runs directly in front of Anubis so that Dennis has to brake hard to keep from running into her. Denise seizes the handlebars from the front and shouts over the sound of the idling motor, "I'm going with you, Dennis. I'm not staying here. I'm going if I have to run after you. I swear it." "Get away, Denise." "No!" "It's no use. Don't you see that?" "Don't talk to me that way. I'm not a baby. I know what I'm doing. Everybody keeps trying to make up my mind for me. But who takes the trouble to ask me what matters to me? Who?" "Move away, Denise." "No, I won't move. The only way you can stop me is to run over me. All right. Go ahead. Go ahead and do it." Dennis looks to his left and sees Sanche de Savigny watching them from his study's bay window. Then he glimpses Seth de Savigny running from the rear door to a garage that stands like the reconverted stable it is behind the chateau. Denise continues to hold the handlebars of Anubis with both hands while she stands almost astride the front tire. "All right, Denise," says Dennis, "Get on." Denise hurries to the rear of the motorcycle, takes her position behind him, and circles his chest with her arms as he puts Anubis in gear and veers under the overarching elms to the main road and then eastward. For mile after mile the sound of the motor is all he hears, all he wants to hear. The scene with de Savigny in the chateau is now joined to the receding dream of his life for the previous twenty-four hours. He finds himself wondering if everything that happened really *did* happen. In the meanwhile, Denise, with her arms around his chest, is occasionally shaken by sudden shudders but otherwise is silent as he. Each time he hears a car accelerating behind him, he half-expects it to be driven by Denise's brother, but each time he is wrong. After driving for more than half an hour, he turns off the corniche halfway between Nice and Monaco and heads inland where he again sees some of the surviving rubble of war—the remains of pillboxes and machine gun emplacements in the sides of mountains, the dynamited foundations of bridges that are now nothing more than a cairn of fallen stones and broken mortar in a chasm. He thinks of his father, of the crisscross of circumstances and choices that have interwoven themselves into a destiny and made his meeting with Denise seemingly inevitable, of the bond between him and the

girl who has her arms around him as he drives at forty kilometers per hour in the quiet, French mountains—a bond whose only reality is the seal of its own silence as he drives. When Dennis reaches a point where the road forks, he stops Anubis and says, "We should decide where we're going, Denise." "It doesn't matter." "But it does. Your father probably has the police looking for us already. Or if he doesn't he will. By tomorrow, everything will be over. And by tomorrow night, I'll probably be deported as an undesirable alien. The whole scenario was made quite clear to me." "It doesn't matter, Dennis. I'll follow you." He turns sideways on his seat as she lifts her face to him. She looks up at him as she has always looked at him, but now he finds that he can return the look and not avert his eyes. He brings his face closer to hers and kisses her on the cheek, then on the lips. "Everything is against us, Denise. You know that." "It does not matter. There is right now. We have right now, Dennis. And later I will follow you no matter where you are." "It may be difficult." "But it is what I want." She pauses and then, without raising her eyes to him, says, "In my heart I am your wife, Dennis. It's how I see myself, how I always saw myself. Now I am sure, and I will do what a wife has to do." "There's not a priest in France who would marry us, Denise." "But *I* can marry *you*. And I do. I'm serious. I marry you. The priest can come at any time. He can come later or never. The feeling is between us, Dennis. We are the ones." "It's not a very beautiful ceremony, Denise. Two people on a motorcycle on a country road. No flowers. No singing." "It's a good ceremony. *We* are the ceremony." She pauses again and raises her eyes to his. She looks at him without blinking. "Do you marry me, Dennis?" Dennis kisses her again on the cheek, the lips, then on each eyelid. "Yes, Denise. I marry you." Adjusting himself on the seat, he makes a U-turn and heads back to the corniche where the traffic is already beginning to thicken with late afternoon drivers. Again, finding himself imbued with a new sense of caution, Dennis keeps to his right before he eventually curves off the road and travels down the small shunt to Eze. The parking lot is empty of cars and tourist buses. Dennis parks Anubis so that it is partially concealed from the road by several trees. Then he and Denise walk slowly toward the restaurant where he has taken her earlier. "Do you still like lemon pie, Denise?" Smiling at him, she answers,

and smiles at him. "It's not much of a wedding present, Denise, but it's all that's available at the moment." "But I love it . . ." She kisses him. "Now let's drink our coffee. It's getting cold." In silence they begin sipping the capuccino like wine from separate chalices until the cups are empty. They are not listening to the sudden thunder, and it is minutes before they hear the rain ricocheting off the windows of the restaurant. Dennis looks at Denise and says, "Even the elements are against us." "It does not matter what is against us. Not any more. Not now." She reaches for his hand and holds it with both of hers. After several minutes the waitress approaches their table and asks them if they want something else to eat. Dennis indicates with a nod rather than a word that they are finished. The waitress returns to the counter, sits sidesaddle on one of the high stools, removes a pack of cigarettes from her blouse pocket, selects one cigarette, and lights it quickly with a wax match. Dennis, his hand still held by Denise, watches the waitress smoke the cigarette halfway down while the rain bounces and pings on the restaurant windows. By the time the waitress finishes the cigarette, the rain has become so intense that it is striking the windows like hail. Dennis leaves Denise at the table and saunters past the waitress to the door. Peeking out, he sees rivulets sluicing into cascades from the heights of Eze to the roadway above the parking lot. The water rushing down past the door of the restaurant reminds Dennis of a mountain river in flood. Then he looks up at the lowered sky where the clouds are shouldering into and over one another like bison. He returns to the waitress and asks, "What time is it, *mademoiselle?*" "Seven. Five after seven." "If the rain keeps up, is there a hotel near here where we can stay tonight?" "No, *monsieur*. I am sorry, but there is nothing." "Where can we go then? You close in half an hour. We have to go somewhere." The waitress shrugs a French no, as if to say she has no idea and, what's more, it's not her problem, really. Dennis heads back for the table but stops when he hears the waitress say, "If you and madame prefer, you may be able to stay in Jean-Luc's apartment. He lives up there in Eze. He is in London since three days to sell his prints, and he will be there for three days more. He left the key with me. If you and madame are, if you will excuse me, prudent, I can let you stay for tonight." "Thank you, but I want you to know that I am willing to pay for the room." "As you wish, *monsieur*, but the payment is not necessary." The waitress removes a single key from a ring of keys behind the counter and gives it to Dennis. "I do not know how you and madame will get up there in this rain. It is formidable. I do not even have an umbrella to give you." "Where is the apartment?" "After you reach Eze, you must go to the church. Jean-Luc's apartment is three doors up from the church. You will see his name and his prints and watercolors in a window beside the door." She steps behind the counter and turns off a hanging overhead light by pulling down on a string. "If you and madame leave early tomorrow before I am open, you may slide the key under the door." Dennis removes several francs from his pocket and offers them to the waitress, who waves him off and smiles. Then he calls for Denise to join him, and they go to the doorway. The waitress turns off the remaining lights in the restaurant and takes a position at the door slightly behind them. The rain shows no signs of slackening. "*Mon Dieu*," says the waitress, slapping her forehead lightly with the palm of her right hand, "This will last all night. This will do damage, this rain." "Do you stay here? "Yes, *monsieur*. My room is upstairs. I am sorry that you and madame have to walk up to Eze, but it is all I can offer you." "No, we appreciate it, *mademoiselle*." "It is nothing, *monsieur*. I am happy to be able to help you and madame. Jean-Luc would not object. I am sure of that." Crowding toward the doorstep, Dennis smiles a last smile at the waitress. Holding Denise by the hand, he leads her into the enfilade of rain. They start to run halfway up the road, their feet drowning in the rushing sluices of water that engulf the road. Almost unable to see ahead, they turn around and begin backing their way up the remaining distance until they reach the cannon-guarded entrance to the village. There they stop under a cowl of rock and look at one another. "Dennis, you look as if you just came out of the sea. This rain is unbelievable." Dennis laughs and jumps up and down in place several times. "In that case, I have to shake the sea out of my clothes. It's making me ten pounds heavier." Denise hugs her sides and tries to stop herself from shivering. "*Froid*. I feel so cold all of a sudden, Dennis." "We still have a little way to go, and then we'll be all right. Just stay close behind me." Once again he steps out into the open where the buckshot-rain forces him to walk close to the walls for what little protection they offer. As they near the passage leading downward to the church, they pass the donkey that they both saw on their first visit to Eze. The donkey's sides gleam in the rain as if they have been oiled. The animal does not look at them as they pass but continues staring passively ahead at the wall to which it is tethered. Dennis keeps walking until he reaches a low doorway beyond the church. Beside the door is a glassed display of an assortment of prints. He points to the door and says to Denise, "This is it." After removing the key from his pocket, he inserts it in the lock and twists. The door swings open, and Dennis leads Denise in out of the rain. After groping for a lamp and switching it on, Dennis sees that he is in an old living room that has been converted into a studio. The original wooden floor, waffled but solid, is covered with a few throw rugs. Across the room is a large fireplace flanked by a studio couch. Tipped against the walls on his left and right are dismantled easels together with unframed prints and paintings. Dennis walks toward the fireplace and says, "We could use a fire." Seeing that several logs are already on the iron grate, he looks for newspapers and matches, finds them, and soon has the logs burning softly but steadily. Denise seats herself on the studio couch and looks at the hatching fire as if she is trying to look through it. When Dennis comes to the couch and sits beside her, she breaks her fire-stare and puts her head against his shoulder. "We're going to get this couch good and wet for Jean-Luc," says Dennis. "Jean-Luc?" "Our host." Dennis stands and watches the shifting shadows of the fire reach and flare across the floor. Denise stands beside him and says, "Will you help me?" "How?" She turns her back to him, reaches around with one hand to lift her hair away from the nape of her neck and says again, "Will you help me with the zipper there?" He draws the zipper of her sweater slowly down until it stops just between her shoulder blades. "Thank you," says Denise before she walks to the fire and pulls the sweater up and over her head. She then stands nude from the waist up before the fire, warming herself. After a moment she drapes the sweater to dry over a basket handle to the right of the grate. Then with the same matter-of-fact motion that she used to pull off the sweater, she takes off her skirt and undergarments and places them beside the sweater. For a few seconds she remains crouched by the fire as if she is alone in the room. Dennis cannot take his eyes from her. Nude, she seems smaller to him. While he watched her undress, he could not help thinking that she reminded him of someone preparing for a sacred ablution or sacrifice. Now he has no other image of her except as herself. As a reflex, he strips the spread from the studio couch and carries it toward her. She does not turn. When he is behind her, he carefully covers her shoulders and back until she is completely tented. "You should hang your clothes there, Dennis. The longer you wear them, the colder you will be." As if he has done it in her presence a hundred times before, he unbuttons his shirt, skins it off, and then rolls down his trousers and soaked underwear and drapes them on the side of the fireplace opposite her. Finally, he removes his shoes and socks and spreads them in a compact quartet in front of the fire. Denise has shifted from her crouch and is sitting on one of the throw rugs. She holds open the edge of the spread like a tent flap and asks him with her eyes to sit beside her. The first touch of his skin against hers chills him, chills them both simultaneously so that for an instant they draw instinctively closer to the fire and clutch the spread more tightly around them. They remain so, like bedouin under a desert shawl, while the fire shadows play across their faces. He places his right hand around her and draws her closer to him as she says, "We are like Romeo and Juliet, aren't we, Dennis?" "What do you mean?" "Doomed." "Is that any way to talk on your wedding night?" "We are still like Romeo and Juliet. We are putting our whole life into one night." "There will be other nights. Other places. This is a big world." "But not for us." "Don't talk that way. If your father has me deported, I'll somehow get word to you. This isn't the Middle Ages. I'll get in touch with you if it takes forever." "Do you mean that?" He pauses and then starts to say, "Denise . . ." But he cannot go on. "Dennis, please talk to me. You have to talk to me, chéri. I want to memorize everything you say to me. It has to last." In response he simply tightens his grip around her shoulder. "Talk to me, Dennis, please." He loosens his grip slightly and says, "I was just thinking that here we are in a place named after Isis. It's almost prophetic." "How?" "The scene. The circumstances. Isis had to wait for her husband after he had to go away. But she found him after all. Even death couldn't stop that. When she found him, she covered him with her wings until he left the kingdom of Anubis . . ." "Anubis?" "The god of death. It's part of the story." "But that is the name of the motorcycle." "I'm going to change the name. I'll rechristen it." He smiles, but she is not smiling. "Dennis?" "Yes." "Why are you telling me this?" "Because the coincidence just hit me." She looks at him directly. "Do I remind you of her, of Isis?" "More than you know." Denise turns to him and, smiling, puts her arms around him, "Can I hold you like this with my wings, Dennis?" He pulls her gently toward him and kisses her. When they part, he sees in her eyes the same look he saw in them in Nice, on the bridge near Eze—the same look she had when she stared at the fire. "You know, Denise, you always look at me like an X-ray. I can't hide from your eyes." She closes her eyes and eases herself toward him with her arms. When she hugs and kisses him, he feels how soft her lips have become, soft and slightly cold. Afterward, Denise turns toward the fire, which is now burning in fierce, orange flames. "I can't understand how my father could do it, Dennis. How could he offer you money like that?" Dennis, knowing that she is really asking herself the question or asking it at large, does not respond. He lets the silence prolong itself between them. Then he says, "Do you remember what you asked me a moment ago?" "When?" "You asked me to talk to you." "Yes." "And I couldn't. I tried, but I couldn't. The words just weren't there." "Are the words there now?" "They may not be the ones you want to hear, but I have to say them, Denise." They both face the fire as he continues. "I'm not proud of the way I've lived, Denise. I don't mean that I'm not happy with what I'm doing. I am. And I'm good at it. It's as worthwhile to me as anything else. After all, everything's a kind of circus, isn't it? But I'm not talking about that. I'm talking about the way I've lived, the way I've looked at people, thought about people, even used people." She is looking directly at him now. "The strange thing that's happened, Denise, is that you've spoiled all that. You've shown me something that I thought didn't really exist, and you've done it without really trying. You've done it just by being who you are. I see it everytime you look at me, so that the only time I feel I'm alive, really alive, is when I'm with you, when I can see you, touch you. Now." He pauses. "What I'm trying to tell you, Denise, is that I can't be what I was any more. But at the same time I don't know where I can go. Or how. I don't know what's ahead. All I'm really sure of is this minute." "But who knows more than that, Dennis? Nobody can go back. And nobody knows what's coming. All we have is right now, and even that is passing as soon as I say it." A log cracks in the grate and splits in its center like an overbaked loaf. Dennis feels the sudden flash of heat against his cheeks before the log settles into a steady smouldering. Shifting position beside her, he starts to speak, thinks better if it, and tries to remain aware only of his arm around her bare shoulder with his suspended hand brushing her right breast just under her armpit. "Silence is really better, Dennis. It has all the answers. It says everything." The cracked log collapses into itself again with a bright shatter of wood sparks. Dennis stands, removes another log from a stack beside the fireplace, and places it carefully over the embers. Denise, watching him, says, "You look like Adonis standing there." "Not Adonis. Osiris. You're mixing the two stories." She draws the spread around her, sits up, and leans forward until she is resting her chin on the knees of her drawn up legs. "Somewhere out there they are looking for us, Dennis. I'm sure of it. My brother is, anyway. That's certain." "Don't think of that now." "I can't *not* think of it." "I've already decided what has to be done. It doesn't matter what they do. Besides, no one can start looking for us as long as it's raining like this." "What are you planning, Dennis? What are you going to do?" "Tomorrow I'm going to give you the key to my house so you'll have it. Then I'm going to drive you home, to the chateau. After that I'll take Anubis and go to Italy. I have friends in San Remo. Later I can find work with the circus in Milan. That should take no more than two weeks. Then I'll get word to you." "But why do you want to take me back to the chateau? What is there for me at home? My mother is the only one who understands . . ." "What else can we do? Where else is there for you to go?" "With you!" "It's no use, Denise. I'm sure your father has every border crossing on notice by now. And every railroad station. And every airport. He would bring you home anyway. The only choice is to go back willingly or else be dragged back." "But I want them to drag me back! I want them to know that I never want to go back there. Ever!" "What would that prove? The result would be just the same." "Not for me, Dennis!" He detects in her voice the same finality and fierceness that were there when she dropped the broken rabbit into the chasm from the bridge railing near Nice, and

he knows enough about this kind of indomitability to recognize it
when he sees it. Crouching in front of her, he whispers, "There's a
real tiger inside of you, isn't there, Denise?" She reaches up and puts
her right palm at the back of his neck. The spread that is draped
around her suddenly separates. As he looks down at her, she appears
foreshortened like a swimmer breaking water after a dive. "You are
all I fight for, chéri," she says to him distantly, "all I fight for." She
reaches up with her left hand and joins both hands behind his neck.
Together they get to their feet and stand before the fire, face to face,
waist to waist, knee to knee, so that the smallest glimmer of firelight
does not whisper its way between them. They do not kiss but simply
stand, his right cheek against her right temple. After a moment she
relaxes her grip and draws away. She walks slowly toward the studio
couch. Dennis notices how the evenly cut lengths of her hair, dry now
after the rain, are curling at their tips and fluttering against her shoulder blades as she moves. She pauses at the edge of the studio couch
and then lies on her right side, drawing her left leg up slightly. When
he sits on the couch beside her and waits for her to look up at him, she
keeps her left arm angled softly across her face like someone trying
halfheartedly to keep the sun out of her eyes. After several moments
he puts his hand on her waist and feels her pull away slightly before
she lets her waistflesh relax against the heel of his hand. Hesitantly he
moves his palm, permitting it to shape itself to her hip, then across
her hip and down the relaxed length of the back of her thigh until his
fingers burrow softly into the damp pocket of her knee-pit. She makes
a slight moaning sound but does not move. Her elbow remains limp
across her eyes. A memory of Yvette insinuates itself into his mind.
He tries to be rid of it, but, like a leech, it will not be removed. The
memory blurs and then focuses—of Yvette supine on his bed and
daring him to arouse her, of Yvette in a tussle with him on the pillows,
of Yvette biting at his earlobe and laughing as they couple before a
pleasure she tries to resist but cannot deny or subvert silences her into
a final few grunts of satisfaction that she swears to him afterward
were feigned for his benefit. And then she laughs again as they separate, leaving him to ask himself what the hell he sees in her, and why,
in the afterward of their mating, he feels an emptiness that is almost
like nausea. And all the time, even when she goes into the bathroom

to wash her groin, Yvette is never more than a breath away from a laugh that is meant to tell him that nothing really matters, that nothing will change, nothing but their glands have been involved in a kind of mutual relief. Now, with his hand on the back of Denise's thigh, he hears Yvette's mocking laughter and his hand freezes. In a moment he withdraws the hand as if it has been involved in a violation. At the same moment, Denise lifts her elbow from across her eyes and looks at him. He has turned away from her and is staring at the fire. "What are you thinking of, Dennis?" "Nothing." "Is that an answer?" "Well, frankly, I was just thinking about myself, and I don't feel very good about it." "I thought we were going to forget about that, not talk about that. My solution is to tell myself that my life started when I first saw you. And it keeps starting again every time I see you. Everything else just fades away." "I'd like to be able to say that, but I can't." "Maybe you don't have the same feelings for me that I have for you, Dennis." "But I do. That's the problem. The man I *was* keeps coming back to bother me. He keeps trying to spoil every minute I have with you." "You shouldn't think that way, Dennis. All you do is make yourself suffer for nothing." "I can't help it. It just happens." "But you *can* help it. All you have to do is let go. Nobody should carry his old life around with him like a suitcase. It's over. Finished." "I know I don't have to, and I don't want to, but there it is anyway." Denise stands, walks slowly to the fire and says, "I just can't seem to get warm." Then she returns to the couch. Outlined against the glow of the fire, she seems to Dennis like a woman emerging from a dream. "You act as if you are ashamed, Dennis. Are you ashamed?" "Of what?" "Of us. Of me." "Only of myself, Denise." "Would it help if I told you that I love you? I love you enough to make my whole family turn against me. But I regret nothing. That old life is nothing to me. Compared to you now, it's like ashes." He stands and embraces her. This time they kiss as they stand closely together. When they end the first kiss, they kiss again before they lie side by side on the studio couch. Kissing her there, he runs his fingers through her rain-scented hair while she, her eyes lidded softly, presses herself against him. Raising himself on one elbow, he looks down the length of her small, flame-painted body. As he looks, she turns supine on the couch, her breasts taut and mounding so smoothly to the nipples that they re-

96

mind him of sculpture. He kisses her again and then eases his body
onto hers. He can feel her breathing quickly beneath him. She keeps
her legs together for a moment, then vees them slowly apart and
draws her knees up against his thighs so that he is able to enter her
without difficulty. Once he is inside of her, he feels her loins tense
against him, feels her embrace him with her legs as well as her arms
so that, together, the two of them form a moving, living knot on the
couch. With his cheek against hers, he feels the tautness in her body
slowly slacken and then regather with a different intensity as she
moves first slightly and then more strenuously against him until she
begins to shudder and whisper, "Help me, Dennis. Help me, please."
He responds by moving in reaction to her own movements. Her
whispering turns huskier just before it crescendos in two or three
little pants as she clutches him with a strength that surprises him.
Then she goes limp in his arms while he continues moving with a
rhythm of his own. After he subsides, he remains lying lightly on top
of her while she slides her flexed legs down on the couch and stretches
against him as if the life of every muscle in her body depends on it. "I
love you, Dennis," she says, "and I even love myself more when I'm
with you. I am not a very good lover, though, am I?" "You're fine." "I
can always learn. We have a long time to learn." He smiles as they
kiss. Then he lifts himself off of her and lies on his back beside her on
the couch. The only sound in the room is the occasional loud snap of
collapsing embers in the fireplace and the monotone of rain against
the windows. Dennis tries to understand his mood. He feels that a
different and better life is suddenly before him, that no one can deny
it to him but himself, that he is experiencing no distaste and not a jot
of regret. Instead, he knows only a pleasant tiredness that is more
than an aftereffect of satiety. It makes him want to talk. Without
turning toward her he asks, "Where are you, Denise?" "Right beside
you. Where else should I be?" "I'm walking on a wire over the Atlantic Ocean all the way to New York. And you're walking on it with
me. We're both walking as if we're walking on a sidewalk. How do
you feel?" "I'm getting dizzy." "Just watch me. You won't get dizzy.
I'll get you across safely. But you have to watch me. Every minute."
They turn toward one another, and she makes herself small in his
arms. In the grate the logs continue to die their occasionally loud but

always beautiful deaths. Dennis continues to hold Denise in his arms
until she is asleep. Occasionally a faint shudder passes through her
body, but she does not waken or move. The last thing Dennis hears
before he sleeps is the rain on the window hitting and glancing like
the weighted tips of a million whips. For some reason he tries to
remain awake. Slowly, so slowly that he does not realize how it is
happening, he listens to the clatter of the rain grow fainter and fainter, and his grip around Denise loosens. He keeps telling himself that
he is walking the Atlantic, that he cannot sleep. In the quick drift of
his dream, he sees the Atlantic change into the bridge that spans the
chasm beside Eze. He is approaching the bridge on Anubis. Before
he crosses the bridge, he stops, lets the motorcycle idle on its kick-
stand in the middle of the highway, and decides to proceed on foot
across. By the time he has crossed one-third of the bridge, he realizes
that the bed of the bridge is overgrown with moss and crabgrass. He
decides to turn around when he sees someone walking on the thin
bridge railing toward him. He recognizes the rail walker as Denise.
She waves to him. Instead of waving back, he opens his mouth to
shout a warning to her, but he cannot hear his own voice. After drawing in his breath, he tries to shout again, but there is only silence. He
starts to wave her away from the railing, but his hands suddenly
become like the hands of a wind-up toy that has already wound down
to nothing. Denise keeps on walking on the bridge railing toward
him. With every step she takes a greater risk. First she balances on
one leg. Then, with both eyes closed, she steps forward on faith alone.
Dennis starts to run toward her, but, as in so many of his previous
dreams, his legs ache with the strain of their own weight. He is like a
man struggling through deep sand or sloshing through swampwater.
The more he struggles, the more he feels that his legs are like iron
stumps. When he is finally within a few yards of Denise, he sees that
she is pirouetting like a ballet dancer on the rail. He keeps watching
as her foot slips off the railing. He reaches for her in an agony of
slowness, but she has already fallen beyond his reach. With one final
effort he hurls himself against the railing and stretches for her with
both arms, but she is plummeting down, down, down, down, her
arms raised toward him, her eyes drawing him after her, her lips
shaped into the hint of a sad smile. The scene does not end. Dennis

keeps reaching, and Denise keeps falling, forever out of the grasp of his hands until, with a choke that is almost the beginning of a scream, he wakes. Denise stirs beside him but continues to sleep. Even though the room is beginning to turn chilly, Dennis finds himself sweating. Instinctively, he retrieves the spread from the floor and covers Denise with it. Then he steps to the fireplace, pokers the few embers left in the grate into a core of fire and adds two more logs. After the logs have caught, he collects his now dry clothes and puts them on. He notes that there is no longer the rattle of rain against the window. When he looks through the smeared panes, he can see clearly out to the sea. The Mediterranean swells slowly and heavily toward the indistinct horizon, its surface spined with waves. Reflections of the ivory moon bleed shakily from wave to wave to wave. Cowling the seascape, the star-busy sky slurs outward from the coast toward the convex and shifting hump of the dark sea and Dennis lets his mind follow it still farther to the coast of Africa and back. When he turns away from the window, he sees that Denise is awake. She has obviously been watching him. "Couldn't you sleep, Dennis?" "A dream. It woke me up. I thought I'd get dressed and survey our kingdom." "Is it still raining" "No." "Will it be morning soon?" "I'd guess in about an hour." He seats himself beside her on the couch and, touching her hair, says, "How is my bride?" "That's nice. It's nice to hear you say that to me." "I'll say it every hour on the hour." Denise slides toward him and rests her cheek on his knee. Then she says, "After you give me the key to your house . . ." "*Our* house." "After you give me the key, is there anything you want me to do while you're in Italy?" "No, not really. I just want you to have the key in case. Later I'll get word to you from San Remo. I might need a few things by then. Some clothes, maybe. No matter what your father does, I'm planning on coming back some day. The house is mine. No one can take it away from me." He smooths her hair with his fingers several times and adds, "Your father is going to ask you all about tonight, Denise." After a pause Denise says, "I know." "It might be rough for you." "I am not ashamed, Dennis. And I am not afraid now." "I didn't mean it that way." "I will face my father. I can face him. I can face anyone, chéri." Silenced, he slides his palm over the silk of her hair. He sees that the fire is almost out. Suddenly there is the sound of a bell. It is a single bell and it is obvious that it is being rung by hand. While it rings, Denise sits up on the studio couch and says, "That must be the bell for the first Mass." Dennis watches her hurry to the grate where her clothes hang limp and dry. While she dresses, she looks at Dennis and asks, "Will you come with me?" "Where?" "To Mass. To the church." "I haven't been in a church for years, Denise." "Will you come with me?" "Is it important that I do? I'm not a very good hypocrite." "It would mean something to me if . . ." She walks to the door and opens it before adding, "I just want to start today with God, Dennis. I want . . . I can't explain it, but . . ." "You don't have to explain. I'll go with you. But let's straighten things up in here so that we don't have to come back. We can leave right from church." Together they shape the spread to the studio couch. Then Dennis jabs out the fire with a poker while Denise repositions several of the shifted throw rugs. Finished, they leave and lock the apartment and walk in the lightening darkness down the rock path to the church. The priest is already saying the Mass as they enter and select a pew. Denise kneels. Dennis sits. The priest turns from the altar, notices them, and proceeds. There is no one else in the church. Dennis concentrates on the two candles on either side of the tabernacle, fascinated by the way each is speared with the same length of orange fire. As the Mass goes on, the candles steadily melt, but the flames maintain an equal size. The priest intones and mumbles at the altar. At a certain point, Denise rises from the kneeler and, with her hands joined in front of her at the waist, she walks to the old wooden rail at the foot of the altar and kneels there until the priest descends, approaches her, and carefully places a white host on her tongue. Denise whispers something to the priest. The priest nods, looks in Dennis's direction and makes the sign of the cross in the air. Denise returns to the pew. Ten minutes later, after they have walked to the stone plaza in front of the church, Dennis asks her, "What did you whisper to the priest?" "I asked him if he would bless my husband." Dennis takes her hand and leads her to the church wall that overlooks the lower road. The early sun is brightening the roofs of the mountain houses below them and across the corniche and the still moist streets are gleaming cleanly. There are no cars parked in the lot beside the restaurant. Dennis can just glimpse the front wheel of Anubis beside the tree where he parked it. "I hope

I can start the motorcycle, Denise. The rain was very heavy and some of the points may have gotten soaked." "May I start it and drive it up here? I'd love to steer up that road at least as far as the gate." Dennis looks at her, laughs, and then sees that she is serious. "Do you think you can do it by yourself?" "Let me try it, Dennis. Please." "Okay." He hands her the keys and adds, "I'll just stay here and watch you." She kisses him excitedly and runs off. He watches her dash out of sight behind the buttress of the church and then reappear seconds later on the road below him. Framed for a moment in the cannon-defended arch entrance to Eze, she waves to him and then starts down the bending road to the parking lot. Watching her, Dennis barely notices a black Mercedes sedan that is parked just below the first bend in the road. When Denise comes abreast of the Mercedes, she glances into it, stops, and is about to retrace her steps up the road when two men emerge from the sedan, seize her by either arm and then pull and drag her into the rear seat. Seeing what is happening, Dennis is too shocked to make a move. He does not hear footsteps behind him. When he turns, he sees Seth de Savigny and another man only several yards away from him. The two of them stop, separate, and approach Dennis stealthily as if they expect him to bolt. "What do you want, Seth?" says Dennis. "Where are you going with her?" Seth de Savigny looks at Dennis with the same scorn that Dennis saw in his eyes at the chateau. "You've ruined my sister, you bastard. You're going to pay for it." "Where are you going with her?" Just then the other man with the young de Savigny makes his move toward Dennis and knocks him back against the wall with a half-punch, half-shove. Dennis avoids the man's second punch and braces himself for de Savigny. He notices for the first time that Seth de Savigny is gripping what looks like a gendarme's club, black at the handle and heavier at its tip than at the base. He approaches Dennis, swings, and strikes him on the upper arm. Wincing, Dennis reels to his left as de Savigny raises the club and prepares to strike a second blow. With a quick spring, Dennis mounts the chest-high church wall and tightropes his way out of range. De Savigny follows him, swinging the club in fierce arcs at Dennis's shanks, but Dennis, like a man jumping rope, times his leaps precisely so that de Savigny's sweeping swings scythe only the air. Finally, cursing him in French and frustrated by repeated misses, de Savigny stands back and throws the club. The butt-end strikes Dennis just below the Adam's apple, and he topples backward off the wall headfirst, flailing with his arms until he crashes into the wiry shrubbery at the base of the wall. He gasps for breath and begins to spit blood. He blinks as if someone has poured acid or thrown hot ashes in his eyes. He keeps blinking, but the light is already fading into a void that progresses from gray to pitch. The core of his right eye begins to smart and ache like a burn. He keeps reaching for something to grip, but the strength is gone from his arms. He feels himself slipping. Instead of struggling, he lets himself go. And that is all he remembers until he hears voices. He blinks several times, but the pain in his right eye makes blinking difficult, then impossible. The voices are closer now, French voices, men's voices, whispers, orders, shouts of caution. Dennis feels himself being lifted. He has the curious sensation that he is a spectator at his own wake, but the burning in his eyes convinces him with every pulsation that he is still alive. Men are holding him under the arms and easing him onto a stretcher. Then he hears the siren of an ambulance, and a man is saying to him in kind but peremptory French that he must remain on his back, that he is in good hands, that he is being taken to the hospital in Cimiez and that, no, he should not put his hands to his eyes. Dennis attempts to respond, but he is only able to swallow his own blood that keeps building up in his mouth like bile. He makes an effort to lift and turn his head so that he can spit, but he feels hands on his chest keeping him flat on the stretcher. He moves his lips to shape words but gives up. At last, all he wants to do is lie back and let himself be carried. He just wants to sleep, to sleep. Once in the ambulance and moving, he loses all sense of time, of place, and he drifts with the motion like a man at sea. Then he feels the ambulance stop, feels himself being lifted from his stretcher to another stretcher, this one more padded and sturdier, and then wheeled over smooth floors to a slow halt. After a long pause he hears himself being told in French by a man he will later know as Dr. Russi that he is being prepared for surgery, that he is in Cimiez, that he, Dr. Russi, will be the surgeon in charge. And that is all he remembers until he wakes hours later in the same darkness and touches the bandages over his eyes and lies spent and nauseated in a seige of exhaustion that is so total that he thinks he will never want to wake or walk again. But he remains awake, and the voices that he hears are voices that he knows. One is the voice of Dr. Russi, and the other, yes, no question about it, is the voice of Sanche de Savigny. Dr. Russi is saying, "But he has said nothing. Monsieur de Savigny, he is just out of surgery. The damage to both eyes was quite severe. You must understand that. This is no time for questions." "And you should understand that this man seduced my daughter." "I am not interested in that. My only concern with this patient is medical." "I'm telling you this, Dr. Russi, because of what your patient might tell you when he recovers. Now I want you to listen to me. And I want you to listen carefully. Your patient deceived my daughter into running away with him and my son followed them and found them in Eze. When my son attempted to rescue his sister, your patient threatened him and attacked him without warning. My son was able to avoid the attack, but the result was that this man could not regain his balance in time and fell over the wall and into the brush where you found him." "Why are you telling me this? This is for Inspector Gagnon to know, not for me." "I'm telling you this so that you know the whole truth of this incident. I'm sure that your patient will give you his own version, but ...." "Are you going to prefer charges against him?" "My son and I have already explained the whole situation to Gagnon as it actually happened. Gagnon is willing to prefer charges, but I have no desire to see the name of my daughter and son and the name of my family involved in a suit. No, Dr. Russi, I am not going to prefer charges." From his recovery cot, Dennis listens to the conversation. He tries to speak out, but the burning in his throat stops him as if he has swallowed fire. De Savigny is saying, "What I have decided to do, Dr. Russi, may seem illogical to you, but it seems to me to be the best solution in light of this accident. I will take care of all the expenses for this man until he recovers. Then I will make arrangements for him to be deported permanently from France." "That is not my concern, Monsieur de Savigny. But why are you accepting these costs? They will be quite expensive, believe me." "Let us just say that I choose to do it. I want my daughter to see her father as he really is, and to see this American as he really is. Frankly, I have no feeling of vindictiveness toward him at all, but I want to make sure that he leaves France with no possibility of returning and bothering this girl again. I hope I can count on your cooperation in this regard, Dr. Russi. And your discretion." "Of course. If Gagnon raises no questions, why should I?" "Very good. But I should add that my daughter may be in communication with you, may even try to see this man. She is a girl of twenty, and I'm not sure she sees through this deception yet. I will do everything in my power to discourage her from any contact with you or him. But it remains a possibility until she comes to her senses. In any case, I am sending her to Paris tomorrow morning." "Your daughter is not my problem, Monsieur de Savigny. This is a purely professional matter for me, purely medical. No information on patients is given out except to next of kin. And she can't very well visit him from Paris, can she?" Dr. Russi pauses and then asks, "Do you know if he has any next of kin?" "To the best of my knowledge he has no family at all. All I know about him is that he is a performer with the circus. He goes where the circus goes." Dennis listens as the voices ebb and fade entirely, and he is again alone in a darkness that is not black but charcoal. Every time he swallows, he feels as if there is a chicken bone in his throat. Each effort is more like a gulp than a swallow, and he grimaces as his throat muscles constrict and burn in even so simple an act. It is days before the pain eases, before the intravenous feedings are discontinued and he is permitted to sip bouillon through a glass straw, before he can finally chew and swallow small portions of ground beef, which he locates on his plate by fingering them into a soup spoon that he lifts slowly and dubiously to his lips. Morning after morning Dr. Russi visits him in his room, converses briefly and impersonally, and warns him to remain as still as humanly possible so as to avoid any further detachment of the retina in his right eye. And all the time, hour after hour, half-hour after half-hour, and often minute after minute, he thinks of Denise, wondering where she is, why she is not with him, whether she has yielded to the strategies of her father, wondering at last if he will see her again, ever. And intervening with these crosscurrents of wish and counterwish are memories of his days in American boarding schools, of days with his mother, of his sessions in clown school in Sarasota, Florida, of his first walk on a wire. His entire past becomes like a phantasmagoria telescoped into a vortex of circumstances that have led him and now leave him supine and bandaged in a hospital in Cimiez and totally stripped of the only present and future that together constituted his life. He struggles to make some sense out of what has happened, struggles to find a meaning that never surfaces for him, relives his times with Denise until the desire for her voice, her nearness, the softness of her hair beneath his palm becomes overpowering to the point of madness so that he shouts her name aloud in the quiet room, shouts again and again and even curses her in English and French until the nurse enters the room and attempts to soothe him while he curses her as well. And the days that are nothing to him but one long day—one long night—pass and pass and become a month, then a month and a half. One morning during his regular visit, Dr. Russi tells him as tactfully as possible that there is some hope for his left eye but that the right eye is quite beyond recovery, adding that in time he might be able to discern images and colors in bright light but will have trouble calculating depth or distance, that his days of walking a wire are over. When Dennis answers that wirewalking is part of the way he earns, not merely his living, but his life, Dr. Russi says nothing for a moment, then asks, "Why did you choose this life? You told me that you went to the university in America. You could have done something else, something . . ." "Better?" "Let us say something different. What did you study in college?" "Shakespeare." "Just Shakespeare?" "I asked every one of my teachers who the greatest writer was who ever wrote in the language, and the vote was unanimous for Shakespeare. So I just thought it was a waste of time to read anyone but the best." "And you read everything by Shakespeare?" "Every syllable. I know a lot of Shakespeare by heart, the way I know my own name." "That's remarkable. You might decide to be an actor. It's worth thinking about." Dennis does not listen to the doctor's remark but lies quietly, his mind alive with Shakespeare. "Do you know what Mercutio says, Dr. Russi?" "Mercutio?" "In *Romeo and Juliet*." "I'm afraid not." "He says, 'A lover may bestride the gossamer that idles in the wanton summer air and yet not fall, so light is vanity.' " Again the doctor is silent. After a long pause Dennis says, "That sounds like me, doesn't it? Except for one difference. I fell. Both ways." After the doctor leaves the room, Dennis remains still. Later, when the nurse brings in his dinner, he refuses it. Still later, he falls asleep and wakes when he hears the door being opened and closed. He expects to hear footsteps, either the doctor's or the nurse's, but there is nothing. Yet he knows that someone is in the room with him. "Who's here?" He turns his head in the direction of the door and waits. "Is anybody here?" He reaches toward the door with his right hand and waits. Nothing. Slowly he eases himself back on his pillow and waits. He holds his breath for a moment and strains to hear the inhaling and exhaling of whoever it is who is in the room with him. He listens. Still, nothing . . .

Eze

Gagnon peers across the gorge. Perched where it has always been, the village seems to have no reason to be what it is or to survive as it is, but there it is, surviving. To Gagnon the place has the beauty and allure of absurdity. Perhaps it is this enigma more than anything else that intrigues him, has always intrigued him. He knows how its history has been a series of resurrections as if the only possible life for it was waiting to be claimed after each inescapable death. Gagnon savors the thought along with his pipesmoke, remembering how the near-fatal wound in his right arm made him rethink his own life, reappreciate the very air, relook at trees and water and cheese, re-create himself. By transposition he understands how Eze became more differently and distinctly itself after every one of its deaths, reviving and regenerating as if every death were merely another birth. Gagnon smiles. Forgetting the two policemen he has stationed near the western end of the bridge, forgetting the staff car where Sanche de Savigny waits with Etienne, forgetting his suspicions and his reasons for being where he is instead of relaxing to Bach in his apartment, Gagnon concentrates through his pipesmoke on the contours of Eze in the near distance and remembers the Eze of his boyhood, Eze of the seaward winds, Eze of the moon, Eze of the ashes of Isis and Osiris, Eze of the Phoenicians, Eze against the Saracens, Eze of the Guelphs, Eze of Provence, Eze of the Grimaldis versus the Ghibellines, Eze of the white stones, Eze dismantled and bombarded, Eze at dusk, Eze by Filiberto fortified, Eze of the House of Savoy, Eze of the Italians, Eze of the French, Eze of the cross inscribed in Catalan—"As I was you will be"—Eze of the captives, Eze of the artists, Eze of Zarathustra, Eze of the lovers, Eze of his boyhood, Eze of the seaward winds, Eze of the moon, Eze of the ashes of Isis . . .

The Isis Flight

After closing the door gently behind her, Denise stands with her back against it and looks across the hospital room. She sees Dennis turn his face toward her, sees the gauze scarf across his eyes, hears him ask if someone is there, sees him reach with his right hand toward her. After a moment he lies back on the bed and settles his head on the pillow bunched behind his neck. Denise suddenly realizes that she is holding the keys to Anubis in her hand. Slowly, without letting the keys jangle against one another, she inserts them into the rear pocket of her denims and remains standing by the door. Her hands are shaking at her sides and she feels that she will at any minute begin to sob. She resists the impulse to run to Dennis until she comes to terms with herself. But minutes pass, and her hands keep shaking, and tears seep quietly from the corners of her eyes and down her cheeks. She finds herself leaning back against the door as if for support. Has it really been a month and a half since the incident at Eze? Denise cannot believe that the intervening days have really passed. It is as if the only life she ever lived began on one rainy night in Eze and then was suspended until this second, as if every day and night before that was, if not a dream, something like a pre-life, almost a myth. Even as she stands she feels that she is at the very frontier of vertigo or pain. Can what happened in Eze and Paris really have happened to her? She reels under the questions and clenches her hands into white fists as if by her will alone she can force them from her memory. The effort seems to work. She opens her fists. Seeing Dennis, she gradually relaxes, and by relaxing she feels more herself than she has felt in weeks. For a moment the mere presence of Dennis across the room seems enough for her, and she forgets her plan, forgets what compelled her to come to this specific room from her apartment in Paris, forgets even what she has become and why and when. She closes her eyes.

The scent and atmosphere of the room put her in mind of another hospital room. It is years earlier. She is not yet three-and-a-half. She

113

is wearing a white dress, and her father is leading her into a room
where her mother, in a pink dressing gown, lies in a bed that has been
slightly inclined. There are many vases of flowers in the room, and
Denise sees that her mother is cradling a baby against her and that
the baby is asleep. Her mother says to her, "This is your brother,
Denise. You have a baby brother now, and his name is Seth. You will
have to help me with him." Denise looks first at her mother's smile
and then at the baby. Then she turns to her father, who is standing on
the opposite side of the bed and looking down at the infant. "He is
asleep, Papá." Just then Clothilde de Savigny, speaking as if Denise is
no longer in the room, says, "You should be happy now, Sanche. He
is a sturdy boy. He looks exactly like you." "The doctor told me you
had some difficulty in the delivery, Clothilde." "It was nothing. I am
all right now." "Well, we should be grateful for that. I've already
made arrangements for a nurse to be at the chateau to help you when
you return with the child. I've taken every precaution." "For me,
Sanche, or for your son?" "For you both, of course. It is important
that you both have the best care, particularly the child. Our future
rests with him, Clothilde." "I've had enough of the future. The future
is just a dream to me, a word. All I know is the present, this minute.
It is enough for me." De Savigny shrugs and walks to the opposite
side of the bed, where Denise is looking down at the sleeping baby. "I
will be back this evening, Clothilde." "Leave Denise with me." "But
you need your rest." "Leave Denise with me, Sanche. I just want her
to be near me." "As you wish." After her father leaves the room,
Denise moves even closer to the child and tries to look at his face, but
the blankets are in the way. Smiling at her, Clothilde draws Denise to
her and slowly peels back the blanket folds as if she is opening the
petals of a rose until, like the bud in the center of the peeled petals,
the baby's face appears. The child is awake now. "Do you like your
brother, Denise?" "He is so small, Maman." "You were even smaller,
chérie. But you ate, and you grew." She shifts the child and says,
"Now it is time for your brother to eat." Denise watches her mother
separate the lapels of her pink dressing gown and reach into the opening. She eases out a mound of soft skin topped with what appears
to be an inverted pink rose. Her mother adjusts herself in the bed so
that the inverted rose brushes the baby's lips until the lips fasten blindly

114

to it and start to tug and suck. Fascinated, Denise watches the little mouth at work. Weeks later, at the chateau, she helps her mother wash and dress and even change the infant, and, rather than grudging the presence of this new requirement on her mother's time and attention, she begins to feel a certain protectiveness, even a certain responsibility, toward her brother. In the years that follow, the bond between them remains and slowly matures. Even her father's unconcealed preference for her brother does not disturb Denise. She knows that it is her brother who will be expected to guide the destiny of her family and she has no wish to change or challenge the arrangement. And so she grows. In her conventional education she is taught the graces expected of a French girl, learns something of the history of Europe, is introduced to ballet, the violin, and choral singing, while her brother is enrolled early in a private Jesuitical school with an almost military code of discipline. One night at dinner she hears her father say to her mother, "If it weren't for the Jesuits, there would be no discipline left in the schools of France. They are the best educators in the world, especially for boys. Let them be hard on him. That's why I sent Seth there. It is good for him, Clothilde." "But he is still a boy, Sanche. Who are we to take his boyhood away from him—those few years?" "He will never miss them, believe me. He will thank us for all we're doing for him. It's what's ahead of him that matters. We must prepare him for the future." "Alway the future . . ." "The future is what matters, Clothilde. Would you be shocked if I told you that I'm already making arrangements for him to be enrolled at St. Cyr?" "An officer? But he's too young. Why must you direct him toward the army?" "These are difficult times for France, Clothilde, and the army is the best place for him. We will be in crisis before we realize it. I know what's coming. Look at the Germans. Look what Hitler is doing for his country by using a strong hand, by discipline. He is making a nation. And what were the Germans yesterday? Rabble. Now they are a nation of soldiers. Even the women. Europe will have to listen to them sooner than it likes. If this business with the Poles is not resolved, there will be war, I assure you. And if there is a war, France will be involved. And if we refuse to discipline ourselves, we will lose." "Please, Sanche, stop talking this way, especially in front of Denise. You'll frighten the child." "France will lose, Clothilde. And why? Because we are not French any more. We have forgotten our history. We have let ourselves be contaminated by people who have no vision. Perhaps we need to be defeated by the Germans to have an awakening. What we really need now is another Napoleon, but there is no one." "Sanche, do you really think there will be war?" "Yes, absolutely. And I only hope that we will not be savaged too much in the losing. It will not be like the last war. It will not be year after year in the trenches. It will be quick. A matter of weeks, even days." "What will we do if that happens?" "We will stay right here. Why shouldn't we? We have no quarrel with the Germans. We will accommodate ourselves to them. We will learn to survive until they leave." Denise listens while the sliced lamb and the buttered asparagus spears cool on her plate. She looks up at her father and asks, "Will Seth be in the war, Papá?" "No, Denise. He is much too young if the war happens now. But no matter when the war happens, it will not be long. It will be quick and decisive. If it happens later, Seth will be ready. Perhaps France will be ready by then. But if it happens now, we will do what we have to do to survive. We must consider Seth's life after the war. That's when he will be needed, and my only concern is to prepare him for that day." "Sanche, please, for the love of God, change the subject. Can't you see that you're upsetting the child." "She is not a child, Clothilde. She is a young woman, and she cannot be protected forever."

The coming year proves her father correct about the war. For months, nothing. Sitzkrieg, say the papers, not blitzkrieg. Then the salient through Sedan, and in weeks the Germans are in Paris. For Denise the war becomes the sound of aircraft over the chateau, the roads glutted with caravans fleeing south from as far north as Normandy, the distant sounds of howitzers and rifle fire in the night. Then it is calm again, and her father is discussing with her mother the necessity of accommodating the new government in Vichy as the best that can be hoped for under the circumstances. In another later discussion her father says, "This de Gaulle! Who is he, for God's sake? Who ever heard of him? Why does he think that he speaks for all of France? Can't he be man enough to admit that we've been beaten? Decisively beaten! The only solution is to try to make life as bearable as possible

bright, pink flare. "I want to fight when I am old enough, Denise. I will be like Napoleon." She pretends to ignore him, but something in her closes like a carnation at night. Whether it is love or fear she does not know. She suddenly sees her brother as a pre-man moving inexorably toward whatever it is that is still unknown to both of them—something more than solitary nights among the wine kegs, more than listening to the midnight guns, more than watching the movement of soldiers in gray field uniforms on the road in front of the chateau, more than feeling the weighty rumble of tank after tank caterpillaring first south, then north as the tide of battle changes. It is still weeks away from the afternoon of the German corporal, months away from the scene with the stoned woman in Cimiez, and half a year away from the first firing squads.

The battles south of the coastal side of the chateau begin moving ineluctably east and north as more and more Americans come ashore. Denise and her family are sleeping nightly in the wine cellar now. Her father carries a pistol with him at all times and rarely leaves the chateau. One afternoon, when the sound of firing has subsided entirely, Denise crosses the fields to an adjacent farm to barter wine for eggs. On her return from the farm by the main road she does not see the corporal slouched against an elm until he calls out to her in German. She stops. The corporal leans on his rifle and, using it as a crutch, hobbles toward her. He is not wearing a helmet, and there is a gleaming blot of blood from his right knee to his ankle. Having been warned of stragglers by her father, she backs away. The corporal calls to her again, pointing to his wound and pleading with her in German. Still leaning on his rifle, he removes his canteen from his belt. After removing the cap, he inverts the canteen and shakes it several times to demonstrate to her that it is empty. Then he offers it to her as he continues to speak in German and she realizes that he is asking her to fill it for him. Hesitantly she takes the canteen from him as he falters and quickly steadies himself with his rifle-crutch to keep from toppling. The corporal appears to Denise to be not many years older than Seth. This surprises her since she has always pictured all soldiers to be contemporaries of her father. But this is her first glimpse of a wounded man, and suddenly the war is no longer a game to her or

119

something waged far away from the chateau. Watching the corporal hobble back to the elm, seeing the wound in his leg continue to ooze blood through his puttees, Denise tucks the canteen under her arm and, with the farmer's box of eggs in her free hand, dashes up the elm-lined driveway to the chateau, leaves the eggs inside the kitchen doorway, fills the canteen at an outside tap, and returns to the spot where she left the corporal. Approaching the elm, she hears voices. She recognizes one of the voices as that of the farmer from whom she has just received the box of eggs. She runs in the direction of the voices and suddenly stops. In front of her by fifteen yards the German corporal stands with his back against the elm. Coming step by step closer to him is the farmer armed with a pitchfork. Behind the farmer is his wife. The corporal is swaying like a man in a coma. His rifle lies at his feet. When he sees the pitchfork, he starts to plead with the farmer in German. Then he points to his wounded leg and hold his hands high in the air in an act of surrender. But the farmer keeps advancing. Rushing ahead and placing herself between the corporal and the farmer, Denise tells the farmer that the corporal is wounded. The farmer shouts at her in gruff French, "He is a Boche. That is enough. Get out of my way, girl." "No. No, I won't. He is hurt. Can't you see that?" But the farmer just pushes her to one side with the edge of the pitchfork and continues to advance on the corporal, who looks as if he is about to faint. When the farmer is only a few feet from the corporal, he jabs the fork at him tentatively so that the tips of the tines just touch him, but the corporal is too weak to parry or avoid the tines. Then the farmer steps back and lunges with all his force toward the corporal and Denise sees the tines sink through the German's tunic and pin him momentarily to the elm. The corporal then lurches away with the pitchfork still in him and sprawls near the road. The farmer follows him, pries the pitchfork free and jabs a second time into the corporal's neck. Again he pries the pitchfork loose and drives it a third and final time so that one of the tines punctures the German's cheek. The farmer is trying to work the pitchfork free when Denise, weeping and screaming, throws herself over the fallen corporal as if to shield his body with hers. The farmer tries to pull her off, saying, "He is a Boche, you fool. Don't waste your time on him." Denise grabs the corporal's arm and holds fast. The farmer releases his grip on Denise, pulls out the pitchfork and stands back. "Have it your way, girl. Besides you are too late. He is finished." As soon as he says the word, the farmer's wife stoops down and removes the corporal's boots, tugging the bloody puttees with them. Denise, still sobbing, stands and backs away from the body before she turns and runs toward the chateau. Once she looks back in time to see the farmer and his wife dragging the German's body by the arms into the shrubbery along the side of the road. Then she runs in tears to the chateau where she sees her mother and father hurrying toward her. "Denise!" shouts her father, "Where have you been? We found the eggs, but there was no sign of you. Why are you crying? What happened?" Pointing toward the main road, Denise describes the incident with the corporal and the farmer. Even before she finishes, she hears her father tell her mother, "Take the child inside, Clothilde. I must go down and bury that body. If the Germans should find him like that, there's no telling what they will do. They are desperate these days. In Oradour-sur-Glane they executed the entire village because the Maquis killed one of their officers near there. In the Vercors it was worse. They turned the Mongols loose in St. Donat. They killed every man in the massif. They raped all the females from children to grandmothers. We can't be too careful."

The memory of the corporal's death stays with Denise for days, for weeks. It drives all other thoughts out of her mind. More than once she meets the whole scene again in her dreams so that she wakes in midscream, her nightgown sweated to her flanks, her hair sticking to her cheeks like wet string.

As soon as the last German patrols have joined the main body of the retreating army west of Ventimiglia, Denise's mother decides to take her to Nice not merely to bargain for necessities but to get the girl away from the chateau for an afternoon. In Nice, Denise sees her first Americans. The city still shows a few signs of bombardment and house-to-house fighting, but most of the stores are open and doing some kind of business, however minimal. Denise follows her mother from a few fruit stalls to a farmer's stand where she manages to buy a brick of cheese. For the first time in weeks, Denise finds herself distracted from her own memories. The mood lasts throughout the afternoon and even continues during their return trip to the chateau. It is only when they reach Cimiez that everything comes apart. The woman they see on the road appears to be leading a small procession, but the scene becomes more bizarre as they draw closer to it. The woman is naked except for a pair of low-heeled black shoes, and what appeared to be a procession is really a gang following her. From time to time a man or a woman will leave the group and, drawing abreast of the naked woman, spit on her or throw what appears to be mud at her. Occasionally the woman stops, turns to face the group, holds them at bay with a few words and then continues to walk on, making little if any effort to protect herself when the spitting starts again. "Maman," asks Denise, "What is happening? What are they doing to her." "I don't know, Denise, but don't look at them. Look the other way until they pass." Denise cannot help but look at the woman as she approaches them. She notices that the woman's hair has been scissored off and she makes out uneven ridges of hair between bare paths of scalp. There is even a long red mark just above the woman's right ear where the scissors must have slipped. When the woman is only a few yards from them, Denise sees that the hair has been roughly scissored or razored off the woman's pubis so that her crease is exposed, making her appear to Denise more naked than she seemed at a distance. As the woman is about to pass Denise and her mother, she stares at Clothilde de Savigny and almost hisses her words, "You have your husband to blame for this, madame. He picked my husband to work in Frankfurt and I had three girls to feed. He made me do what I had to do. Why do they blame me?" One of the women in the group draws abreast of the naked woman and says, "Shut up, you bitch. You let the Germans fuck you any time they wanted." "They gave me food. What else was there to do? I had three girls to feed." "And what about you? You ate better than any woman in France. Well, see how this tastes for a change." The woman pitches a pail of manure before the naked woman can dodge, and the filth pelts the side of her face and her shoulder. Seeing this, Denise edges closer to her mother and cowers against her. The woman who has emptied the pail is shouting, "It will take you a long time to wash that shit off your face, you whore." A man from the group joins the woman and prods the naked woman on so that she trips and lands on her knees on the road. Pretending that she is a beast of burden, the man straddles her and then sits down heavily on her back, smacking her hard on the right buttock as if to get her to move ahead. Then, with a laugh, he dismounts, and the woman struggles to her feet and tries to run out of the group's range. She heads for the woods adjacent to the road. One of the other men in the group picks up a stone from the berm and throws it at the fleeing woman. Then everyone in the group seizes a stone and throws it. Most of the stones miss, but one hits, and the woman collapses, tries to get to her feet, cannot, and crawls into the shelter of the trees as the stone throwers slowly disperse and head back to Nice.

All the way back to the chateau, Denise says nothing to her mother, says nothing for days to anyone. The memory of the German corporal and the pursued, naked woman of Cimiez overshadows everything she attempts to think or do. And she keeps wondering why the woman at Cimiez singled out her father for blame. What could he have done to her? The question remains a question for days, for weeks and even for months as the war in the south of France gradually but reluctantly becomes part of the past. Seth returns to school with the Jesuits and Denise completes her studies at the lycée and, at the age of eighteen, matriculates at the Sorbonne. Following her first academic year, she returns to the chateau for the summer. Her brother, also summering at the chateau, has reached that point in adolescence where he starts to treat Denise as his junior. He has also developed the habit of speaking his sentences like pronouncements, and he spends much of his time reading the historical and military annals of the de Savigny family in the study of his father. Her mother has become decidedly more religious over the years, attending church services regularly and punctually, participating in parish causes, and hosting the curate, Monsignor Lascaux, at the chateau at least twice a week. Her father resumes his role as overseer of the family business and holdings, flying periodically to Paris, London, Milan, or Rome when business demands it. Each month that passes sees him becoming more and more cryptic about his affairs, more insistent that his son realize, truly realize, what the future holds for him, more indifferent to and sometimes dismissive of Denise's mother while remaining almost casually aware of Denise herself and her studies. Once, when they are alone, he asks Denise, "Why biology?" "Because it has to do with life, Papá, with . . ." "But are there many women involved in this profession?" After a pause Denise answers, "No, Papá." "Are there any other women in your class?" "No, Papá. I am the only one." "Doesn't that in itself tell you something?" "But it is all that interests me, Papá. It holds all the drama in the world for me. There is a mystery about it, a challenge." "Very well, very well. As long as you're interested, there's no harm in it. It's as good a discipline as anything else, I suppose." Later that same day, while she is reading in her room, she decides to call a classmate of hers who is living in Antibes. She lifts the receiver and is about to dial when she realizes that her father is already on the line. She is about to return the receiver to its cradle when the sound of her father's voice makes her pause. He is not declaiming but conversing, actually conversing. It is a tone that Denise has not heard in his voice for years. He is saying, ". . . difficult at best, Madeleine. Perhaps on Monday, but not today or tomorrow." "But it is impossible for us to continue like this, Sanche. Who means more to you? You have no feelings for Clothilde any more. Why keep up this pretense?" "This is the only possible way that I can arrange my life, Madeleine. It's not as simple as you imagine it. You even took a chance calling me here. Suppose I had not answered the phone?" "I really don't care any more, Sanche. This boredom is insufferable." "Wait until Saturday then, Madeleine. Clothilde and Denise will be spending the day in Cannes and I will send Seth on an errand to Nice. I should be able to see you late in the afternoon at the usual place." "It is harder and harder to live without you, Sanche." "Until Saturday, Madeleine . . ." Slowly, ever so slowly, Denise fits the receiver back on its cradle. She cannot quite believe what she has heard. This is obviously not a recent thing. From the sound of the conversation, her father and the woman named Madeleine have been maintaining a secret life for some time. Denise cannot help wondering if her mother is aware of it. Several days later on a trip with her mother to Cannes, Denise observes her closely, but there is nothing in her mother's expression that betrays anything to her. "What is Papá doing today, Maman?" "What is today, Denise? I forget so easily lately. Isn't it odd? I am never wrong about the month, but I have to think twice to remember the year, the date, the day." "It's Saturday, Maman." "Then he is going to Nice with Seth. They have something to do there." "What, Maman?" "It's their business, Denise. I am never curious, you know that. Why do you ask?" "I was just wondering, Maman." After a protracted pause, Clothilde asks Denise, "Is there something you want to tell me?" "No, Maman." She waits and adds, "Just that I love you, Maman." Clothilde smiles, reaches for Denise's hand and squeezes it affectionately before saying, "You have the best heart of all of us, Denise. You are the only *real* one. I love you for that. But I fear for you because of it." "But why?" "Because love makes you too vulnerable, Denise. You have to make yourself harder, at least on the outside. You have to learn what to ignore . . ." "But I cannot live that way, Maman." "Then you must learn, chérie. Experience will teach you that. Then, when you have questions, I will be there to help you, if God spares me." "But how can you learn to be hard and learn to love at the same time? Isn't love what everyone really wants?" "It's not that simple, Denise. There are other considerations always. Especially if you are a French woman. You must learn to be patient, to be tolerant. You are too young yet to understand. But there is your whole life still ahead of you. You will learn what you must learn. Come now. We are talking too much. I almost forgot that I must stop at the hospital in Cimiez. I must leave a package for the monsignor there." Once they are parked in front of the hospital, Denise remains in the car while her mother heads for the chaplain's office in the hospital wing. Seated, Denise looks out at the familiar facade of the hospital. She knows that this is the place where she and her brother were born and where, in the latter days of the war when the Germans were retreating slowly to the east and north and when the fighting in Italy was at its deadliest, it was used as an infirmary and convalescent center for wounded American soldiers. But the Americans she expected to see when she visited the hospital with her mother turned out to be Japanese. All the soldiers she saw were small, muscular, serious men with close-cropped black hair. They seldom spoke. Once she walked with her mother through a ward reserved for the most seriously wounded and she heard nothing—not even the least audible whisper or moan. Now as she studies the repainted facade of the hospital, she sees, as if in a dream, a group of Japanese on the lawn. One is missing an arm from the elbow down. Another is compensating for his amputated leg by leaning on an aluminum crutch. A third has a bandage over his right eye. A fourth, legless, is seated in a wheelchair. She remembers her mother's having told her that these men were organized into a single division and sent to fight in Europe rather than in the Pacific or in Asia where there would have been problems of misidentification in battle. Her mother also mentioned to her that these men had a reputation for extraordinary bravery. "The monsignor told me, Denise, that this division received more decorations for valor than any other division in United States military history." "But they are not Americans, Maman. How can they fight for a country that is not their country.?" "But they are Americans, Denise. It is not as it is in Europe or in France, chérie. In America you can become a citizen if you are loyal to America, no matter where you originated. It has nothing to do with family or money or tradition or such things." "But I think that is very good, Maman. It is good to be able to choose your country. That way, everyone is equal." "Some think it is the best way. But America is a young country. All it sees is the future. It makes light of tradition and family. But here these things are important to us." Denise recalls how she looked at the Japanese men as her mother kept on talking and how she felt a new and serious admiration for a country for which small, quiet men from the Orient were willing to sacrifice parts of their bodies without so much as a murmur. Somehow these men seemed freer to her, more complete even with their shocking wounds, than any people she had ever seen in her life.

When her mother returns from the chaplain's office, they resume their drive to Cannes and subsequently to Antibes where Denise visits her classmate, Thérèse, while her mother shops. Seated in Thérèse's living room with Thérèse's older brother, Pascal, Denise cannot forget her visit to the hospital in Cimiez years earlier and her reaction to the Japanese there. "But there were many Oriental men there, Thérèse. In fact, the hospital was used for them exclusively. It took me so long to understand how they were willing to fight and even die for a country that was at war with their country." "Maybe they had no choice, Denise." "Ever since then I've thought about America differently. It must be a great country to inspire that kind of patriotism . . ." Pascal, who has been reading a newspaper and smoking a pipe, folds the paper and slaps it flat on the table beside him, saying, "Thérèse is correct, Denise. Maybe these men had no choice. As American citizens they had to serve in the army, or they would be punished." "But I learned that they had received more decorations than anyone else." "Propaganda," says Pascal. "No, it is true. I verified it, Pascal." "It's still propaganda." Thérèse interrupts and says, "Pascal knows more about these things than we do. He says we should not take what we read or hear so seriously." "But if it is true, doesn't that say something to you about America? Before, I just thought that . . ." "Forget your new attitude, Denise," says Pascal, sounding more and more like Seth, "because America is nothing but a huge bourse, a dynamo, a marketplace. The dollar is king. Now we have to show them a good face because they are protecting us from the Bolsheviks, but they are really just protecting themselves. I know all about the Americans. In their hearts they only respect you if you become like them. And we can never become like them. We have more history, more breeding, more everything. We have everything that they lack." "But I like what they lack, Pascal," interjects Denise. "It gives everybody a chance, the same chance to achieve something." "Denise, you are talking like a child about a fairy tale. Believe me, the Americans have faith in nothing but themselves. They think the world turns around them. Look at the American soldiers when you are in Paris. They are like big boys. Last month I asked one of them how he liked his trip to the south. He said he only saw Antib-ee. That's the way he pronounced it. I asked him if he knew that Antibes used to be called Antipholus, that it was named by the Greeks. He didn't know what I was talking about. He just said it looked like any other Frog tourist town to him. Can you imagine that? And he was talking about Antibes!" Pascal picks up the folded newspaper and slaps it again on the table top as if for emphasis and stomps out of the room. Denise turns to Thérèse and shakes her head and manages a faint smile, "Your brother is just like Seth, Thérèse. They carry all of France on their backs." "Why do you blame them for that? At least they are becoming French men. They both see what is ahead of them, what is expected of them." "But why are they so sarcastic, so intolerant? They seem like such slaves to the future, and everybody who differs from them is wrong. I don't know about Pascal, but Seth is starting to live like a train on a track. Everything is marked. Everything is fixed. Everything is so predictable. There is no room for any movement from one side to the other." "Why do you want to change him?" "Because lately I've started to think that life is more than that. I don't want to marry someone who is a train on a track. And I don't want to have children and repeat the same pattern with them." "But that's the way men are. Don't you want to marry someone who is reliable, who will be good to you, who will be a good father?" "I don't know, Thérèse. Lately I've been wondering about that more and more. All I know is that I don't want a life where everything is mortgaged to the future, where everything in your past and the present has to mean something in the future." "But that's life, Denise." "Is it? What about right now? This minute? Today? What's wrong with wanting a life where the present keeps becoming the present, where you live and not just live *on* or live *for*?" "That's just childish, Denise, and you know it." "Then I want to stay childish." "Maybe that's why you like the Americans. Have you ever thought of that?" "If it is, then I want to be like the Americans. I want to marry an American." "Speak for yourself. I couldn't marry anyone outside of my nationality. After that I don't care. Just so he is someone who is reliable and who will be good to me." "Don't you want to love him?" "Trust is better than love, Denise. My mother's been telling me that for years, and she knows what she's talking about." "Well, for me love is everything. It is by itself." "You're still talking like a child." "Perhaps. But that is how I am."

Denise does not see Thérèse again that summer. It is not until the following winter that they meet in Paris, where they are both studying in different programs at the Sorbonne. Sitting at an outdoor table near the Place Michel, they exchange news of the intervening months until they are joined briefly by another student whom Thérèse introduces simply as Sexto. Denise notices a change in Thérèse as soon as Sexto appears. She becomes nervous, deferential, defensive. After Thérèse gives Sexto a key from her purse, he leaves without saying a word to Denise. When they are again alone, Thérèse says matter-of-factly to Denise, "His name is Sexto Suares. He's from Barcelona."

Then she adds after a pause, "I live with him. Or, rather, he lives with me." Denise's only answer is to look down at the tablecloth. She is trying to reconcile the Thérèse of Antibes with this new Thérèse of Paris. "Are you shocked, Denise?" "No." "Then why don't you say something? Why are you so silent?" "I don't know what to say. What do you want me to say?" "Poor Denise," says Thérèse with an indulgent smile, "you are still too Catholic. You live with blinders on your eyes." "It has *nothing* to do with that." "It has *everything* to do with that." Thérèse takes a cigarette from her purse and lights it. Denise watches her, trying to understand how security-minded Thérèse could be transformed into this Thérèse in less than seven months. Finally she asks her, "Do you love him, Thérèse?" "Frankly, I haven't even thought about it that much. I enjoy him, and he enjoys me. That's enough for now. Besides, love is passé today. Who believes in love any more? Who? People have desires. They satisfy their desires. Love has nothing to do with it." "I never thought I would hear you say that, Thérèse." "Does it surprise you?" "How can you really separate desire from love, Thérèse?" "You still talk like a child, Denise." "But how can you?" "It's simple. It's the way things are. Try it. You'll see how easy it is." "I always thought that if you separate the two, then anything is possible. And if you find out afterwards that you were wrong and they couldn't be separated, you couldn't go back." "What's wrong with believing that anything is possible? Look at us, Denise. All our lives we've lived as if everything is not possible, as if the right things are determined for us. We were like little dolls. Well, I learned from Sexto. He showed me that anything is possible now, that you can have everything if you want it. All you have to decide is that you're going to break loose and find out about life *for* yourself *by* yourself." "But what if you find out that you're wrong, Thérèse?" "What's the difference?" "I mean you can't go back and erase your mistake. It stays with you. You have to live with it. It will spoil your happiness later in your life." "Later? Who knows if we'll be alive later? Give me an answer to that." Denise is silent, and after a moment Thérèse resumes, "Don't you want to make your life happen instead of have it happen to you? That's what I want. And I'll take all the consequences. And don't talk to me about happiness. Happiness is for children. Who is really happy, Denise?" Denise looks down at the tablecloth and purses her lips. When she looks up again, she sees Thérèse in tears. Wiping her eyes with the back of her hand, Thérèse stands up and hurries across the Pont St. Michel. Denise pays the check for their half-sipped coffees and follows her, catching up with her half-way across the bridge. "Thérèse, what's wrong? What happened? What can I do?" "Nothing. Nothing, Denise. Just leave me alone. Please." "Thérèse, I'm your friend. Talk to me. Are you sick? What's the matter?" Thérèse just shrugs her shoulders helplessly and looks at her feet until her tears stop. When she faces Denise again, she says, "It's something between Sexto and me." "Yes." "Well . . ." Again Thérèse looks down and then up again. "Well, I was going to have a baby by him." Denise meets Thérèse's look before Thérèse averts her eyes. Thérèse leans against the railing of the bridge and peers down at the Seine. Sidling toward her, Denise asks, "What can I do for you, Thérèse?" "Nothing. There's nothing anyone can do." "Did you lose the baby?" Thérèse nods slowly yes, and Denise responds. "Maybe it is better, Thérèse. Sometimes when everything is not as perfect as it should be, the body . . ." "You don't understand, Denise. I made arrangements to lose it. It didn't just happen. I made arrangements." With that, Thérèse faces right and walks back across the bridge to the Place St. Michel and keeps walking. Denise follows her at a quick step and comes abreast of her on the Rue de la Huchette in front of the church of St. Severin. Without a word Thérèse enters the church and sits near one of the empty confessionals. There is no one else in the church, and the afternoon light speckles the convoluted swirls of the pillars behind the altar with beams reflected in rich rainbows by the stained glass windows. As she approaches the pew where Thérèse is sitting, Denise notices that Thérèse's shoulders are quivering and the tears are again running freely down her cheeks. Quietly she sits beside the weeping girl and holds her left hand in her own right. As if the assurance of her hand in Denise's hand has stabilized her for the moment, Thérèse says, "It's been terrible for me, Denise. You can never understand how terrible . . ." Squeezing Thérèse's hand, Denise says, "Don't talk to me about it if you don't want to. You don't have to say anything." "But I have to talk. For months there's been no one I could talk to. Sexto thinks I did the right thing. The only thing. But he leaves the room every time I bring up the subject. He tells me that he'll tell Pascal if I don't shut up. He holds that over me . . ." "But doesn't he see that Pascal would hold it against him if . . ." "And me as well, Denise. Pascal would look down on me, and Sexto knows that. And what does Sexto care? He could find someone else and just disappear. He's good at that." "Then why do you stay with him?" "I don't know. I don't know." Thérèse puts her hands over her face as if she is washing it. When she returns her hands to her lap again, she looks ten years older, and she resumes speaking, but now in a monotone, "I was almost five months along, Denise. You know what that means. You study biology." Denise has the impression that Thérèse is not really speaking to her but to herself. With every word her tone becomes more deep-seated until it finally seems that she is soliloquizing. "When a woman is five months pregnant, the baby is already formed, Denise. It's very small still, but it is complete. And that's when I decided to make arrangements. For weeks I'd been thinking about it, but I didn't have the courage. It went against something in me. It went against everything I ever learned, everything I felt. You understand what I mean, Denise. But it was a fact that I was pregnant and in my fifth month, and I was starting to be obvious no matter how I tried to hide it. That's really what decided me. I was all right as long as it wasn't noticeable. That way it was still my little secret. That's the way I thought. The only ones who knew were Sexto and myself. My parents knew nothing. Pascal knew nothing. I hadn't seen them since the end of summer and I kept making up excuses why I didn't have the time to go home. But the real thing that decided me was that I was sick. I used to get up in the morning and vomit or else just sit on the toilet and moan. I kept telling myself that I had no reason to suffer like this, and day by day I started to believe it. And besides, what did I have to look forward to? More sickness? And who could tell what else was waiting? And everything I'd been reading in Paris made it seem all right. There were singers and actresses who'd had it done, and they were even open about it. I kept telling myself that this was my body after all. I had some rights. This wasn't the Middle Ages. What was I hesitating about? Anyway, that is what I told myself until the decision finally just seemed to make itself. So Sexto took me to a doctor that he knew, and he examined me and told me to come back the following day." She clenches her hands in her lap and takes a deep breath. "That night I was really frightened, Denise. And I was more than frightened, really. Despite all the vomiting in the morning and all the nausea and the rest, I felt something . . ." She opens her hands in her lap and clenches them again. "I felt something for the baby. I can't explain what I mean, but it's what you feel when you're like that. But I was determined, and the next day I went to the doctor's office, and he examined me again and told me that he was going to give me an anesthetic that would not be complete—just from the waist down. He said he wanted it that way so that he could talk to me in case he needed my help as things went along. I was numb, Denise. I just nodded, and the next thing I knew was that I had the feeling that my legs no longer were my legs. And then the doctor and the nurse started to work. You may know about these things, but I didn't know what they were going to do. I've learned a lot about the whole method since then. In fact . . ." She starts to cry again but manages to blink back her tears. "In fact, Denise, I've really become an expert on the subject. I'm a real authority, believe me." She stops and weeps into her hands until she is able to continue. "Do you know what they do, Denise? If it happens in the first month or so, they just open the woman with one of those spreading instruments, and then they use a suction machine and just suck everything right out of her. They say it's very simple, and the woman is able to walk right out of the office after she's had it done to her. But when you're in the midmonths the way I was, they can't vacuum it out. They have to use stronger techniques. Sometimes they use a needle, a hypodermic. They go right through your skin here until the needle goes into the womb, and then they inject a fluid. After that, they just wait for the fluid to work. It takes a little while before there are spasms, and then the convulsions force out everything like . . ." She pauses and does not look at Denise as she resumes. "For me there was another way. The doctor told me that the baby was very small. He said he didn't anticipate any problems. I watched him reach for his instruments. They have an instrument that opens you and keeps you open as if you were going to have a baby. That gives them room to work. But with me they ran into problems. I could see the doctor beginning to perspire. Then I heard him tell the nurse that he was going to try to work it out with his hand. But when that didn't work, he asked the nurse to bring him some other instruments. Even though I couldn't feel a thing, I was starting to get hysterical. I could hear myself screaming, but it was as if the screams were coming from some other woman. It's hard to explain, Denise, but I even felt that I could observe what was happening to me. Then I heard the doctor swear and tell the nurse that he had to . . ." Thérèse comes to a full stop, and for a moment Denise does not think that she is going to speak again. But she does. "I found out later what they did, Denise. They had to take the baby out of me piece by piece. That's what they had to do. They dismembered him while he was still inside of me, and they took him out in pieces. Like parts of a chicken. That's what they did to my baby, Denise, and I can't forget it. I try to put it behind me, but I can't stop imagining how they cut him up while he was still inside of me. I tell myself that he wasn't alive when they did that, but it tortures me. It stays with me, and I don't know how to live with myself." Thérèse stands and edges out of the pew before she says, "And I'm afraid, Denise. I don't know what I'm afraid of. Maybe, it's God. I don't know. Sometimes I'm so afraid that I won't leave my room, not even to go to my classes." Standing at the edge of the pew, she seems to be waiting for Denise to respond, but Denise simply returns her look and says nothing. "I don't know why I'm saying all this to you, Denise. All I see in your eyes is that Catholic look, and it goes right through me." "That has nothing to do with it, Thérèse." "Well, why are you looking at me that way? What are you thinking?" After a pause Denise says, "I was just thinking of the baby. He was so helpless through all this. And now? Now he's gone. That's what hurts me." "Well, what would you have done if you were in my place?" "I couldn't have killed it, Thérèse. I'd have died myself before I would have done that." "That's easy for you to say. But you don't know what you'd really do if you were that way." Denise does not answer but stands and joins Thérèse in the aisle. Thérèse is saying, "Do you know what would have happened to me if I would have had it? Do you know what my parents would have done, what Pascal would have done? Just imagine." "But if you and Sexto loved one another, you could have lived with that, Thérèse." "Damn it, Denise. Why do I talk to you? You haven't understood anything I've said." "I told you that you didn't have to tell me anything. I didn't ask you."

"Well, I had to talk to somebody . . ." Thérèse faces Denise as they reach the church door. "You won't tell my parents or Pascal?" "Of course not." Together they leave St. Severin and move into the ruck and the aromatic scents that intermingle in the concourse. As they pass the open doors of the different restaurants on the Rue de la Huchette, the scents separate into a single scent that varies with the flavor of the cuisine being prepared within. "Does Sexto love you, Thérèse" "Sexto? Love me? He loves me four or five times a week. Like a clock. Does that answer your question?" "How can you stay with him? After what you told me, I don't see how you can live with him." "Sometimes I ask myself the same question. Do you know the only answer I can find?" "No." "Maybe it doesn't matter . . ." "Doesn't matter?" "I mean, maybe, the feeling doesn't matter. Maybe Sexto and I are just getting from one another what we need. And maybe that's all there should be, all there is. Ever." "I don't understand you, Thérèse." "Why do I have to love him? Can you imagine how I might have been if I really loved Sexto and then let the doctor do what he did to me? It's hard enough living with myself as it is. Thank God that love had nothing to do with it. I don't know what would have become of me." "You don't really mean that, Thérèse." "Of course, I mean it. I never loved Sexto, and I don't love him now. He's just a good convenience. Besides, nobody loves anybody any more. Haven't you heard? Love is really a myth, Denise. Men and women just use one another when they have to. We're one another's conveniences. That's all. And if you don't get careless the way I did, you have about as good an arrangement as you can expect." "When I think of the way you were last summer and how you are talking now, Thérèse, I can't believe it." "Last summer was another life, Denise. You'll change too. It happens sooner or later. You'll see. *Au revoir*, Denise." Denise watches Thérèse hurry back to the Place St. Michel and disappear into the crowd.

For weeks Denise remembers everything that Thérèse told her. In detail. Whether she is in the laboratory or studying in her room, she is disturbed by images of Thérèse's abortion. Again, in detail. But she mentions this to no one. When she returns to the family chateau in the south of France at the beginning of the summer, she decides that

she will not go to Antibes at all and risk a meeting with Thérèse's
parents or Pascal. The details of the conversation with Thérèse in St.
Severin remain as clear to Denise as they were when she first heard
them. Even when she tries to distract herself by studying or practicing
on the piano, she finds that she becomes too depressed to persevere. It
is this depression more than anything else that makes her decide one
afternoon to go to the circus at Monte Carlo in the hope that the acts
and atmosphere of the circus will change her outlook, her perspec-
tives. In the main tent she sits through two complete performances,
watching the lions paw at the tamer's flickering whip until they roll
on their sides like kitchen cats on a warm floor, smiling at the chim-
panzee that careens around the ring on roller skates, laughing out
loud at the Russian bear that tries to do the same thing, gasping at the
trapeze swingers, looking away as the young wirewalker, without a
pole, seems to dare the wire to disobey him. Then the clowns parade
by her, blowing kisses to the crowd, tripping one another, collapsing
in place like laundry falling from a clothesline. She watches a clown
on stilts pass like some extraordinary human stork. Then she sees the
clown whose eyes she cannot seem to ignore. She saw the same clown
during the first performance and, primarily because of him and the
way he looked at her and she at him, decided to stay for the second
show. It is not his patched coat and oversized trousers that intrigue
her, not his lightbulb of a yellow nose, not the white ring around his
vermilion mouth, not the open-ended top hat that always seems on
the verge of falling but never quite falls, not the blue, pillowy slippers
that flap up and down on the sawdust with every step he takes—not
any of these. It is his eyes. They do not seem to match his appearance
or his performance. They are not even sad, which would serve as a
contrast with the rest of his appearance. They are simply the eyes of
someone who seems bored but still perceptive of everything near and
far—aviator's eyes. And there is something else that is present in his
eyes, something that says that nothing matters, that the world is just
a circus so why pretend, that we all meet as clown to clown, and, after
all, why shouldn't we, why hide, why worry about taking false faces
as true and true faces as false? At one point the clown's eyes meet
Denise's. For an instant she looks away but then returns his look and
holds it. Eventually he is the one who breaks the stare. Later, as he

cavorts on around the ring, he keeps glancing back at her. The second time he begins his orbit of the ring, he looks for her again. Everyone around Denise is laughing as the clown on stilts trips the patchwork clown with the yellow nose and top hat so that he sprawls like a rag doll on the floor of the tent. Denise does not laugh. Instead, she feels the impulse to dash into the ring and help him to his feet. After the clown sprawls for the third time and lies spread-eagled like someone about to be nailed to a cross, Denise rises from her seat and heads for the exit. Just before she leaves, she turns around. The clown's eyes are on her, and she gives him one last, long look and ducks under the tentflap into the heavy afternoon air. All the way back, she is troubled by the look in the clown's eyes. More than anything else, they are what kept returning her to all the realities she wanted to forget. Now they are all she remembers from the entire afternoon. Later that evening while she is washing before dinner, she looks closely at her face in the mirror and surprises herself by glimpsing in her own eyes the same look that she saw in the eyes of the clown—a mixture of melancholy and a kind of resignation that is not quite complete, that still hopes for the resurrection that will eventually save everything. She promises herself that she will not return to the circus, not place herself in a position where she will be at the mercy of her own vulnerabilities, not even think of the clown again. Days pass, and the memory of the clown's eyes blurs and decomposes and gradually loses its grip on the present perfect. The decomposition is so complete that the young man who confronts her on a street corner in Nice seems at first simply an annoyance. It is only when he persists that she is compelled to look him full in the face. And it is the eyes that stop her. "You!" she exclaims, "You are the comedian, the clown!" And he nods with a smile, and within five minutes they are sipping capuccino at an outdoor cafe near the Negresco. The fact that she has never spoken to an American, face to face, except to exchange a word or two makes her listen intently to him as he speaks to her in his awkward French. Occasionally he lapses into his own language when his French vocabulary comes up short. There is a freedom in his manner that is new to her, and she finds herself drawn to it. In some ways he reminds her of the Japanese soldiers she once saw in Cimiez. He is only slightly taller than she is, but he is proportioned like an athlete, wide in the shoulders and trim at the waist and hips. Yet, though lithe and compact, he regards and executes every movement of his body or of his limbs alone with something approaching abandonment, as if his body knows what it must do without his worrying about it. His face is more square than round and his brown hair falls forward and to one side from a natural part above his right temple. When he smiles, he smiles with his whole face, not all at once but gradually, with the lips setting the tone and the eyes following. He speaks slowly, not because he has to think about what he is about to say but rather because he wants to make sure that what he is saying is right the first time he says it without any subsequent need of amendment. For the first time in months she feels that she is really *conversing* with someone, really speaking to someone who is listening to her and her alone and then responding to what he has just heard. Days later when he invites her to ride on his gleaming black motorcycle named Anubis, she feels that same sense of intellectual and emotional hospitality in his manner. But the speed of the ride terrifies her and shows her something in his personality that does not match what she already knows about him. They swoop up and around the mountains of the Esterel as if speed limits do not exist, as if there are no limits at all except those the driver imposes upon himself. The final arbiters seem to be nothing external, nothing but the skill of the driver and the capacities of the machine. It is this wild courage that frightens her. She begins to think that he is not what she thought he was at the cafe but that the real man is the one who veers pell-mell on the mountainous dips and curves. Gripping him around the chest as he steers, she feels the unyielding fact of his own will pitted against the road, provoking him to extend himself to the farthest limits of danger not as a matter of necessity but as a matter of choice or spite or even anger. This repels her, but she cannot bring herself to tell him why. Finally, when she sees him balance on the rail of a bridge below Eze and walk the length of it as if to impress her, she finds the courage in her to berate him and then is surprised when he responds not with annoyance but with a kind of innocent dismay. After that, as if in deference to her, he drives Anubis much more slowly and with some sensitivity to the fact that speed and daring are as terrifying to her as they are animating to him. And it is only then that she notices that he is again the man with whom she can converse. And from that time he studiously avoids acting in front of her in a way that she might construe as a performance for her benefit. They speak now almost exclusively in his language rather than French, and she becomes more and more impressed by how much he appears to know and how she, almost involuntarily, becomes a sharer in that knowledge so that her viewpoints slowly, imperceptibly, ineluctably change. He makes no effort to persuade or convince her of his views. Instead he speaks frankly and plainly, like a man who is saying to her what he committed to memory years earlier. She often feels that she is listening to a kind of diary named Dennis Holt, and word by word by word she is able to reconstruct in her own mind and in her own time the hopscotch patterns of his early years, the anecdotes about his mother and father, the reasons why he chose to be a clown rather than anything else on earth, the legacy that summoned him to France, the challenge of the wirewalk and the perspective he has developed toward his own country as a result of his being abroad, not as a tourist or a mere itinerant, but as someone who is forging out a private destiny. Once, in the cactus gardens of Eze, he tells her of all these matters as if he has to say them for her and for her alone once and for all, and Denise listens to him for more than an hour, letting the portrait drawn by his words realize itself and evolve until it becomes complete. Suddenly, interrupting himself as if he has overlooked the most important point of all, he says, "Gravity! The more I think of it, the more I think that gravity is what we have to resist to stay alive." "Gravity? Do you mean real gravity? What pulls us down?" "Gravity. Weight. Whatever you want to call it. I started to feel it when I was in college. Everything I studied made me feel, not enlarged, but smaller and smaller. I felt as if I had to sponge up everything until I was weighted down. Every year I felt that gravity was winning." "But that is how we are, Dennis. We have to absorb our past. It tells us what we are, where we come from, where we are now, everything." "Like hell. I used to think that way, but it's just a lie. We don't learn about ourselves that way. Do you know what we really want? We want to rise above what we are. I don't mean social climbing or anything like that. I mean more than that." "I don't understand, Dennis." He pauses as if looking for examples to make his statement clearer. Finally, he says, "We know, we all know that we're going to be disappointed some time or another, that we're going to suffer, that we're going to die. What I'm saying is that all we want is to rise above that somehow." "Instead of accepting it, you mean?" "Instead of accepting it *in advance* and then living with the acceptance. We *have* to accept it when it happens. Isn't that enough? But the trouble with all the people I know is that they feel that they have to accept it before it happens to them. They make what's inevitable a fact before it's really a fact, and that just weighs them down. They never really live." "Is that why you walk in the air?" "That's part of the reason. It gets me away from sea level for a while. And clowning does that too, believe it or not. I get out of my own skin for an hour or so. For me, wirewalking and clowning are my two ways of suspending gravity." "But you always have to come back down. What do you feel then?" "I feel like my weighted-down self again, and I don't like it, so I jump on Anubis and go zooming along the coast or up into the mountains. That gets me through the rest of the day." "And the nights?" "They are always the hardest." After a pause, Denise asks, "Do you have a girl?" "Having a girl is like gravity sometimes." "Should I see something in that?" "I don't mean you, Denise. You're just the opposite, believe me. What I meant was that having a girl, having any girl, can weigh you down. It's the same kind of gravity unless . . ." "Unless you love her. Is that what you're trying to say?" Dennis grimaces as if the question is beyond his capacity to answer it. Then he says, "I don't know if I really believe in love, Denise. I don't know if it's really possible. I'd like to think that it is, but I don't know." "But you seem to believe in it. Isn't love the opposite of gravity for you? Isn't that what you're really saying? You even said that you really come alive when you walk the wire in the circus or when you turn into a clown and pretend that you're somebody else. Isn't that a kind of love?" "Maybe. I don't know. I never thought about it like that. I just know that something in me wants to beat gravity, wants to get close to the sun like that old Greek and his son. Of course, you can't get too close, or you're finished. But if you don't try, you're finished anyway. So you might as well try." He stands and strides about, his hands pushed into his pockets. "That's what drove me out of America, Denise. There was no real lift in my life there. Everyone around me just wanted to go on. Everything around me just wanted to go on.

No life. Just living on. Longevity. The whole country's that way. And that's why it's starting to come apart, not just at the seams, but in the places where there are no seams. In the fabric." "I don't accept that at all, Dennis. The whole world wants to be like America. Just look around you. Everything is becoming American." "Then the world's in for a big surprise." "But how can you say that about your own country?" "It's the truth. The whole country just reminds me of my mother." "Dennis, please. It bothers me to hear you talk that way." "Then it will just have to bother you, because that's the way I see things. My mother started out fine, but then she didn't know how to get along without cutting corners here and there. And her life started to shrink away. Her *real* life, I mean. And America's just the same. It keeps backing away from its real life. It keeps shrinking. It keeps diminishing, but it doesn't realize it, doesn't admit it. It's not what it was even ten years ago." "You talk as if you're ashamed of it." "Ashamed? Why should *I* be ashamed? If I haven't contributed to its shame, why should I feel ashamed?" "It's different here in France, Dennis. Here we have a deep pride in our country. We're raised that way, taught that way." "That's just as bad, Denise. If you haven't contributed to the good of the country, how can you have the right to be proud?" "Oh, Dennis, why are you so cynical? You talk as if you were fifty or sixty years old." Dennis tries to break her mood by saying, "I'm really seventy, Denise. See. I have one white hair already." Denise looks at his smile and wants to smile in return, but she cannot. Knowing that he's meant everything he's said to her, she just looks out to sea and says nothing. He returns to her side and sits down. "I'm not as cynical as all that, Denise. All I want is to be free, to be who I am. Do you know why I'm doing what I'm doing? Do you want me to tell you?" "Of course I do." "I just couldn't be part of the lockstep in America. Job, promotion, success, retirement, death. I didn't want that. I didn't want anything to do with status or anything like it. And in America that all adds up to one thing. Money." He pauses. "And I didn't want to play a role every day that went from promotion to promotion so that my life was always waiting for me somewhere in the future. That seemed just like luring a rabbit with a carrot. So I looked for something else. I tried clowning, and I liked it. And I was good at it. And I got better at it after I went to a school for clowns in Florida. And that's what I want to keep on being, Denise. No promotions, no wanting to have power over somebody else, no ambitions, no competition. There really isn't any competition, you know. No one can be the kind of clown I am. Tomorrow I can't be the kind of clown I am today. All I want to be able to do is to be what I create, to create myself. And I want to keep on doing it whether the people in the audience like it or not. Of course, if they like it, that makes me feel good, but that's not the reason why I do it." He pauses and looks at her and asks, "Does this make any sense to you?" "It just proves to me that you're not like anyone else I've ever met. You don't think like other people." "Maybe I'm all wrong, Denise. Maybe I'm just a fool. But at least I'm my own fool. I can always say that much about myself." Denise watches him as he starts to smile, thinks differently of it, looks seaward and lets the breathing sea hold him like hypnosis. It is this certainty about himself, this sense of acceptance that intrigues her and makes her always want to know him better, know as much about him as possible, know everything there is to know. And it is the overflow of this interest that leads her to discuss him with her father and mother and, finally, her brother. Eventually she invites Dennis to the chateau to meet her family. There she waits for him in the gazebo while he and her father tour the estate. Once he joins her there with the others, she waits for her father and mother to see in him what she sees in him, but her mother remains deferential, her father baronial and almost suspiciously correct, her brother dismissive. And she notices how Dennis reacts to them, how his expression congeals from pleasant to determined. After the monsignor's questions, Dennis simply holds his ground, not trying to win agreement as much as establish a certain position, a certain distance. Days later Denise detects a change in him, a brusqueness, an inclination to hurt her in ways that she does not understand at all, a crudeness that is almost exaggerated for her benefit as if he wants to appear overnight less attractive to her. At first she thinks that he is merely trying to test her, and she remains silent, not wanting to provoke him further or give him the vaguest pretext of carrying his tactic to the point of outright rejection. Then when he takes her to his cottage and when she sees Yvette for the first time, she realizes that he is trying too hard to sunder things between them even though she does not fully understand why. But it is the overseriousness of his attempt that convinces her that it is a matter of the will and not the heart. And even when she stands naked in front of him at his suggestion, she knows intuitively that he is just acting, but she does not know how far the act will go until, in the end, he hands her her dress and turns away as if he cannot or will not embarrass her by looking at her. From that moment on, he changes. And they both know, without saying a word about it, that what exists between them is not only undeniable but irrevocable.

Knowing now how her father regards Dennis, she arranges to see him more or less secretly. These meetings are not things she disguises, but she no longer discusses Dennis with her family. Once, during one of their weekly shopping trips to Nice, her mother raises the subject with her, "Do you still see that American from the circus, Denise?" "Yes." "Is it serious with him?" "I don't know, Maman. I think so, but I am not sure." "Is it serious with you?" "Yes." "You know what your father's attitude is, do you not?" "I think I do." "He is against it absolutely. If it goes on, he will approach you about it." "What should I do?" Clothilde does not answer for several minutes. When she does speak, she speaks more as another woman than as Denise's mother, "I'm not sure, Denise. But I've been thinking about it a great deal. When it becomes truly necessary, we will talk about it. I am not opposed to this boy. I want you to know that. But I am, how shall I say, still wondering." "Do you like him, Maman?" "That is not the point, Denise. The only point is what you feel and what he feels and what decisions will come of this for both of you." "But do you *like* him? It matters to me, Maman." "In some ways, yes. In some ways, no. But I love you, Denise, and I know in my heart immediately when someone else loves you." She pauses and looks at Denise. "He is doing his best not to admit it to himself, but he has feelings for you, Denise. He has real feelings. I can tell that much. And he has courage. So, something will happen between you. Of that I am sure, but I have no way of knowing what it will be or how you'll deal with your father. Nor do you, really. Nor does he. But nothing stands still in love. We shall just wait and see what happens." After another pause, she adds, "I am not opposed to this boy, Denise, if there is something real between you. I want you to know that now." After Clothilde finishes speaking, she manages a reassuring smile. Denise, remembering the conversation she overheard between her father and the woman named Madeleine, feels a different solidarity with her mother than she has ever known. She wonders if she should tell her mother what she overheard on the telephone but decides against it. The silence between them takes over until they arrive in Nice, and the subject does not come up on the return trip.

Her mother's words are still with her when Denise sees Dennis again. He seems more somber than usual and is walking with a slight limp. "What happened, Dennis?" "Accident. The bike slid and came down my leg. It's nothing." "For a minute I thought you fell from the wire. I thought you made a mistake." "I never make a mistake on the wire." Denise frowns and says, "Don't say it that way, Dennis." "Why?" "Just don't. Please." "Do you think it will bring me bad luck?" "I don't know, but I worry when I hear people say they will never do this, never do that." "Okay. I take it back." He reaches out and closes his fingers around a fistful of space and brings it back toward his mouth and pretends to eat it. "There," he says, "I've just eaten a 'never sandwich.' Very good." Later, when they are returning to the chateau, she ask him, "Dennis, why are you more serious than all the other people I know?" "I'm not serious. I just pretend to be. Or maybe you just take me more seriously than most people do." "No, you are more serious. You look into things longer, deeper. You see behind things. Why are you that way? It spoils so many things for you." "If you think I'm serious, you should meet my friend Ramuz." "Ramuz?" "He's with the circus. He used to do what I do. Clowning. Wirewalking. He's too old to walk the wire any more, but once in a while he puts on the paints to clown for the crowds, but his heart's not in it." "Why is that?" "It's hard to say, Denise. He tries to tell me, but he doesn't have the words for it. What's at the heart of it is that he can't separate himself from his part as a clown now, and that depresses him. When he was younger, he felt that he was just playing a part. When he took off the paints and the costumes, the part was over. Now the part just keeps on going. One of the things you learn in clowning is that humor is possible only when there is a kind of distance between yourself and what you're trying to present as comic. If there's no distance, then there's no humor. It's like the old story of someone who slips on a banana peel. It's not funny to the person or to the onlookers when it happens. But later, assuming that no one was hurt, it's funny, even to the person who slipped. Distance . . . Well, that's Ramuz's problem now. He tries to clown, but it's not funny for him or for the people who see him. He just can't laugh in character. But he still dresses up once in a while, hoping he'll find the distance again, but he hasn't found it yet." "What else does he have? How does he live?" "He just does odd jobs around the circus now. That's all he has. And that's all he has to look forward to. Sometimes he talks to me because I'm the only one who listens to him. He tells me about his life. Yesterday he told me something that's been on my mind ever since. He told me straight out that it's getting harder and harder for him just to get up in the morning. He hates to do the little things he knows he has to do like going to the bathroom, washing himself, shaving, getting dressed, eating breakfast, drinking coffee. He hates to do what he's done a thousand times, a hundred thousand times before. It just bores the hell out of him now, but he can't *not* do it. He has to go to the bathroom and do all the other things. He told me yesterday that he's just become a slave to his needs, a slave to himself." "Doesn't he have anything else to live for? Family? Some person?" "Nothing. He's just getting older and older all by himself. If it weren't for me, he would have no one at all to listen to him." "You must not ever ignore him, Dennis. Not if you're the only one he talks to. Without you, he might do something desperate. People do desperate things when they feel they are absolutely alone." "Don't worry. I won't turn my back on him. But I hope to God I never get that way. I'd rather die than end up like Ramuz." He pauses. "It must be terrible to get old. But once you're old, what can you do about it? That's the hard part. You just can't do anything about it, can't stop it. Ramuz told me that being old is not being up to what you want to do. You feel yourself slipping. All the things that were your life just desert you, little by little, and when you try to hold on to them, they don't stay with you any more. Life just betrays you. And what does it stick you with? Memories. Just memories. And the memories make things worse." "If he had someone to care for, it might be different for your friend." "That's the answer, huh? Someone to care for, worry about?" "What else do we have? Doesn't everyone have to feel necessary to somebody else? If I knew that I wasn't necessary to someone else, I'd feel useless. No one to live for, to live with." "Well, Ramuz is a perfect study in uselessness. He has nobody. He tries his best to make the children laugh at him when he clowns, but all he makes them do lately is cry. He frightens them. Yet at one time he was one of the greatest clowns on the whole continent. He was as well known in France as Footit and Chocolat. Now? No one remembers him." Dennis lapses into a seriousness that walls him away from her. She has become familiar with this seriousness. More and more she feels herself lapsing into it with him so that her point of view starts to change. The familiar becomes suddenly unfamiliar, leaving her confronted not only with a different world but with a different sense of herself. The first time she became sensitive to it was when he visited her family at the chateau. Sitting in the gazebo beside him, she watched him as he watched her father, her mother, the monsignor, and her brother. Knowing that the conversation was forced, the hospitality merely correct, the circumstances awkward, she felt herself changing. Drawn from the orbit of her own family and into the orbit of Dennis, she no longer felt as if her previous life was a part of her any longer. For a moment she regarded her father as just another man, her mother as just another woman, her brother just another adolescent, and the visiting monsignor, whom she had known since childhood, merely another ecclesiastic whose language and inflections had an institutional unctuousness and rhythm that she had never before noticed. She suddenly felt alienated from an environment that had been until that moment as real to her as her own name. The words of her father and the monsignor became just so much talk. She felt that she could predict what they would say before they said it. But with Dennis she could predict nothing. She found herself listening to his answers the way she might listen to his breathing if he were asleep—with that much care, that much silence. He seemed to be creating his meanings just as he spoke so that the only criterion was his own honesty with himself and not any prudential instinct about how his words would be received or what effect they would have. Denise felt in this the magnetism of life itself, and she could not distract herself from it even if she tried. Her previous life suddenly appeared to her as something she had lived

145

through and not really *lived*. When it came time for Dennis to leave the chateau, she dreaded having to return to her roles as daughter and sister and function again in them. All at once they appeared to her like clothes that she had outgrown overnight. When she walked with Dennis to Anubis, she was really unprepared for what he was about to say to her. Noticing that he seemed grim, she asked, "What's wrong, Dennis?" "Nothing." "You did not like my family?" "I think it makes better sense the other way around." "Was it something anybody said?" "Nothing direct. But enough." He paused as he started Anubis and then said to her, "Tell your father I won't breathe on his jasmine. It might make him happy to know that." The remark left her confused, and she remained perplexed for days. She tried to see Dennis, but he avoided her. Finally, she did see him, and she remained with him even when he tried to leave her, convinced that her determination would eventually be rewarded. And in the end it was. When he said to her, "There's really no hope for us, no future," she knew that all his brusqueness was not meant to brutalize her but to brutalize his feelings for her, to quell his love for her by abusing it, degrading it, punishing it. It was only when he realized that this was hopeless that he was able to face her as he was . . .

". . . if I remember, I'll show you some pictures I have of Ramuz in costume when he was in his prime. Then, you can see . . . Denise, are you listening? You look like you're centuries away from me." "I'm sorry. I was just thinking about how serious you are sometimes." "Come on, I'll take you back to the chateau. That's enough talk for one afternoon." When they return to the chateau, Sanche de Savigny asks to see both of them in his study. Denise remains for the beginning of the conversation until her father asks her to leave. She waits in her room, hoping to see Dennis before he returns to his cottage on Anubis. But somehow she misses him. The following day she hears the sudden sound of Anubis in midafternoon and she wonders why Dennis has returned to the chateau. Then she hears her brother call her name from the hall. Before she answers, he tells her that she is wanted in the study. She dresses in a rush, passes a comb through her hair, and descends the stairs. From the very first second she enters the study, she feels that she is walking on stage in the middle of a play. It appears to her that everybody has already been assigned a part except her. She sees her father seated behind his desk and her brother standing beside him. In front of the desk stands Dennis with a flat package in his hand. Denise senses that there have been earlier scenes in this play and that they have involved her. She seats herself quietly to one side of the desk and listens while her father tells her in a few words that he has had a previous discussion with Dennis that is directly involved with her future and that Dennis now has something to say to her. From that point on, she feels herself sucked into the play, and everything accelerates. She hears Dennis speak not to her but to her father. He is telling him that he is returning his francs with interest and that he can use the surplus to try to buy back the respect of his daughter. Suddenly Denise realizes with horror that her father has attempted to bribe Dennis to stay away form her. She sees Dennis slam the package of francs on the desk and then stride out of the study. For several moments after that Denise remains seated in a kind of paralysis. Her fingers are on her cheeks, and she is attempting to say something through the baffled fury of her tears, but the words, when she actually hears them, are not her words, not hers at all but her mother's. And the words are addressed not to her but to her father. Clothilde de Savigny, who must have entered the room without Denise's having seen her, is saying that she is outraged by the presence of the francs on his desk as well as their purpose, that this is the worst thing that could have been done. And Sanche de Savigny, sweeping the francs to the floor with one hand, is saying that this whole matter is none of her business, none at all. Clothilde walks toward him and, after a pause, asks him in a straightforward but still slightly defensive tone if Madeleine is none of her business either. Clothilde says nothing else to de Savigny. Then she turns to Denise and asks her if this is what she wants, if she is satisfied to see Dennis walk out of her life this way. Immediately Denise says no. Clothilde then asks if she is brave enough to follow him. Denise nods her head yes. Then Clothilde asks her what is stopping her, why she is still standing, why? Denise runs past her mother and out of the chateau toward the circle where Dennis is revving Anubis, and in minutes she is astride the motorcycle behind Dennis, and they are traveling in silence along the coastal and mountain roads, and she shudders less and less from the aftermath of the confrontation in the study until at last she is calm, and the steady motorsound of Anubis becomes as relaxing to her as a lullaby . . .

Later in Eze, after the lemon pie and the capuccino, after the slow and sometimes backward mounting of the road to the perched village through the scrimmage of rain, after the opening of the locked door that admits them to the artist's apartment, after Dennis starts a slow but reliable fire, Denise is even more relaxed, and she kneels before the fire and stares at it as if she is determined to learn by sheer staring what fire really means. For the first time since childhood, she feels completely at home in these strange surroundings, and the fire crackles and radiates its heat like the sun of a new and more familiar world. Still later, when they are both naked, she wonders why she does not blush or look away. Instead she finds herself looking at Dennis as she might regard her own body in a mirror. When she feels his hands on her hips and thighs, she does not become tense. She does not withdraw. She simply lets her body go out to him as calmly as an exhalation, and when she holds him against herself with her arms and then with her arms and legs simultaneously, she feels, even beyond the compulsion of clasping and pressing, a new life whose geography and language she is learning even as she is experiencing them for the first time. Any comparisons are no help to her. Is she descending into another life slowly, certainly, evenly as a body might fall through space or through the sea? If so, why isn't she afraid? Instead of feeling any dread or apprehension, she feels as if the descent will never end, and she does not want to have it end. She is like a feather in a vacuum, beyond gravity, beyond buffeting, beyond everything but the wordless and windless silence of the moment. Even the strength and focus that gather in her loins only intensify what she is feeling. She turns and wrestles and almost immobilizes Dennis against her, but she is not grappling with him as much as she is at the mercy of the crest of whatever passion it is that is making her body more hers than she has ever known it and at the same time less subject to her. She cannot turn away if she chooses. She is like a woman in labor and in irresistible ecstasy at once. She hears quiet but unfamiliar cries gathering in

148

her throat, and they emerge from her lips as short, forced whimpers, beginning softly and intermittently until they become more frequent and almost guttural while she embraces Dennis with the tightness of death itself. Their bodies kiss and strain against one another as if one wants to exchange places with the other. For Denise the memories of the morning at the chateau evaporate like rain water in the sun of this new hemisphere. Where she felt rancor toward her father, she now feels nothing at all. For her brother she feels no deep resistance, only solicitude. For her mother she feels a different bond that has nothing of daughterhood about it any longer. All this she remembers as she rocks and whimpers with a slowly increasing effort in his arms while he remains silent, moving only when and if she moves, letting her forge the way and make him the follower. Somehow this merely intensifies her desire for him, and she presses up against him as if her entire body depends upon the closeness of his for survival, for life. And still he says nothing, and she remembers how silent he was on an afternoon in Nice when he told her about his father and his mother, about his days in college, about his toying with the idea of becoming a clown until the decision really made itself. He told her that he simply awoke one morning and knew that being a clown was what he could give himself to, that everything else for him was a predictable route that led to a future that was always about to happen but never actually happened, that the circus was to him—with all its noises and sawdust and greasepaint and tiger dung—more real than what most people casually but dogmatically referred to as the world. And she remembers his telling her softly but with the seriousness of someone phrasing a vow that life for him had to mean *life* and not merely living the day through. And now with her body fastened and linked to his, she feels what she had merely taken for granted when he made the remark. She feels *alive*. It is as if the past and the future have suddenly released her into a present that she is herself creating merely by living it, living it fully. Now for her there is only what's happening and what's about to happen. Everything else becomes merely a part of the prose of time. Even while she thinks of this, she feels a wildness gathering in her for release, and she begins to move and shudder almost involuntarily against him, straining to free herself from the soothing torture that is mounting within her, that is discovering itself not only in her groin and thighs but in every part of her body, that makes her forget herself little by little, then completely. At last, she feels that the tension in every nerve in her body is peaking, steadying, aching for that second when the clash of pleasures she is only now imagining will somehow spend itself. And it's already happening. She feels her shoulder blades twist into the couch cushions as she pushes like childbirth at Dennis's body that is centering her to the spread. And suddenly she feels tears rush to her eyes, and she looks toward the ceiling without seeing it, and her right hand begins fisting and unfisting in the night air without her knowing or caring about it. And the quick sharp cries she hears are hers, and she wonders when the warm loosening rush through her body will end while it keeps on forcing her back against the spread in one diminuendo after another. She feels herself clamping her teeth tightly together as if there is a deep itch at the root of every tooth that she must ease. By degrees her fisted hand opens and relaxes like a spent thing against the cushion, and she hugs Dennis to her breasts while her uplifted legs slide down his hips and rest finally on the spread itself, and the ceiling that she looked up at but did not see shrinks relentlessly into itself again. And she lies back and stretches, relishing the calm that she feels, a calm so utterly itself that she feels at peace and almost in communion with the posted furniture in the apartment, with the diminishing fire in the grate, with the whole silent Mediterranean just beyond the window. When they are again side by side and Dennis asks her how she feels, she smiles at him and says she would love to have an apple—a large, cold, firm apple. He leaps form the couch and returns with a still life that was propped against the wall. Painted on the taut canvas are several bananas, a peach, a clutch of green grapes, and one apple. "This is the best I can do under the circumstances, Denise." She smiles and studies the painting before he props it back against the wall and returns to her side on the couch. "Have you ever noticed, Dennis," she muses, "that no painter can ever really capture the color of fruit. The real color." "It's untranslatable." "What is?" "The color of fruit." He smiles and looks at her and adds, "God has the patent." She returns his look and says, "That's the first time I ever heard you speak about God." "A slip of the tongue." "But there *is* God, Dennis." "Only if you believe." "Your believing creates God." "Not for me, Denise."

"You're different." The following morning when she receives the sacrament at the dawn Mass in the church of *Les Pénitents Blancs*, she remembers their midnight talk about God and impulsively asks the old priest if he will give Dennis his blessing. And that is the last calm act that punctuates the day for her. She walks alone to the spot where Anubis is parked and waves up to Dennis who is leaning against the church wall so that he can keep her in sight as she goes. Then she sees the parked Mercedes. Before she can turn, she is gripped by two men who drag her into the car and pinion her between them in the back seat. She recognizes Monsignor Lascaux in the passenger seat and hears him tell the driver to return to the chateau at once. She struggles with the men on either side of her and screams at the monsignor to stop the car and let her out. But the Mercedes speeds on along the corniche and no one in the car says a word to her. By the time they reach the chateau, she has not so much banked her fury as exhausted it. While the monsignor remains in the car with the driver, Denise is led by the two men into her father's study. Her father is waiting for her there alone. After the two men leave, de Savigny tells her to go immediately to her room and wait there until he calls for her. When she asks him why, he mutters that he wants no further problems with her in this matter, none whatsoever. She turns, leaves the study, goes to her room, flings herself face down on her bed, and sobs in a fury of helplessness and misery. It is at least four hours before her father has her brother summon her to the study. Seth looks preoccupied and nervous, but he says nothing to Denise. Together they walk to the study where the door is ajar. Hearing voices within, they wait. Denise can see that there is another man with her father in the study and that they are both standing near the French doors that lead to the garden. De Savigny is saying, "I can assure you, Inspector Gagnon, that this was an accident. A regrettable accident, but an accident nonetheless." "But there are several things that are quite ambiguous here, Monsieur de Savigny. Excuse me for these questions, but it is necessary, you understand." "Of course. I will help in any way I can." "You say that your son just went to Eze to warn the American that he was making a nuisance of himself with your daughter. And they had a discussion. And the American somehow fell." "That is what Seth told me." "But it is difficult to understand how the man could have fallen from that point." "I can only tell you what Seth reported to me. My son is not a liar, I assure you." "Very well. There is nothing I can do about this at the moment. Perhaps we will have to reconstruct the whole scene at a later date." He pauses, scribbles something in a notebook, and resumes, "But the waitress in the café said that the American had a girl with him. Could that have been your daughter?" "If you check at the circus, Inspector, you will find that this American was well known to several women there. It could have been any one of them." "But it was none of them. My men have checked already." "Then it could have been another girl. Who knows?" "But not your daughter." "Of course not. She's been in the chateau all night, and she's here now." "Very well, Monsieur. I will take you at your word, at least at this time. Later I might have to ask you if your daughter might appear for an identification by the waitress. I am sure you will not mind that. We have to be correct, you understand." He slips the notebook back into his suitcoat with his left hand. "You are sure there is nothing else you wish to tell me, Monsieur de Savigny?" "Yes, nothing." "Thank you for your cooperation. If I have any further questions, I will contact you. Please remember me to Madame de Savigny." "Good night, Inspector Gagnon. I will help you in any way that I can." Denise sees the man leave through the French doors. Seth then precedes her into the study. De Savigny faces them and starts to pace back and forth. "Papá," says Denise, "why was the inspector here? Where is Dennis? What's happened?" "Sit down, Denise," mutters de Savigny. "There's been an unexpected accident, and I have to discuss it with you." "Papá, why did you send those men after us in Eze? Why couldn't you leave us alone after what you tried to do? How can I face you any more?" "I did it for your own good, Denise, not my own. Some day you'll understand that and thank me for it." "But how did you find us?" "That was really quite simple. Seth went to the circus this morning early and made some inquiries. He has a girl friend there, your American. Her name is Yvette. She was quite sure that the two of you would be in Eze. And, as it turned out, she was right." "Did you pay her as well, Papá?" "That was not necessary, Denise. And I can do without any further accusations from you, if you don't mind." He pauses, looks at Seth, who is standing nervously beside the desk, and continues, "After you entered the car with Monsignor Lascaux . . ."

"I did not enter, Papá. I was forced into the car. I was pulled . . ." ". . . after you entered the car, your brother and Pierre from our factory . . ." "Seth? Was Seth there?" "Seth and Pierre found this Dennis in Eze and tried to explain to him that it was in his interest and in the interest of our family for him to stay out of our affairs." "But it is my affair, Papá. It is nobody's affair but mine." "In any case, there was a scuffle, and the American suffered a fall there. He seems to have lost his balance and . . ." Denise rushes to her father and screams, "Where is he?" De Savigny does not respond to her mood but resumes his account in a monotone, ". . . and he was taken to a hospital in Cimiez." "I'm going there now, Papá, this minute." "You will do nothing of the sort, Denise." "I'm leaving now if I have to crawl to Cimiez. You can't stop me." "Will you still want to go if it means that your brother might be put in serious trouble?" "How? What trouble?" "Seth told me that the American fell while they were talking. But what is to prevent the American from saying that Seth pushed him? What is to prevent him from inventing any story? As far as Inspector Gagnon is concerned, he accepts what I told him just now. All he thinks is that Seth went to Eze to see the American, and somehow there was this accident. They detained Seth for a few questions at the scene and then released him. They think that the American was alone or with another girl. At least, I hope they do. They don't know that you were there. And I know some people who can persuade the waitress in Eze to say that you were never there with him. And I think it is best if it remains that way. But if you visit him in Cimiez or write to him or call him or contact him in any way, that will only convince the police to continue their investigation. And they will ask questions that will lead directly to your brother." "But I don't care, Papá!" "You don't care? What if the police are told by the American that Seth did more than talk to him in Eze? Do you want to see your brother taken into custody? Do you want to see him in jail? Do you want him to be tried?" "But if he is telling the truth, he has nothing to fear." "You don't understand the mentality of the police, Denise. Even if there is only an interrogation, it would be damaging to him and to all of us. To you as well." Denise turns away and begins to shake her head from side to side slowly. Then she faces her father and asks, "Is Dennis hurt badly, Papá?" "From what I understand, it is not serious, but it will

153

take time. Possibly a month or a little longer." He waits for several moments while Denise sits down. Then, in a change of tone, he says, "This is what I want you to do, Denise. I want you to leave for Paris this evening and stay in our apartment there. The rest of us will join you in a week or so. I've already made arrangements at the hospital that all the expenses of this accident will be borne by me. And I've told the doctors there that I want this American to have the best care possible." He pauses deliberately until she looks up at him. Then he says, "If you and this boy still feel as you do when he is released from the hospital, I will personally see to it that there will be no obstacles in your path." "Have you told this to Maman?" "I'll talk to your mother about this later. Last night was not easy for her. I told her to rest, but she refused. She took a sedative just before dawn, and she's still sleeping. But when she wakes, I'll explain everything. Now it is important that she rests and that she knows you are well." "Does she know about Dennis?" "No. Not yet. But that will change nothing. You will leave tonight for Paris by train, and in the meanwhile you will not be in touch with this American in any way. And I've already warned Seth not to discuss this matter with anyone. And tomorrow I'm sending Pierre with a truck to get the motorcycle from Eze and bring it here for safekeeping. I will take care of everything, Denise, but you must do exactly as I say." "But I must see him, Papá! I can't just vanish like this." "Denise, haven't you caused us enough trouble for one night? You will do as I say! Do you hear me? I've told you that you can live your life any way you choose in a month or so! Isn't that enough? But in the meanwhile I want you to think of the possible consequences to your brother and your family and yourself and to this clown as well if the police begin to suspect that this was not an accident." "You keep saying it was just an accident. Was it an accident, Papá?" "Do you think Seth would lie to me, Denise?" "Well, Dennis is not a liar, Papá. Why do you keep saying that he will tell the police something that didn't happen? Has he said anything to the police, anything at all yet?" "No. Not yet. Perhaps you are right. I doubt if he would do anything that would make you choose between him and your family. Perhaps I spoke too hastily. But to prevent any indiscretion, I still want you to return to Paris this evening. Go and pack. I'll take you to the station myself." "Please tell me you're not lying to me again, Papá. Please. I want to believe you." De Savigny strides toward Seth near the desk and says to him peremptorily, "Tell your sister exactly what happened." Seth looks at his father several times before he tells Denise, "We were just talking by the wall near the church, Denise, and he lost his balance. I don't know how it happened. He just fell." "But the wall is higher than my waist, Seth. It comes up to here. How could he just fall over it?" "I don't know, but he did. It happened so quickly." "Look at me, Seth! Look in my eyes! Make me believe you!" "Why should I lie to you?" "Seth, you're not talking to a stranger. I'm your sister. Tell me the truth!" Seth looks at his father with a futile gesture and shrugs. "Why can't you look me in the face, Seth?" shouts Denise. "Why? Just tell me the truth, for the love of God!" "Very well, very well! The truth is that I hated him! I hate him now! I hate what he's done to you, what he's made of you! I went to Eze, hating him, and I . . ." "Seth, you pushed him off that wall, didn't you? Didn't you?" "Yes, I pushed him. And I'd do it again if I had another chance! The only thing I regret is that he didn't die when he fell. Is that what you want to hear?" "Oh, my God, my God . . ." De Savigny takes Seth by the arm and leads him to the door of the study, "Go to your room, Seth." "No, Papá. I'm staying with you." "Go to your room, Seth, until I call you. And be quiet. I don't want this to waken your mother." Seth exits without another word. De Savigny closes the door firmly behind him and crosses slowly to Denise, who is now sitting limply in her chair and weeping softly, hopelessly. "Now, now you know, Denise." "I knew it from the beginning, Papá. But why? Why did he do what he did?" "I was trying to hide it from you. I was hoping you would never . . ." "I would have found out sooner or later. Oh Papá, why didn't you leave us alone? Why didn't you stop Seth? Why?" "It's too late for that now, Denise. We have to deal with the facts as they are. And they are serious. The police had no proof, so they had to let your brother go. But if they learn what actually happened or if they suspect that something really exists between you and the American, then the situation will become difficult. It will be devastating to your mother. This is why you must go to Paris immediately and stay there until this man is released from the hospital. I'll take care of all the details, and I promise you that there will be no interference from now on. If you feel in a month or so as you feel now, I will not stand in your way." "But I must get word to him, Papá. I must do something." "You must put that out of your mind, Denise. It's too dangerous. Even as things are, I have no idea what the police might do. They are naturally suspicious. I think the only reason that Gagnon is holding back is that he doesn't want to impose a hardship on your mother. He still feels indebted to her. She saved his life, you know . . ."

Several hours later, after she has packed her bags, Denise asks herself why she is doing what she is doing. Why doesn't she just break her bonds and go directly to Cimiez? She feels she ought to be there. But the impediment created by her father's words stops her. She tells herself that she will wait a month, that a month is nothing, really nothing, that her life will start a month from now. Once aboard the train from Nice to Paris, she keeps trying to distract herself by looking at the darkening landscape. The hills and flatlands repeat themselves past her window in the lowering dusk until it finally becomes dark enough outside for her to see her reflection in the pane. She studies herself as she might study a bad painting. Then she looks through her reflection into the darkness beyond, which is punctuated occasionally by the racing lights of farmhouse or village or town. By the time the train reaches Lyon, she is again in the grip of the conflicting impulses to go on or to return. She is about to reach for her bags and detrain when the memory of her father's warning paralyzes her, and she sits down again, perplexed. Should she go to Dennis, regardless of the police, regardless of Seth, regardless of the consequences? Is Dennis asking for her even at this minute? What is she doing on a train heading for Paris? Why can't she make a complete break and do as she chooses? Debating these alternatives with herself, she wishes she had spoken to her mother before leaving the chateau, but there had been no time. Now, cornered by question after question, she puts her head back on the seat cushion and closes her eyes as if the mere shutting of her eyelids will condemn everything else to silence. She feels that she is drifting, drifting, drifting without course. Slowly, so slowly she cannot stop it, sleep takes her. And then the dreams come. Darkness. Darkness as absolute as ink. Suddenly a spotlight lensed with a pink gel. It focuses on a man in a brown business suit. In his left hand are five knives, which he holds deftly downward in a bunch by the tips of their blades. The man turns toward Denise, and she immediately recognizes him as her father, a younger version of her father but undeniably her father. The spotlight shifts, banishing de Savigny to the darkness. It snoops like a hound across the floor until it stops at Denise. She blinks at the pink brightness. Then she realizes that she is standing with her back flush against a wooden door and that she has her hands clenched at her sides. She hears her father call to her from the darkness, "Denise, you must not move at all. It is imperative that you do not move. Do you understand me?" Then she hears the first knife sing through the darkness and stab the door just below the clenched fingers of her right hand. She can even feel the knife quivering in the wood. Shuddering, she tries to step away from the door, but her father repeats, "It is vital that you do not move, Denise." She tries to answer him, but she cannot. She tries to scream, but she cannot. Then she hears the second knife. It sticks in the door just below her left hand. But this time the tip of the blade has come so close that it separates her index finger from her middle finger. She can feel the cool blade between her finger joints. She tries to go completely limp, hoping she can collapse out of her standing position, but she is helpless against the door as if she is crucified against it. Then, the third knife. It strikes an inch to the side of her right cheek and quivers still like an arrow. She hears her mother calling her name from the darkness, and she tries to answer. Again, nothing. Then, the fourth knife. The blade comes so close to her cheek on the left that it makes a small slit in the skin. She can feel the blood tracking down her cheek like a slow tear. All of a sudden she sees Seth standing in front of her, removing the knives one by one from the door before he leaves her alone again. Now she hears the fifth and last knife. Now she can even see it, cartwheeling through the air toward her chest. It is aimed directly at her heart; it is coming faster and nearer, nearer, nearer ... The pink spotlight goes out. Darkness again. Dennis is talking to her, and she is answering. They are not only talking but are in the midst of lovemaking, and she is luxuriating in the presence of his body in hers. She hugs him to her as if she intends to break him with her thighs. She feels her body tense with an energy that is totally new to her, and she is saying things to him that she never dreamed

157

she would be able to say to any man. "Do you know the name for where you are, Dennis?" "What name?" "For where you are now, right now?" "I think so." "I mean in Latin?" "Does it start with the letter between *u* and *w*?" "Do you know what it means?" "No. Does it matter?" "It means sheath." "Sheath? For a sword?" "You are my sword . . ." The train stops and jostles her awake. Stretching her way out of her dreams, she looks out of the window at the gathered lights of Paris. Is she really here in Paris? Why? For days after her arrival she lives in an atmosphere of both dismay and regret. The people and ambience of Paris pass by her with the same grayness that character-ized the French landscape that she viewed on the train ride north. She has the feeling that she is waiting for things to stop and focus themselves, but they never do. She seems to herself to be the only permanence in the flux around her. Occasionally she finds herself in tears without reason or provocation, not only when she is alone but in public as well. She remains so until her classes commence at the Sorbonne. But there, even the discipline of her studies offers no relief. Yet her work gives her the excuse to be out of the apartment and away from her parents who have joined her in Paris. Neither her father nor her brother speak to her about the incident in Eze, and her mother postpones any conversation with her until they are alone. Even then their words veer away from the subject that both find somehow be-yond words for them, but her mother tries to be helpful by telling her to be patient, that she is young, that there is time. When Denise does ask her father about Dennis, she is told that his recovery is continuing but that the need for avoiding any contact or communication with him is still necessary, even by telephone. The result is that Denise retreats into her studies so completely and with so little regard for time that she does not even notice that her period passes without happening. One day. Two days. Four days. Finally, two weeks late. Actually, after the first week, she knows what is happening to her. It is not calendar days that convince her but a signal from some deeper personal pulse that informs her of a change in her temperament, her outlook, her sensitivity. At first, she becomes almost possessively se-cretive about herself, overly careful in ways that are not and have never been natural to her, evasive of the eyes of her parents, her brother, her fellow students. It is as if all the events of the preceding weeks have suddenly turned upon her physically so that she has to think, actually think about holding herself together. Otherwise she fears that she will simply yield to a yet unknown but powerful centrifugal force that will tear her to pieces like a prisoner drawn and quartered or ripped asunder by the black horses of execution. At the Sorbonne she listens to lectures with such an act of will that she ends up by overconcentrating on what is being said. In the laboratory she finds herself unable to dissect the toads that she must examine. The simple act of slicing the skin of a preserved specimen makes her shudder. But she finally forces herself to do it, ordering her right hand to its simple deed like a general issuing to a lieutenant an obvious, logical and irrefusable command. For more than two weeks she locks herself into a regime of study, occupying and inundating her mind so that it is almost too spent to think about anything else. But at night, just before she sleeps, she must contend with all the waiting devils that she has managed to keep at bay during the day. She thinks of Dennis in Cimiez, of her father's warning and how his words have now become so many bricks in the wall that separates Dennis from her, of the life that is infinitesimally shaping itself inside of her. And she feels so trapped from within and from without that she sleeps fitfully and wakes long before dawn and lies supine in her bed, listening to the soprano racket of the birds outside her window, waiting for the ransoming sun to brighten the blue ceiling. Then she dresses and leaves for her classes. One day becomes indistinguishable from predecessors or successors until the day of Anubis . . .

As the day reaches noon, she is examining a slide of rabbit tissue beneath her microscope. It reminds her immediately of the broken rabbit that she dropped into the gorge when Dennis insisted that it would only suffer by her attempts to nurse it. But she puts the memory to sleep by concentrating willfully on the slide and the slide alone. She suddenly sees the tissue smear and fuzz out of focus. After trying to dial the slide into definition again, she finds that the tissue remains blurred. When she pushes her laboratory stool back from the table and blinks, she notices that the faces of the students around her are out of focus as well. At the same time she feels the clogged hiccough of nausea at the base of her throat. Leaving her station in the labora-

159

tory, she rushes for the door and hurries down the hall to the women's lavatory. Once there, she feels the nausea gradually leave her, but she fears that there will be a recurrence, and she remains. After five minutes, she rinses her face with cold water, returns to the laboratory, and asks to be excused. Outside, she walks for several blocks along the Boulevard St. Germaine. Her legs grow weaker as she goes. By the time she reaches the Place St. Michel, she is perspiring freely. She locates an empty table at one of the outdoor cafes and orders a glass of orange juice. When the waiter finally brings the juice to the table, she drinks it so quickly that she chokes on it. She unloosens her blouse buttons around her neck and, opening the collar, sits back in the chair and closes her eyes and keeps them limply closed until she hears someone call her by her name. She opens her eyes and turns. Thérèse, accompanied by Sexto, is bending toward her and asking, "Denise, what's the matter? Are you sick?" Denise tries to sit erect in the chair, but the nausea returns, and she remains slightly bent over. Thérèse says, "Is there anything wrong, Denise?" "Nothing. Nothing at all. I'll be all right in a minute." Thérèse turns to Sexto and says, "You go ahead, Sexto. I'll meet you later. I'm staying with Denise until she feels better." "Where do you want me to meet you?" "Not at the apartment. You know why." "Where then?" "I'll call you at the brasserie in an hour." Sexto slouches away, and Thérèse seats herself beside Denise and says, "Are you feeling a little better now?" "Yes. Yes, it's going away. I think I'll be myself in a few minutes." It is actually fifteen minutes before Denise can sit erect in the chair. Then, still perspiring, she leans forward and rests her elbows on the tabletop. "I've known you long enough," says Thérèse, "to know when something is bothering you, Denise. You're not yourself. You look changed." "I'm still the same, Thérèse. I just felt a little faint, that's all." "When did you ever feel faint, Denise?" "I'm no different than anyone else." She looks down at the tabletop between her elbows and sees the palest reflection of her features in the scratched but burnished marble. She does not speak or change position. After several minutes Thérèse says, "I think I know when I'm not wanted, Denise. I might as well be invisible." "Don't leave, Thérèse, please. It's just that I have so much on my mind lately. My mind goes its own way sometimes." "I thought I was the only one who had problems." "No, you're not the only one, Thérèse." Denise lets her arms fall into her lap and slouches gradually back into the chair again. For a second she feels as if she might lose consciousness entirely. Then the malaise leaves her. "Denise, you look as if you're going to fall over." Denise again sits up in the chair and faces Thérèse squarely, "I'm pregnant, Thérèse. I think I'm in the second month." "Pregnant?" "Yes. I am sure." Thérèse opens her mouth in surprise, and for a moment Denise does not know if she is going to laugh or scream. Instead Thérèse lets her mouth close into an expression that is neither a smile nor a frown. "That would have been the last thing I would have suspected, Denise." She pauses for a moment and then adds, "I can't think of anything to say, really. Pregnant? Are you sure?" "Yes." "Do you need to see a doctor? I can give you a name of one." "No, Thérèse. I don't want to see that kind of a doctor." "You mean you really want to have it? You want to be pregnant?" "Yes." "How far along did you say you were?" "A month. Maybe a little more." "Shall I ask you who the father is or mind my own business?" "Someone you don't know. An American." "Does *he* know?" "No. He's been in an accident. He's still in a hospital in Cimiez." After a pause Thérèse says, "It all sounds very complicated." "You're the only one who knows, Thérèse. About the baby, I mean. You must promise not to tell anyone." "You needn't worry about that, Denise." Denise attempts to stand and actually makes it to her feet with little if any dizziness. "There," she says, "I think I can make it home by myself now. I'm feeling better." "I'll walk with you just to be sure." Together they leave the table and proceed across the Pont St. Michel. At one point Denise stops when she feels a surge of vertigo, but it passes almost immediately, and she goes on. She only takes a few more steps when she sees it, and she stops so quickly that Thérèse goes on for several yards before she realizes that Denise is no longer beside her. Thérèse turns and asks, "What's the matter?" Denise is staring straight ahead. It is exactly as she last saw it when it was parked against a tree in Eze—the gleaming black metal body and white-striped fenders, the black seat, the white-tipped handlebars. Even without moving closer to examine it, she knows that it is Anubis. But here? In Paris? How? And the final enigma is Pascal, Thérèse's brother, who is standing beside Anubis in a helmet and goggles and smiling at both of them as they approach him. Thérèse follows Denise's stares and says, "Pascal? I thought you were going back to An- tibes!" "I had some things to do. I decided to leave tomorrow." Denise is walking slowly toward Pascal, looking alternately at him and then at the motorcycle. "Pascal, where did you get this?" "Do you like it?" "But where did you get it? I have to know." "Come on, Denise. I'll give you a ride." "Tell me, Pascal. Where? I have to know." Pascal looks at her suspiciously before he says, "From your father, actually. Your father's foreman called me ..." "You mean Pierre?" "Pierre called me and told me there was a motorcycle that your father wanted me to keep for a while. The real owner had had an accident or some- thing like that and asked your father to store the motorcycle for him until he recovered. He wanted your father to keep it for him rather than the police or somebody else. Anyway, I went with Pierre to Eze, and we loaded it on a truck and brought it to Antibes. Then we had a mechanic make a key for it, and I asked if I could drive it until they wanted it back and Pierre said it was all right with him. So here I am. I drove it all the way from Antibes to Paris three days ago to see Thérèse, and I'll be taking it back tomorrow." "Pascal," says Thérèse, "you're impossible." Denise interrupts with, "Did Pierre tell you any- thing else about the real owner?" "No, not really. But he told me that the real owner might be leaving France and that if he didn't claim the motorcycle in a month, it might be mine. Your father would see to that, and ... But why are you so interested?" Denise feels another rush of vertigo and holds the handlebars of Anubis for support. Pas- cal turns to Thérèse and asks, "What's the matter with Denise?" "She's just not feeling well right now, Pascal." Denise releases the handlebars and walks away from Thérèse and Pascal. Step by step her strength returns to her as she goes. Pascal shouts after her, "Den- ise, don't tell your father I'm in Paris." Denise does not answer. Thérèse calls after her, "Denise, where are you going?" Denise keeps walking. She heads for the family apartment on the Ile St. Louis. The sight of Anubis has stirred all her memories alive again. By the time she reaches the apartment, she has already determined what she will do. She hurries to her room and closes the door behind her. Immediately she goes to a drawer in her dresser, opens it, and removes a tight wad of francs and unrolls them carefully. Inside the roll is the key to Anubis that Dennis had given her in Eze on the day of the accident. She holds the key in her hand for a moment before rewrapping it in the roll of francs. Just as she is replacing the francs in the drawer, she hears a knock on her door. "Yes?" "Are you all right, Denise? I heard you come back early." "Yes, Maman." "Why are you home so early?" Denise does not answer. After a pause her mother says, "I want to talk to you, Denise." "Yes, Maman. Come in." Clothilde de Savigny opens the door and walks slowly into the room. As she passes Denise, she touches her gently on the cheek, then crosses to the bed and sits down on the edge. She crosses her arms over her breasts and lets a moment pass. "This has been very difficult, Denise. This has been very difficult for all of us." "I know it has, Maman." Clothilde uncrosses her arms and lets them rest in her lap. When she speaks, she speaks like a woman who has rehearsed for this moment for some time. "Do you remember, Denise, when we were driving to Nice once, and I told you that the time would come when we would have to talk?" "Yes, Maman." "I think that time is now. Right now." Clothilde pauses, grips the edge of the bed with both hands and looks at Denise. "This is not easy for me to say to you, Denise, but I want everything to be honest between us now. We must talk like two women now, and we must be honest." Again she pauses, looks down at her lap, raises her eyes, and says, "When I told you to follow this American boy after that scene in the chateau, I took a position I've never taken before in my life. It was the first time I disagreed with your father in your presence. But I want you to know that I knew what I was doing. I want you to understand that from me. I knew every minute what I was doing." Denise nods her head yes before Clothilde continues. "Your father and I have been together but not really together for many years now. It's reached a point now where we have no illusions about it. At least, I have no illusions. Not any more. There is a woman named Madeleine who has been a part of his life for the past eight years. I've known about it almost from the beginning, but I said nothing about it. He thought I was blind to what was happening, and I let him think it. I just couldn't bring myself to face him with it, do you understand? I kept telling myself that he was not really a bad man. I said that he was just weak. And he is not a bad man, Denise. It's just that he is absolutely rigid, inflexible. He sees the role he thinks he must play, and he plays it to the letter, and he thinks everyone else should do the same. He wants everyone to conform to what he thinks is right. He doesn't see the other side at all. When I was your age, my parents told me that a man with qualities like Sanche would make a good husband. And I believed them. I did what I was told. It's taken me all my life, Denise, to realize that I wasn't told the truth. I was told what my parents thought was the truth, but it was just a lie. There must be love, Denise, real love. It must be like breath itself between a man and a woman. When I saw that you had that kind of feeling for this boy and that he had the same feeling for you, I decided that this was more important than anything else. As long as you had that between you, everything else was possible. That's why I spoke up and told you to follow him. It had to be, or else you would live a life of regret until the day you died . . . If it was to be my last act on this earth, I would not let that happen to you." "I know that, Maman. I felt it long before I really understood it." "Thank you, Denise. It means something to me that you have that feeling, but I would have done it regardless. Of course, I had no way of knowing what was going to happen, so, really, the true problems are still ahead of us. I don't know how badly Dennis has been injured. I have tried to find out, but the doctor communicates only with your father, and your father just says that he is recovering. In fact, he says very little to me, and he says nothing to anyone else because he fears that the police might want to interrogate Seth again. Seth claims it was an accident, but . . ." "It was no accident, Maman." Clothilde de Savigny rises from the bed and paces the room for several minutes before she says, "Are you sure it was not an accident?" "Yes, Maman." "How do you know?" "Because I faced Seth myself, and he admitted it to me." "Then he has not told me the truth. Does your father know this?" "Yes, Maman." Clothilde shakes her head sadly from side to side. Denise comes to her side and says, "It makes no difference now, Maman. I don't really blame Seth. He's young. And he has always been quick-tempered. I'm sure he didn't fully realize what he wanted to do. In his own way I believe he was thinking of me. But I'm sure he is safe from the police. I know that Dennis will not tell the police what really happened. If he hasn't done it already, he won't." "How do you know?" "I just *know*. When he recovers, he will leave the hospital, and no one will ever know except us." Denise stands in the center of the room while her mother keeps pacing. Finally, Denise states, "I have decided to go to the hospital in Cimiez myself and see him, Maman. I want to find out how he is myself. I can't go on living this way. I don't know what is happening behind the scenes. I must talk to Dennis myself. I don't care what anybody else will think if I go ..." "But don't you think it would make the police suspicious of Seth?" "I don't know, Maman. But I will lose my mind if I have to go on this way. I can't worry about the consequences. It's gone beyond that for me now. You said that we had to be honest with one another, and I'm being honest with you." "Why do you say that it's gone beyond that for you?" Denise faces her mother, who has stopped pacing and is looking at her unswervingly. Denise starts to speak and then stops. Her mother says nothing but waits without moving. "Maman," says Denise and stops again before she adds slowly and quietly, "I think I am pregnant, Maman." Clothilde does not respond. Then she nods slowly to herself and walks to her daughter. She puts her right arm around her and leads her to the bed where they both sit down. They sit in silence until Denise says, "Today I was so sick I could barely walk home." "Have you been sick before this?" "No, Maman. This is the first time." Clothilde stands, walks to the door, opens it, looks up and down the hall, closes the door again and returns to the bed. "Does anyone else know, Denise?" "Thérèse. I told her today. I don't know why. I just had to tell someone." "Have you seen a doctor?" "No, Maman. I thought the doctor might tell Papá, and that would only make matters worse than they are." "I think it is essential that you see a doctor immediately. This is a very delicate time, these first weeks and months." "The doctor will have to wait, Maman. I have to go to Cimiez first." "Don't be hasty, Denise. Nothing will change in one day. I'm talking as your mother now and I don't want to see you do something foolish. I will make an appointment for you with Dr. Jacob. What time is it? I think I can arrange for him to see you immediately. I'll drive you." "Dr. Jacob is a good friend of Papá's. I'm sure he will tell him everything." "No! No, he will not! *I* will tell your father myself. You will leave that entirely to me, Denise, do you understand? And you will not worry about it. That will be my business." Denise nods as Clothilde goes to the telephone, calls the doctor, and arranges for an appointment within an

165

hour. For the first time in her life Denise observes a new independence, a new severity in her mother. She seems surer of herself. With every word and act she gives Denise the impression that she knows precisely what she is doing and what must yet be done and why. Denise notices how the set and line of her mother's jaw now seem as definite as the look of a queen's face profiled on a coin . . .

The image of the determination in her mother's jaw remains with Denise hours later as she mounts the stone steps to the doctor's office. Her mother has driven there but, at Denise's request, has remained in the car, reluctantly. When Denise enters the anteroom, she passes the only other patient there—a young woman in the final days of pregnancy—and approaches the nurse-receptionist on duty. The nurse looks up from her charts and asks, "Are you Denise de Savigny?" "Yes." "Did you bring the specimen?" "Yes." "May I have it, please?" Denise removes the clear, capped cruet of urine from her purse and stands it like a chessman on the desk in front of the nurse. "Thank you. Be seated, please, until the doctor can see you." Denise sits directly across from the other woman in the anteroom, who is scanning with casual interest each full leaf of a glossy magazine spread-eagled in her lap. The woman seems to be in her late twenties. She sits with her pillowy legs slightly apart so as to allow her unwieldy, puffed abdomen to rest on her thighs. The woman's blue dress barely contains the abdomen, which continues to swell upward until it curves to a finish just underneath the woman's breasts. Swollen and pendant, the breasts lounge on the roof of the abdomen. For several moments, Denise regards the woman as the stranger she actually is, but little by little she starts to feel a kind of solidarity with her as if the woman is a prefiguring of what Denise imagines she herself will be in time. Once the woman looks up, catches Denise in midgaze, smiles and keeps on roughly flipping the shining leaves of the magazine. By then the nurse returns and calls Denise to her desk. She begins asking her a litany of questions—age, weight, date of last period, etc.—and entering Denise's answers on a yellow sheet of lined paper in front of her. When she is finished, she leads Denise into an examining room and says, "Please remove all your clothing except your shoes and put this on." She hands Denise a white medical gown and leaves, closing the door behind her. Holding the gown over her arm like so much fabric, Denise inspects the room. To the right of the door is a table on which there are spools of gauze, several urns of ointment, a baker's dozen of glistening instruments lined side by side like silverware. In the center of the room is an examination table topped with black leather. At one end of the table is a pair of stirrups. On the right wall is a chart of a woman's body in progressive stages of pregnancy. Denise is studying the chart when the nurse reenters the room, sees that she has not undressed and says, "You must remove your clothing. The doctor will be ready for you shortly." "I'm sorry, I . . ." "Is this your first examination?" "Yes. I've never had to have an examination before." "I see," says the nurse and smiles, "but there is really nothing to be apprehensive about." "Yes, I understand that, but I am apprehensive anyway. I am a student of biology, so I know what to expect, but it's one thing to know and another thing to have what you know happen to you." Denise makes an attempt to smile, but the nurse ignores it. "After you remove your clothes, you may fold your dress and undergarments and leave them on the chair behind you. Leave your shoes on, and slip into that robe." Again the nurse leaves the room. Denise unzips her dress, takes it off, and then slips out of her underwear as if the walls are eyes. For the first time she becomes sensitive to the coldness of the room. Carefully she dons the gown, which tents her like a small sheet with an opening in the center for her head. Then she stands beside the examination table and waits until the nurse, after a tentative knock on the door, enters the room. "Seat yourself on the table, Denise. Yes, just slide on the table. There. That's fine. Now lie back so that your head is resting on that small leather cushion. Very good. Now place your feet in the stirrups at the end of the table. Just let your heels slide into the supports. Yes. That's fine. A little adjustment. I will help you." The nurse arranges Denise's feet in the stirrups. Self-consciously Denise attempts to let the folds of the white gown cover her lower abdomen. "Now when the doctor comes to examine you," the nurse is telling her, "you must slide down as close to the bottom edge of the table as possible so that your buttocks are right here. And please, you must relax. Try to be as relaxed as possible." When the nurse leaves the room this time, she keeps the door ajar. Denise looks up at the ceiling. Supine and stir-

ruped, she feels all at once like a victim. She makes an effort to concentrate on her new identity as a patient, but the idea repels her.
Tilting her head to the right, she studies the instruments aligned on
the white table by the door and tries to solve their purposes. She can
feel the leather top of the examination table beneath her shoulder-
blades as unyielding as a sheet drawn tight over a board. To distract
herself, she starts counting to a hundred by fives. She is only at sixty-
five when the doctor, followed by the nurse, enters the room. He is a
heavy man with thick gray hair combed straight back from his forehead. Denise remembers him immediately from the war days in Nice,
but this is the first time she has seen him since. He picks up her chart
and scans it quickly before handing it to the nurse. "Well, Denise,"
says the doctor, "do you remember me?" "Yes, Dr. Jacob, but it is
many years." "It was another world, wasn't it? A different world."
He stands beside her and says, "Have you been lying here thinking of
all the terrible things that I'm supposed to do to you?" "I don't know
what to think." "Well, just think that you are here because your mother
called and thought it would be a good idea." He looks down at her
with a purely medical expression. He seems suddenly converted into
a stranger to her. Reaching under the gown, he touches her breasts
with his heavy but gentle fingers, then her abdomen. "I suspect that
the tests will be positive, Denise. Based on what you told the nurse
and what my fingers tell me, I would say that you are pregnant.
Probably in your second month." The nurse leaves the room and
returns after several moments with a yellow slip in her hands. The
doctor reads it and nods to Denise. "They rushed the tests for us."
"The tests?" asks Denise. "The tests with the urine. We are seldom
wrong. It only confirms what I just told you." Again his expression
becomes professional, all familiarity removed from it. "Have you had
any sickness with this, Denise?" "Not until recently. This morning
as a matter of fact." "Nausea?" "Some, yes." "Pain? Are you in any
pain?" "No, no pain. I was just dizzy, and I felt I had to vomit."
"Have you passed any blood, any at all? Do you have spotting?"
"No." The doctor turns his back to her for a moment and then faces
her with a different look in his face. It is the look of a friend of the
family who is not attempting to be curious but who needs to say
certain truths. "Your mother was deliberately vague with me, Denise,

and I did not question her, but am I right in assuming that the father is not your husband?" "No, he is my husband. He's been in an accident. He is in the hospital in Cimiez." "An accident?" "He is recovering." "Well, that's good. He is your husband then?" "Yes." The doctor pauses. Denise can see from his expression that he does not accept her answer but that he has decided to change the subject. "The nurse told me that this is your first examination." "Yes, Dr. Jacob." "Well, there has to be a first for everything." He pauses and adds, " I want you to tell me if you have any sensitivity here." He places both hands on her breasts and begins to knead them softly through the gown. "Anything, Denise? Any sensitivity?" "No." "Good." He nods to the nurse who quickly wheels a small stool to the foot of the examination table. "I will have to give you an internal examination, Denise. It's purely routine. The main thing for you is to be as relaxed as you can be." Denise grits her teeth as the doctor sits on the stool and positions himself between her arched, spread legs. "Will you move just a bit closer to me, Denise?" Assisted by the nurse, Denise inches down the table. The doctor says, "That's fine." The nurse removes a transparent glove from a sterilized white towel and helps the doctor fit it on his right hand. After much flexing of fingers and tugging, the doctor works his hand into the glove. The nurse then lubricates the doctor's gloved thumb and index finger with a colorless ointment from a blue-and-white tube and stands back. Denise tries to concentrate on a specific spot on the ceiling. As she feels the doctor's finger enter her, she recoils slightly on the table, and the doctor hesitates. Denise suddenly realizes that she is holding her breath and that she has been holding it for more than half a minute. The doctor removes his finger and waits. "Please try to relax your muscles, Denise. This should only take a little time." "I try, but I just can't, Dr. Jacob." "Please try a little harder. Take a deep breath and release it slowly, very slowly." Denise draws in a breath and then exhales as the doctor probes with his finger again. For some reason Denise is overcome with a sense of defeat, and this feeling is followed instantly by a flashing image of herself as a tabled specimen. The doctor says to the nurse, "The uterus is quite soft." Denise feels his fingers press in and up until she feels pressure against her pelvis. The doctor nods to the nurse who lifts one of the instruments from the table and hands it to him. "This might feel a bit cold to you, Denise, but I have to have some dilation. Just stay relaxed for a little bit longer." Again Denise draws a full breath and releases it as she feels the spoonlike tips of the instrument enter her and remain there. Applying counterpressure to the handles, the doctor spreads the spoons, and Denise feels the expanding pressure of the metal within her. Again she realizes that she is holding her breath, but she cannot help it. Only when the expansion eases does she exhale. She can barely hear the doctor and nurse conferring in medical terms that are foreign to her. Lying there, staring up at the ceiling while the doctor resumes his work on her, Denise feels her eyes cloud with tears. The tears slide out of the corners of her eyes and streak toward her ears and then across her neck. She does not bother to wipe or dry them. Just then she feels the slightly distended spoons being closed inside of her and slowly withdrawn. The doctor adjusts the gown over Denise and rises from the stool. After removing the glove from his right hand and discarding it into a white receptacle, he stares for a moment at the yellow card that the nurse left on the table. Denise can hear a telephone ring in the outer office. The nurse leaves the room and, after answering the phone, returns and whispers to the doctor. "Excuse me, Denise," says the doctor, "I must take this call." After the doctor is gone, the nurse says to Denise, "You may sit up now, but the doctor would like you to remain on the table until he returns." Removing her right and then her left foot from the stirrups, Denise swings her legs to one side of the table and sits up. She watches the nurse place the doctor's instrument in a sterilizer, then turn toward her and ask, "Is your husband seriously injured?" "He is almost fully recovered now." "But I notice you are still using your family name." She gestures to the yellow card on the white table. Not knowing how to respond, Denise keeps still and lets an interval of silence build up between the nurse and herself. "Is the doctor seeing the other woman now?" "What other woman?" asks the nurse. "The woman who was in the waiting room when I came in." "No. He saw her just before he saw you. She was just waiting for her husband." "Am I the last patient then?" "Yes. There is no one after you, if that's what you mean. Excuse me for a moment, please. I have to make sure that the office door is locked now." Again Denise is left by herself. She grips the leather edge of the examination table and holds on tightly.

She does not know if tears or the dew of sweat are glazing her cheeks. She has the feeling that her body has now taken on an identity and will of its own and that she is now subject to its commandments and has no choice but to obey. What she wants to do or say seems to her to mean nothing any more, nothing whatsoever. Her night in Eze with Dennis preempts what is crossing her mind. Dennis's face appears before her with a clarity that almost makes her cry out. She feels again the warmth of the studio fire, sees the black, flecked arch of the Mediterranean in the blanched distance, feels Dennis's hand on her hip, feels too the crumpled serge of the couch cover under her shoulder. Her fingers tighten on the leather edge of the examination table until they cramp, and the memory of Eze shatters like a kaleidoscope gone mad. Facing her is a gestation chart. Each sideview of a female figure shows a foetus in successive stages of growth. Denise scans each stage from the cramped, one-eyed crescent to the fully developed infant with shut eyes, drawn-up legs and the loose lariat of the umbilical cord curled under one of its arms. She has just reached the final stage when the nurse and doctor reenter the room. The nurse stands beside the table. "My nurse mentioned to me," says Dr. Jacob, "that you are studying biology." "Yes, I am." "It's not often that I meet a woman in this field." "I never really wanted to study anything else. What is more interesting than life?" "Of course." The doctor shifts away from the table. He brings his right hand to his chin and strokes an imaginary beard. Instead of making him appear thoughtful or prudent, the gesture only betrays a certain nervousness. After several strokes, his fingers move more rapidly. Sensing this, he stops and puts his hands to his sides. "Denise," he says, and the fingers return to the beard that is not there, "I have something I have to explain to you. I'm going to explain it slowly and scientifically so that you understand what I mean. It's important that you understand." Denise becomes more erect on the table. "Is there something wrong?" she asks. When the doctor does not answer immediately, she asks again, "Is anything the matter?" "Nothing is the matter with you, Denise. You will be able to leave this office in perfect health. It is not that kind of problem." "What kind of problem is it? The doctor waits and says, "There is a problem with the conception itself, with the tissue." "With the baby? What is it?" "I think it would be better now, Denise, to refer to the

171

conception as the tissue, not the baby. It will make everything in the
long run clearer and easier, believe me." The doctor turns to the chart
on the wall, seizes it at the center of its base like a windowblind, gives
it a slight downward tug, and lets it roll itself up toward the ceiling.
Then he reaches up and pulls down a second chart, holding it to its
full extension until the roll locks in position. When Denise looks at it,
she has the impression that she is looking at an elaborate ink blot, but
she realizes at once that the chart is a cross-section of the female
reproductive system. "I'm sure, Denise," says the doctor as if he is
conducting a class, "that you are familiar with this from your university studies. Normally, I would not be this detailed with any of my
patients, but I know you and your family, and I want to explain
everything to you so that you see how unique this is." He taps the
chart with his finger for emphasis, then says, "If I say to you that you
have what is medically called an ectopic pregnancy, does that have
any meaning to you?" "Yes, but I want you to tell me, I want to hear
it from you." "Very well. An ectopic pregnancy is a pregnancy that
occurs somewhere other than the uterus. It may happen here near the
ovary, here in the Fallopian tubes or elsewhere. But the point is that
an ectopic pregnancy is not a normal pregnancy. Many of them mis-
carry naturally. By that I mean that many of them abort themselves
without any intervention. But this can't be counted on in every in-
stance. The fact is that ectopic pregnancies are doomed pregnancies
because of the positions in which the conceptions happen to develop."
For some time Denise says nothing, does nothing, and her face resembles the face of an athlete after a race of maximum intensity. Then she
says tonelessly, "Do you mean I will lose the baby?" "I'm afraid I
mean more than that, Denise. I mean we ought not to wait for you to
lose it naturally. That leaves too much in doubt. Fortunately, we have
detected the problem early enough. The easiest procedure now would
be curettage. Because of the position of the tissue, we will not have to
make any kind of incision. There is very little risk." The doctor turns
to the chart again. "What has happened is that you have conceived
here, almost in the cervix itself. There is no way it can survive there.
It can grow for a time there, but the longer we wait the more serious
a threat it will be to you." "Do you mean there's no way it can be
saved?" "No." "What if I remain in bed? What if I keep as stationary

as possible?" "Come, Denise, you know better than that. You know enough about the body to know the truth when you hear it. It's not a question of bed rest or anything like that. Cervical pregnancies are rare, very rare, but they do happen, and they are by definition doomed." "What is it you want to do, Dr. Jacob ?" "I suggest removal of the tissue by suction curettage as soon as possible. We could even do it right now. In fact, we should. It's not a complicated procedure like a salpingectomy or an ovariectomy. It involves no surgery and no convalescence. In fact, you can go directly home from here and feel a minimum of ill effects." "You make it sound so final, Dr. Jacob." "I'm sorry, Denise. All I can say is that the language of science was not intended to alleviate human feelings. Facts are just facts. In this case, there is no hope, no hope whatsoever. But I don't think you should look so sad. It's not a question of life or death. It's simply a matter of relieving you of an improperly located tissue. Try to look at it that way." "But I can't." The doctor rolls up the chart. He approaches Denise and puts his hand on her shoulder and says, "I'll let you think about it for a minute or as long as you like. Really, Denise, there is no choice. The time to act is actually right now. As long as these pregnancies are aborted before the end of the twelfth week, there are really no problems. But after a twelve-week period, it can involve hospitalization and so forth. Now to be perfectly candid with you, you could go home and come back tomorrow or the day after that, but the situation would remain exactly the same. And the longer we wait, the larger the tissue becomes. Time is really our enemy at this point. Tonight you're here. You seem to be in good health otherwise. If you want my professional opinion, the curettage should be done right now." The doctor pauses and waits for Denise to respond, but she still has the expression of an athlete in exhaustion. "Do you want to talk to your parents? Or your . . . husband?" "No, not my husband." "Your parents then?" "My mother is downstairs waiting for me, Dr. Jacob. I didn't want her to come with me. I wanted to see you myself. I wanted to see . . ." She stops speaking in midsentence, brings her hands to her temples and begins to sob in a series of soft, sucking gasps. The doctor nods to the nurse, who steps next to Denise and puts her arm around her. Denise sobs on for several minutes. Even when the sobs stop, she still has the expression of a woman in the midst of tears. She begins to fidget with her gown, straightening and smoothing it across her lap again and again. When she stops fingering her gown, she says, "There's no possiblity that you might be wrong, Dr. Jacob?" "None. None at all." "You're sure it's hopeless then?" "Absolutely." "Then," says Denise with a resoluteness that seems to surprise the doctor and the nurse, "then I think we should do what has to be done now. I don't see why we should wait." "I think that is a wise decision, Denise. As I said before, the procedure is very simple, actually. Within an hour you can leave the office with very little discomfort. Are you sure that you don't want to call your mother to wait for you here?" "No. No, I don't want that." "Very well then. I should tell you that you may have some bleeding for a day or so, but that will pass. In the long run . . ." "Please, Dr. Jacob, I don't want to know the details. Just do what you have to do before something makes me change my mind." The doctor shrugs a French shrug at the nurse, then says to Denise, "As you wish."

Several moments pass, and the nurse helps Denise lie supine on the examination table again and fit her feet exactly into the stirrups. The doctor is busying himself with several instruments that he has removed from a lower drawer in the white table. With his back to Denise, he examines each instrument in turn and says to her, "You're old enough to know, Denise, that pregnancies are rather simple to avoid these days. Extremely simple, as a matter of fact. You could have spared yourself this problem if you had come to see me earlier. I could have suggested something for you or fitted you with one of the new devices, and you could have been as active as you wished without any concern for the consequences." Denise looks up at the ceiling while the doctor continues to speak. "It's a different kind of morality these days, Denise, and the medical profession has adjusted to it very well. Of course, what I'm telling you is what I've told many of my patients, and some of them have even returned to thank me. It's not really . . ." "But you don't understand, Dr. Jacob. I wanted to have the baby." The doctor again shrugs, turns, and approaches her with the instruments in a steel tray. He seats himself on the stool at the stirrup end of the examination table while the nurse stations herself beside him. The nurse reaches down and slides a white pail flush against the base of the table. "Denise," says the doctor, "can you slide down a bit more toward me?" Again Denise shifts on the leather until she feels her buttocks reach the table's edge. Then she shuts her eyelids with the same effort she might use to clench her fists as she feels the chill spoons enter her and begin their expansion. "I don't think it's really necessary, Denise, but I'm going to give you a pubic block to numb the area. It serves the same purpose as novocaine." Denise waits for the pin jab of the hypodermic. For a moment, nothing. Then, when she does not expect it, she feels the quick pressure of the needle in her groin and she twitches involuntarily on the table. In a moment a numbness spreads in her loins so that she barely senses the slide of the suction nozzle into her. She reclenches her eyelids as she feels the pull of the suction within her, slightly at first, then stronger. She can hear her fluids spilling from her body into the white pail on the floor at the foot of the table. At last the suction eases. The doctor says, "There. It is finished." He speaks quietly and briefly to the nurse, who is already applying unguent on gauze to Denise, helping her out of the stirrups, sheeting her with the gown. When she is satisfied that Denise is comfortable, she removes the white pail from the room. Denise asks the doctor, "How long before I can leave here? I want to leave as soon as I can, Dr. Jacob." "Are you feeling any discomfort?" "No." "Then just try to relax for another fifteen minutes. Then my nurse will help you dress. My only advice is that you should not do anything strenuous for a day or so or even longer if necessary. As I said, there may be some discharge and some bleeding. You should wear a shield. Nothing internal, though. The curettage was quite simple, and this was an early removal . . ." The doctor continues to speak, but to Denise his voice sounds more and more like a voice from beyond the grave, from another life. She finds herself thinking only about her body, her emotions, her condition. She feels something more than the usual clinical aftereffects. She tries to find a word for it. Is it fear? No. Shame? No. Then the word comes to her. Humiliation. She feels diminished. Had she been raped on the examination table, she thinks that she would not have felt much differently than she feels now. Lying motionless on her back with the gown pulled down and tucked under her, she pictures herself as a cadaver or as something that has served some specific medical purpose and then

175

been ignored. Her body seems no longer to be her private body but simply a body that she had known intimately as recently as an hour before. It then had suddenly alienated her, taken on its own destiny, divorced her. Now she wonders how she will live with her body again. She hopes that it will be her friend, but she knows that it will be a friendship with a difference. And still the doctor continues to speak, telling her that she should suffer no aftereffects, certainly nothing permanent, that her life is ahead of her, that these removals are routine to him, purely routine. She tries to shut the words off, but the words continue until the doctor leaves Denise to his nurse, who helps her to dress before she escorts her to the door of the office and then to the street. Standing outside the doctor's building, Denise suddenly wonders what she will tell her mother and how. After the nurse leaves her, she stands still for several moments before she walks slowly to her mother's car across the street. She sees her mother seated behind the wheel. She is looking directly ahead like someone driving through maximum traffic. She does not look in Denise's direction until she actually hears her open the car door and enter. Denise closes the door behind her and waits tensely for her mother's first question, but there is no question. Clothilde simply looks at Denise and waits. At last Denise mutters, "The baby is gone. There will be no baby, Maman." Clothilde de Savigny shifts on the seat and begins to drum her fingers on the steering wheel. "Did he tell you that you were not pregnant? Be frank with me, Denise." "He took the baby, Maman. He told me that it was forming in the wrong place and that it was doomed, that there was no hope, that it would be dangerous for me if nothing were done." "This soon? Was he sure?" "He said there was no doubt of it." She turns and looks at her mother. Then the tears come, but they come slowly. Her mother's face suddenly appears to her like an image at the bottom of a sea. She tastes her own tears on her lips. "It's just so hard for me to accept, Maman. Dr. Jacob kept saying that the whole procedure was so simple. And it was, really. Very simple. And I know from what he told me that it was necessary. But why do I feel so cheated? Why do I feel like something that's been used and thrown away? Why am I so empty, as if I'll never feel another thing as long as I live? What's happening to me? Tell me, Maman. Hold me, please. I don't know who I am or what I mean any more. I keep feeling like

176

I'm slipping away, Clothilde, like I'm drowning." Having called her mother by her first name for the first time in her life, she embraces her mother the way a drowning woman might embrace the last buoy in a wild sea. Her mother responds by returning the embrace and then smoothing Denise's hair with the palm of her hand. Then she simply holds her and pats her reassuringly on the shoulder. They remain so. At last Clothilde de Savigny says, "It's beginning to be dark, Denise, and I do not drive well when it is dark." She pauses as Denise shifts to the passenger seat and wipes her eyes with her sleeves. "Very well, Maman," says Denise, again the daughter. "Do you want to wait here a little longer until you feel better? I'll do what you want, Denise." "It is all right, Maman. We can go now." Clothilde starts the car, steers out into the sparse traffic and stays almost ten miles below the speed limit. She ignores the badgering horns and klaxons of impatient drivers who dawdle helplessly behind her before they have the opportunity to pass her. When they are halfway home, Clothilde says, "I told your father where we were going and why. This was something I wanted to do myself, and I did it." "Will I have to face him when we reach home? I don't think I am able to do that now, Maman." "I will take care of that, Denise. As soon as we get there, I want you to go directly to your room and rest. Leave everything else to me. Later I will bring you some warm broth, but first you must rest." "I don't think I'll be able to eat anything later, Maman. The way I feel now I don't feel like looking at food." "You will feel differently after you've rested. It has not been easy for you, Denise. Not at all. And it all happened so suddenly. Somehow you must tell yourself that this was the will of God, that it was the hand of God that was guiding you and will continue to guide you. You must believe that. There will be many more years, Denise. You will have beautiful children. You will have very beautiful, healthy children." Denise stares ahead at the linden trees on both sides of the street. They remind her of soldiers at attention. She thinks of herself as a bride walking beneath an arch created by the upraised, poised, and touching swords of twin ranks facing one another. Then the image is shattered by her recollection of the ceiling of Dr. Jacob's office, and the lindens become themselves again. Denise says quietly to her mother, "Doctors work on women in those offices as if they were sheep, Maman. I felt just like that. I could feel what he was doing to me. He even had a bucket there to catch what came . . . I felt just like a sheep being slaughtered, but I didn't die. I couldn't die. I wanted to die, but I kept on living and listening to the doctor, and I felt like a stranger to myself, and I still feel that way. If you weren't waiting for me when I came out of the office, Clothilde, I don't know what I would have done." "Try to forget what happened. It will be better for you if you forget as soon as you can. Remember that God is generous. Think like that. He does not permit us to suffer for nothing." "This was for nothing, Maman." "God is generous, Denise. But you cannot see that now. You need to rest. Things will look changed to you after you've rested." Clutching the steering wheel with both hands, Clothilde steers carefully down a darkening street before she parks in a secluded court adjacent to their apartment. Quickly, she steps out of the car, almost runs around to the passenger side, opens the door, and helps Denise to her feet. "Hold my arm, Denise, until we are on the elevator. Try not to let your weight down, if you understand what I mean." Together, both women sidle into the elevator, where Denise grips the bronze handrail while her mother presses the floor button and the elevator begins to rise slowly. The ascent leaves Denise with vertigo, and she breathes deeply several times to counteract it. She is remembering how she descended in the same elevator that morning, how she walked to the university, how she felt the first nausea in the laboratory, and how everything from then to now simply leaves her gripping the bronze handrail in the elevator while the still raw memories of the afternoon bludgeon her. The elevator stops, and she takes her mother's arm and enters the apartment. In these surroundings she feels much more relaxed, until she sees her father. Standing in the hall, he looks at Denise as he might look at an unwanted guest at his door and then, without a word or a nod or a change in expression, he strides past her into the living room. Denise lets her mother help her into her bedroom. Some time later, after she has undressed and gotten into bed, Denise tells her mother, "You must be tired also, Maman." "It is nothing. Now you must try to rest. Even if you can't sleep, just rest here. Don't think about anything but that. Don't worry about your father. I will deal with him. I will explain matters to him. It is time he listened. He's done enough. If he had listened in the beginning, this might have been . . ." "You are the only one who understands, Maman. I love you more than I can tell you." "Try to sleep, chérie. I will be back later. If you need anything just call me." Clothilde closes the door and Denise listens to her diminishing footfalls down the hallway. She keeps her eyes open, but they are veiled by the darkness of the room, and the darkness now seems more soothing than disturbing to her. It blacks out everything she does not want to recall, making it appear momentarily so unreal that she thinks of everything as a dream. Only her body remains real. But it still seems to her like the body of someone else, a body that has yet to forgive her, a body that is deciding why this, what next, who says so? As she tries to make a private peace with herself, Denise imagines that the darkness around her is no longer the familiar darkness of the room but the darkness of the inside of a well, and she is falling down the shaft, falling without a sound, falling. It surprises her that she is not screaming. Instead, she lets herself fall, and she feels herself descend like a sky diver, but at every foot of her fall she gives up something of her possessions or of herself. The first things to go are her books and school supplies. They flutter upward and away from her like terrified birds. The next dispersion includes dresses, coats, combs, brushes, shoes, slippers, stockings, nightgowns, jewelry, soaps, scents, powders, belts, keys, pens, pencils. She continues to fall. Now she imagines that an infant is being torn from her embrace, not by anybody or anything that she can see but by the suction created by her fall. She reaches desperately for the child, but it swirls upward into the tornado of things toward the upper reaches of the well. She continues to fall. Now she hears a voice that she recognizes as her father's. At the beginning, his words seem to come from a distance like the echo of an echo. But gradually the words become clearer until at last there is no doubt at all about what he is saying. "You! You are no longer Denise de Savigny, daughter of Sanche and Clothilde de Savigny, sister of Seth de Savigny. You no longer carry our name. You are nothing to us." The voice fades into an echo again and Denise's soft plunge continues. Stripped of her books, her possessions, her child, and her name, she imagines that she is starting to fall faster. Then her nightgown shreds like a sail in a high wind, and she falls thereafter naked, nameless and merely female in a void that is hers alone. When she tries to check her fall with her hands, she feels only the cold slime on the walls of the well. She looks down and can see no bottom. Now she is about to scream, but she can hear voices. Again they are like echoes. But they keep becoming clearer. One is her father's, and the other is her mother's. The voices are grappling with one another like wrestlers, but Denise cannot make out what is being said. She reaches out again for the sides of the well, but instead of slime her hands now touch the wool blanket of her own bed. She sits upright in the bed while the dream continues falling farther and farther away without her. But the voices of her mother and father do not fade. Partly awake and partly in the grip of her nightmare, Denise strains to listen. For a time it is only her mother's voice that she can hear, and from the drift and pitch of it she knows that her mother is not in her bedroom but still in the study on the floor below. There is an anger in the voice that startles Denise with its intensity. She can hear her mother say, ". . . unbelievable. It's absolutely unbelievable, Sanche, that you could do such a thing and then stand there and tell me. Don't you have any blood in your veins?" "Why unbelievable? What else was there to do? What else could be done?" "Done! Haven't you done enough already? For the love of Christ, Sanche, I can't believe what you've become." "Keep your voice down. Do you want the world to know what you are saying?" "I don't care what the world knows! I hate you! I hate the very sight of you!" "Be quiet, I said!" "I won't be quiet! I'll never be quiet again. Never. For all the years you were with Madeleine, I was quiet. When you treated me like part of the estate, I was quiet. I'm finished with being quiet. Now you've interfered with your daughter's life—with her *life*, Sanche— and I won't be quiet! How could you tell Dr. Jacob to take the baby from her? How could you call him yourself and tell him that.?" "And why not? What else was there to do? Let her have the baby of a man who has no future, no history, nothing? Let her ruin her whole life for one mistake? Is that what you would have preferred?" "*Yes,* if that was what she wanted! And *I know* that that was what she wanted!" "How do you know?" "I know. I know because she told me. And I knew before she told me. I could feel it." "Well, it makes no difference now. And don't worry about the details. I told Jacob to tell her that the pregnancy was imperfect and had to be taken. That is all that will appear on the records. Denise will never know anything but that."

"You animal! You fool! What if she learns the truth? Do you know what effect this will have on a girl like Denise?" "Jacob will never say a word. After all, if it weren't for me, Jacob and his whole family would have been sent to Germany to work for Krupp. I saved them. I! And I never asked a thing from him in return until five hours ago." "And now the record is straight, is it? You force him to lie to your own daughter so that he can take her baby from her, and you think everything is even. You, you bastard!" "He will say nothing. He would never betray me." "You betrayed him! You've made him a liar and a criminal, and now you have a daughter who might lose her mind if she learns that she lost this baby for nothing! And the truth is that she did lose it for nothing! For nothing but *your* idea of the way her life should be. Mother of God, Sanche, don't you see how monstrous this is?" "Monstrous or not, I had to act. What did you expect me to do when you told me she was pregnant?" "But I was thinking of her. I wanted the doctor to be sure for *her* sake." "The day will come, Clothilde, when you will thank me for what was done." "May God strike me dumb if I ever thank you for this!" "Lower your voice, Clothilde. I'm not going to tell you again." For a moment Denise hears nothing. It is not a dream. The bed and blankets are real. She *is* in her own bedroom, and the voice she hears now is her mother's, and the words are spoken slowly and with the emphasis of phrases in a vow. "Sanche," her mother is saying, "I will lower my voice permanently, I assure you. I hate what you've done. I can't live with it. I can't live with you a moment longer. I can't bear to look at you. Tonight, right now, I'm walking out of your life. I will sleep in Seth's room, and tomorrow I will take Denise away from here. I don't know if I'll ever come back. You can tell Seth and your friends and Madeleine whatever you want. I don't care what you say. All I'm concerned about is Denise. She is going with me tomorrow, and when she is well enough, I am taking her myself to Cimiez to be with this American if that is what she wants to do. He has shown more courage and more feeling for her than you can possibly understand. But I want *her* to decide what she wants to do with her life. And don't you dare to interfere with me. Don't you dare to stand in my way." "Interfere with you? How long do you think you can exist by yourself?" "Forever. Forever if I must!" "And I suppose your son's life means nothing to you as well." "It means everything to me. You are the one who put those thoughts in his head about the American. Now look what you've made of him." "Don't you realize that he will be questioned again and arrested for assault if the police begin to suspect that there was really something between Denise and that clown. If you take her to see him in Cimiez and if it is *reported*—and it *will* be—then you are making the case for the police against your own son. That's all that your inspector friend Gagnon needs. He's been trying to discredit me for years now." "I don't care about the consequences, Sanche. It's too late for that. All that I am saying to you is that tomorrow morning I am leaving with Denise. I am taking her out of here before you or anyone can do anything else to her. I want to make sure that no one so much as suggests to her that her visit to Dr. Jacob was what it really was. That would kill her. And finally . . ." "Well, I am going to have something to say . . ." "Don't interrupt me! Don't you ever interrupt me again, Sanche, as long as you live! I'm not listening any more. Do you understand that? I'm not listening to you. For the first time in my life I see what you have made out of yourself, and you disgust me. I don't know how I never saw it until now, but I see very clearly now. Maybe I just wouldn't let myself see it before. I don't know. But I swear to you on the grave of my mother and father that you'll never interfere with that girl's life as long as I'm alive to prevent it." "You can't mean what you're saying, Clothilde. Can't you see that I was thinking of her good from the beginning? Believe me when I tell you that. In these times you have to protect your children from themselves sometimes. You have to intervene before things go too far, before their lives are ruined permanently." "And how far is that, Sanche?" "Who knows exactly how far? It's not something you can put in so many words, but I know it when I see it. Do you think I hate Denise? She's my daughter. She's my own flesh and blood. I love her more than my own life." "But you love her the way you love everything else—on your terms, on your own terms. Can't you see that? And look what it's led you to do!" "I've kept her life pure. Is that something to be ashamed of? She's been spared having a baby at her age. Should I be ashamed of preventing her from ruining her life? The doctor is pledged to silence. She never has to know the real facts of the matter." "But why did you decide to tell *me*? You made it sound as if she just had a splinter removed from her finger. It was nothing to you . . ." "I never imagined that you would behave like this, Clothilde. I simply thought that you'd see what I did as the humane thing to do. Even now I can't understand your reaction. Did you want her to have a baby to this clown? Didn't you see anything wrong between them?" "I want what she wants, and that's all I want. This was not a casual thing to her. She loved him. And he loved her. Are you so blind that you refuse to see that?" "Infatuation, Clothilde. Pure infatuation. A girl of twenty often mistakes infatuation for love. You know that as well as I do." There is a pause before Clothilde says definitively, "There is no sense in discussing this any further." "Clothilde, sit down. Don't be ridiculous. You're carrying this too far, much too far." "I'm leaving you, Sanche. That's final. I'm taking Denise away from here . . . I don't care what you do or where you go, but I never want to see you again. Never!" "Are you giving me an ultimatum in my own house? "Don't go near that girl tonight, Sanche. Let her sleep. Don't try any more of your strategies, or I swear by the mother of God that I'll expose you. I'll expose what you did during the war. I'll call Gagnon myself and tell him about Seth. I'll do anything if you deceive me one more time. I swear it." "You are a very accomplished enemy, Clothilde. I never thought I'd live to see the day." "Good night, Sanche."

From her bedroom Denise can hear her mother walk through the front hall to Seth's room on the opposite side of the apartment. Denise sweeps the covers from the bed and takes a step toward the door. Suddenly the walls seem to be wobbling. She tries to steady herself. The next thing she knows is that she is on the floor, her right cheek against the high, smooth weave of the rug. It is so soothing that she just wants to remain there. Then she remembers the conversation between her father and mother and she curls up in a foetal knot on the rug and remains there until the wool beneath her cheek is damp with tears. Standing carefully but unsteadily, she hobbles back to the bed and sits on the edge. She waits for five minutes. Ten minutes. Her initial dizziness passes. She sees by her bedroom clock that it is six minutes after four. Through her window she notices that the moon is in its third quarter. Beside it float a few stars. There is not a cloud in sight. Without realizing it, she begins murmuring to herself. "I must leave here. I must leave here tonight. I can't wait until tomorrow." Rising, she walks with assurance to the bureau and switches on a lamp. After opening the top drawer of the bureau, she removes a purse and inverts it. Out fall francs in a tight wad secured by a twisted rubber band, a clutch of coins, and a key. Recognizing the key as the key to Anubis, she picks it up and squeezes it in her palm like a symbol. Then she returns the francs, the coins, and the key to the purse, quickly removes her nightgown, and dresses for the street in a gray turtleneck sweater and denim slacks. Twice while she is dressing she feels her dizziness return and she has to sit on the bed and wait until it passes. But once dressed, she awakens a new confidence in herself. She tests it by pacing the length of the room several times. Then she opens the bedroom door, looks up and down the hall, and waits. Nothing. She returns for the white purse, turns off the bedroom lamp, leaves the room, and hurries on her toes quietly down the hall. Expecting at any moment to be confronted by her father, she descends the circular staircase to the front door, eases it open like a thief, and slips out. After closing the door with the same stealth she used in opening it, she decides not to use the elevator for fear that the motor might be heard by her father. Still on her toes, she descends the stairs to the dark and quiet street below. Again she finds that she is murmuring to herself, "I will go to Thérèse. She understands. I will walk very carefully. I will not become dizzy. I will not become dizzy. I will not become dizzy. I will stay with Thérèse until I am stronger. Then I will go to Nice. Somehow I will go to Nice. Dennis will be waiting for me in Nice." She keeps murmuring to herself as she walks. She has the fear that she will collapse if she stops talking to herself. Once she passes a gendarme who is checking the locked doors of a row of boutiques. The gendarme looks at her with casual suspicion and continues to check the locked doors. Denise walks with short steps and stays close to the walls of buildings. From time to time she wonders if she is bleeding. A taxi rattles by. The driver slows down while he passes her as if anticipating a fare, but Denise does not look at him and the driver accelerates away from her. When she is within a block of Thérèse's room, she stops and leans against a utility pole. It is not vertigo this time, not nausea, not even fear. She is simply tired—no, fatigued. It is not a sensation that makes her hunger for sleep. Mysteriously, she is not at all sleepy. She tells herself that this is something that the old must feel daily—a certain falling off from a once known strength, a weariness that is beyond removal or renewal. But her body contradicts her. As quickly as the weakness overcame her, it now evaporates. No longer unsure of herself, clutching her purse under her arm, she strides down the empty street and enters the small courtyard adjacent to Thérèse's address. Just then she sees what she has almost forgotten. Its fenders and wheel rims glisten even in the darkness. Denise is drawn to it as if it has a life of its own. She holds the hand grip with her left hand, then releases it. The touch of it further reassures her. Turning, she looks up at the shuttered window of Thérèse's room. Now she realizes that Thérèse is not alone, that Pascal is probably sleeping there. Still gripping the purse under her right arm, she runs her palm along the length of Anubis as the idea slowly begins to lure her. Then she circles the machine like a bass around a bait. After touching the familiar black saddle and the pouched tools and helmet behind the driver's seat, she kicks up the parking stand and guides Anubis out of the court like a groom taking a horse from its stall. She pushes it for almost half a block before she removes the ignition key from her purse, inserts it into its switch, and starts the engine. The motor catches, roars for an instant, and settles into a powerful, low idle. Like a horsewoman Denise straddles Anubis, revs the motor with a few quick turns of the hand accelerator and cleaves down the turning boulevard that is bright with the gathered moisture of the night. As soon as she can veer to the south, she does, following the directional signals to Fontainebleau and beyond. The strong, steady thrust of the motor has a consoling effect on her, and she relaxes on the machine as she reviews step by step the lessons Dennis gave her about accelerating slowly, braking, taking a hill, descending, curving. The clean air against her face further revives her and she inhales deeply as she steers confidently on. Only a few cars and trucks are on the road, and most of them are coming toward Paris rather than away from it. When she reaches the outskirts of Fontainebleau, she stops at a service station where she has Anubis fueled and checked while she plots a route with the help of the attendant and his posted map from her present position to Nice. The attendant tells her that the distance is more than four hundred kilometers. Then he looks at her and the motorcycle and shakes his head and smiles the smile of a skeptic. Denise asks the attendant for a folding map to take with her and a pair of goggles. After paying, she opens the map and studies it. Of the various routes to the south, she immediately rejects the one through Limoges, not merely because it is more circuitous but because she notices by chance the name of the village of Oradour-sur-Glane on the map southwest of Limoges. The very name chills her suddenly, drags her back to memories of the war, of the pitchforked German corporal near the chateau, of the stripped woman from Nice who was smeared with spittle and the waste of cows, of the postmidnight conversations between her father and the officials from Vichy, of the accusations against her father after the war. It was her mother who told her reluctantly about what happened at Oradour-sur-Glane—how the Germans held the entire village responsible for the death of certain officers, how they herded all the villagers into Oradour's lone church and then set fire to it, how the surrounding German soldiers shot any villager attempting to flee the church, how the houses, barns, and shops were burned to the ground and left as an example to other villagers in the area with similar ideas of resistance. Straightening the map before her, Denise tries to distract herself from Oradour and its summoned memories, but her eyes keep returning to it, and she remembers having heard that the French government after the war decided not to rebuild the village but to leave it as a monument to those martyred in its name. No, she cannot afford to think of Oradour-sur-Glane now, cannot think again about the war and what it made, has been making, and is continuing to make of her life. She wants to think of what is ahead of her. She wants only to arrive in Nice as soon as possible and as secretly as possible, to take Dennis from the hospital and drive to . . . Drive where? To Spain? To Bordeaux? To Italy? Yes, eastward to Italy where she has friends in Savona, friends who will shelter her and Dennis before anything worse happens. At least they are people she can trust. As she studies the map, the sweat that has been gathering above and on her eyebrows drips on the paper. She wipes her forehead with her sleeve and looks up at a small white flag that is masted on the roof of the station. The flag lifts and rolls in the damp, warm wind like a piece of drowning laundry. Denise feels as if she is breathing through a wet sheet. She stands erect and gulps the wind, then folds the map back to its envelope size, slips it in the leather pouch next to her purse, brings the engine to a quick roar, and pulls out onto the highway. Re-creating the map in her mind as she goes, she reviews the route she has chosen: south to Orleans, then southwest along the Loire to Chateauneuf and Nevers and Roanne until she reaches Lyons, then south again along the Rhone to Avignon, then east through Grasse to Cimiez. She estimates that she will be able to complete the trip in less than ten hours. The possibilities of fatigue or accident never occur to her. If she has no problems, she tells herself that she should be in Cimiez by three in the afternoon. Even if she has to stop and rest or eat, she will certainly be there in the early evening at the latest. Her plan is to go directly to the hospital, explain her idea to Dennis and then, after waiting for nightfall, travel with him to Savona. She knows that she cannot delay much more than that. She suspects that her absence will be discovered early in the morning, perhaps when her mother comes to her bedroom. Then the search for her will begin, but it probably will be confined to Paris. Her father will check the airports and depots. And that in itself might take the entire day. On the other hand, if Pascal reports the loss of Anubis to the police and if either he or the police report it to her father, it just might be that her father might conclude that it was she who, even in her condition, took it. But why would Pascal not try to hide the theft of Anubis from her father? After all, Pascal was not even supposed to be in Paris, and certainly not with Anubis. No, despite even the worst logic of events, Denise feels sure that she at least has the whole day as a head start, that she will have time enough to reach Cimiez, that she will be able to cross the border into Italy with Dennis late at night when the security is reduced and the screening perfunctory.

In Orleans she stops for coffee and croissants at a brasserie. While she eats, she waits for the fatigue she expects, but there is no sign of it. Before returning to Anubis, she stops in the lavatory. There she notices that she has a slight issue of blood. With nothing available to use as a pad, she removes several paper towels from the dispenser, folds them into pad-size and tucks them carefully between her thighs. Except for a slight soreness in her groin, she feels no internal pain. Then she washes her hands and face with cold water over and over and dries herself vigorously. Before leaving the lavatory, she withdraws several spare towels from the dispenser and carries them with her to Anubis. When she finally leaves Orleans, she hears a church bell in the misty dawn ring seven times. Assured that she is on schedule, she heads for Chateauneuf and Nevers. Accompanying her on the left is the Loire. She can see its meandering, flat flow from the road as she goes, and it calms and encourages her to know that it is there. Is it some unadmitted atavism that has made her follow this route? She has no answer, but she does know that something more than the selection of the shortest route to Cimiez made her choose the river roads, first the road beside the Loire and farther south the road adjacent to the Rhone. A curious alliance grows between her and the river currents. They, like her, are going relentlessly in a given direction. Their channels keep them fixed in their courses and there is no turning back. Glimpsing the Loire always on her left flank, she feels that it is her ally, that it is constantly reminding her of her purpose, strengthening her resolve, keeping her headed in the right direction. When she speeds past the few palaces and castles and chateaux along the Loire east of Orleans, she regards them as mere ornaments. Only the river seems real, and the duplicated and reversed pictures of the palaces reflected in the river come alive for her because of what the currents do to them. Yet, in themselves, they seem like so many gravestones, monuments of an era that is as dead as the monarchy. To her father they were symbols of the real France, the real glory of its culture, the France of wealth, of munificence, of largesse, of breeding, of stature. He would speak the names of Cheverny, Chenonceau, Blois, and Amboise with a pride that was beyond justification or even explanation and then add the name of de Savigny in the same tone of voice. Denise had no doubt that he wanted her to realize that her family name was on a par with the most famous family names in all of France. Then he would pause and explain that the de Savigny family was represented in the armies of Charles Martel and Charlemagne. Now as she passes the museumlike structures, most of which are empty except for caretakers, she sees them in all their obsolescence. Like her father's words about them, they become part of a garbled and disintegrating tradition in her memory. Beside the meandering Loire, the chateaux seem like scattered bones in a desert while the river, merely by flowing on, triumphs as the only permanent thing in the landscape.

By noon she reaches the outskirts of Lyons. She senses now that it is not mere distance that is behind her. It is an identity that has been hers since childhood but that is becoming less and less hers with every kilometer. Until this moment she has accepted it as unquestioningly as she has accepted her name, the color of her eyes, the shape of her face. It was what made her herself, and she thought of herself as the sum of what those factors and forces told her she was, and she always assumed that she would grow older as that kind of Denise de Savigny and would never deviate from it. Now she knows that she was wrong. Down the highway beside the Rhone she speeds, and kilometer by kilometer she sheds the history of her childhood, the role of the *jeune fille* she fulfilled before she met Dennis, the etched memory of that final morning in Eze, even the memory of the things that were done to her in the office of Dr. Jacob. The last, searing argument she overheard between her father and her mother also becomes part of a life that is fading, fading. Now there is only the highway that keeps passing like history itself under the wheels of Anubis. There is only the knowledge that the distance between herself and Dennis in Cimiez is diminishing. The presence of the accompanying Rhone on her left has the same effect on her as did the Loire, and it even makes her fear the time when she will have to veer eastward toward Grasse, when there will be no more rivers but only the hills, vineyards, and flower orchards of the Esterel, when she will be completely alone on the lacing roads. But between now and then, there is the possibility of fatigue, and she is just starting to feel the first twinges of it. In an effort to gain time she increases her speed as she enters the outskirts of Avignon. It helps only momentarily. The thrum of the motor is transformed into a numbing chant of dumb power, and she feels herself drifting. She blinks hard behind the goggles like a helmeted deep-sea diver on the verge of collapse. She keeps blinking and shaking her head to keep the fatigue at bay. Later, as she negotiates her way through the Avignon traffic, she revives slightly, but once she begins heading east for Grasse, the tiredness becomes so total that she knows she must stop. She pulls Anubis into a small grove beside a stream and parks it among the trees. She leans forward, letting the sense of motion release its grip on her body and her nerves. After removing the helmet and goggles, she lets her head loll before she looks down. She gasps. The knob of the driver's seat is painted with blood, and there is a slowly enlarging blot of blood reaching from the crotch of her slacks upward almost to the pockets. She feels no pain or discomfort, but the blood is there, and it is undeniable. "My God," she says aloud, "I'm hemorrhaging!" Carefully she eases herself off the seat and almost tiptoes toward the stream. When she reaches the bank, she stops and then moves downstream by almost ten yards to a spot that is shielded from the road by an overhanging willow. Without pausing, she wades into the cold, clear water. The rocks and pebbles under her soles shift like smooth pieces of ice, and twice she almost loses her balance. Finally, she stops when the water reaches the level of her waist. Chilled by the fast currents pushing against and between her legs, she grabs her left bicep with her right hand, then her right bicep with her left hand and hugs herself like someone trying to keep warm in a blizzard. She wants to return to shore, but she knows from experience that the cold water needs time to dissolve and wash away the blood. Standing and shuddering, she winces at a flash of pain just to the right of her belt buckle. It fades and returns, fades and returns, fades and returns like a small pulse of warning or alarm. Fearing that she might faint or be doubled over in midcurrent, Denise slogs her way to the bank. Once ashore she sees that the water has removed all traces of the fresh bloodstains form her slacks. She returns to Anubis, locates the paper towels she packed away when she was in Orleans, and brings them with her to the willow-shaded spot downstream. Still shivering, she removes her slacks and underpants, rinses them by twisting them into a taffy knot and splays them on top of the sunny side of a privet beside the willow. Then she pads herself with the paper towels and waits. After five minutes she inspects the padded towels. Even though she finds no further bleeding, she replaces the towels between her thighs as a precaution. It is only then that she notices the doe. It is stepping nimbly toward her, pausing from time to time to dip its mouth into the stream and lap the sluicing water. Denise is startled to see a doe so far south, and she draws back into the shade of the willow. The doe stands statue-still, its foreleg lifted. Then it splashes softly through the shallows, and with each sure but delicate stop it comes close enough to Denise for her to touch it. Her eyes and the eyes of the animal meet before the doe turns dismissively away. Denise almost reaches out to stroke the doe's pelt, but she restrains herself. Instead, she sits down beside the shrub where she has spread her garments in the sunlight. A moment later the doe decides to nest not more than five yards from her. Again their eyes meet. This time the doe keeps looking, and it is Denise who has to drop her gaze. When Denise looks up again, she sees that the doe is still watching her. It is only then that she notices that the doe's flank is bulged with foal. Somehow she did not notice it when the doe was standing. Seeing it now, she feels an almost purely female solidarity with the animal. And the feeling saddens her, plunging her mercilessly into a memory of the examination table and the instruments and the stirrups and the white waste pail. Tears come to her eyes, and she lets them brim and fall without caring. And all the time the doe continues to regard her as if she is simply a part of the surroundings. Denise leans back against the willow's trunk and closes her eyelids on the tears. All that she can hear is the steady eddying and rush of the currents. She moans twice and opens her eyes. The doe blinks at her but does not stir. The rough bark of the willow suddenly seems more comfortable than a bed and Denise relaxes against it. Her third moan is softer than the first two, almost a sob. She rests her head against the bark and breathes deeply. The fatigue of the journey overcomes her like ether, and she sleeps . . .

In her dream she sees the fawn. Spotted and licked clean, it looks toward her and bleats. After trying to rise, it collapses into the soft nest of itself while the doe stands above it. When Denise moves, the doe bolts but halts after just a few feet and turns her head. It is not dismissive of Denise but apprehensive. Denise ignores it and watches the fawn. The white of its forehead is whiter than anything she has ever seen. She smiles at the brightness as if it is miracle enough. The fawn makes a second attempt to stand, collapses, tries again, and is about to fall when Denise rushes to it and embraces it. Holding it against her, she feels the muted bell of the fawn's heartbeat, sees the innocence and terror in the wild eyes, feels the unbelievably soft first fur on her bare arms. The doe comes a step closer, but Denise does not release the fawn for several moments. Hugging the new life next to her feels so right that she does not want to let go. Finally, she kneels down and cautiously lets the fawn put its weight on its legs. Then she releases it. When the fawn starts to cave in to one side, she seizes it gently and sets it upright again. This time, when Denise takes her hands away, it stands by itself, although its legs seem as brittle as broomstraws under even such a small weight. The doe comes closer and closer to the fawn as Denise backs away. Denise draws back a step at a time as the doe stands directly over the fawn, covering it with its body. The fawn does not fall . . .

It is the roughness of the willow bark between Denise's shoulder blades that wakes her. Blinking, she looks up at the dusk between the willow branches. The doe is gone. She notices, as if for the first time, that she is naked from the waist down, and she instinctively reacts by drawing her knees up to conceal and protect herself. She stands and retrieves her garments from the top of the privet. The underpants are dry, but the slacks are still slightly damp. Regardless, she pulls on both garments. After buckling her belt, she turns around abruptly, hurries through the thicket where Anubis is waiting and picks up the helmet that is lying like a huge, hollow clam shell near the rear tire. After adjusting the goggles over her eyes, she wheels the machine to the road, starts the motor and drives off in the last light of early evening toward Grasse. Unlike the river roads, the road to Grasse is one with the contour of the mountains and valleys, dipping, circling, climbing, banking. Denise is constantly accelerating, decelerating, and braking. It reminds her of her first ride with Dennis and how he took the curves with a sense of impudent expertise. She felt that he was daring the road or Anubis to betray him. She remembers how frightened she was then. She compares herself as she was on that first ride with herself now, mounted on the same motorcycle, veering alone through the fringes of the Esterel and heading for . . . For what? Not where, but what? The question repeats and repeats itself. She renews her concentration on the undulating road and flicks on the headlight. She thinks about her father and mother and wonders where or if they

are searching for her, wonders whether Pascal has informed her father
about Anubis, wonders finally what she can expect at Cimiez. What
if Dennis is no longer in the hospital? Should she stop at his cottage
first? No, why should she? No, certainly not. Each question begets
another, and at one point she is concentrating more on the question
than the road—so much more that she underestimates the sharpness
of a curve and almost careens into a seaward barrier of rocks before
she regains control of Anubis.

After more than an hour of night driving, she reaches Grasse, passes
the quiet houses on the outskirts, speeds quickly through the town's
center, skirts the Fragonard perfume factory where her father's various crops of jasmine have been distilled into perfume extracts for as
long as she can recall, then leaves the eastern edge of Grasse for the
dark, narrow roads again until she reaches the four-lane sea-road that
leads to Nice. Instead of going faster as she draws nearer to Cimiez,
she finds herself going slower, deliberately slower. She is filled, not
with fear, but with a stealthy prudence that is strangely exciting to
her. It occurs to her that thieves must feel this way when they are on
the verge of their thefts and have to prethink what they are conniving
to do just before they do it. Her breaths become shallower and more
frequent and she feels a delicious weakness in her arms and loins.
The closer she comes to Cimiez, the more this weakness allures and
overcomes her. After she reaches the hospital, she parks Anubis near
the side of the building and then lingers near it. Having come so far
on the motorcycle, she feels a certain bond with it and is almost reluc-
tant to leave it. Then she walks slowly to the side door of the hospital.
She still feels as she felt during her drive through the Loire countryside—that she is moving not only through space but through time
past. She remembers the times she accompanied her mother to this
very hospital, remembers the long hours of waiting while her mother
visited the monsignor, remembers too the Japanese soldiers and how
they sat erect and unsmiling in their wheelchairs or spoke in whispers
to one another. Now as she opens the side door and looks down the
white-tiled corridor, she feels the past and the the present collide so
that for an instant she does not know what time it is, what month,
what day. The corridor becomes the same corridor it was five years

ago, ten years ago. As she starts down the corridor toward the lighted stairwell at the end, she feels like the child she was when she first paced the identical floor, first smelled the aroma of alcohol and bandages and pain, first passed rooms where patients in tipped-up beds lay on their backs and stared passively at her as she walked by. Step. Step. Step. She dreams she hears a child's voice that used to be hers saying, "Maman, I can't walk as fast as you can. Wait for me. I will be lost . . . Maman, I saw a man with one leg today. He was walking on a pair of wooden helpers tucked under his arm . . . These men are not Americans, Maman. Someone told me that they are Americans, but they are Oriental. How is it possible for them to be Americans, Maman?" The dream dissipates as she reaches the stairwell. She pauses and then mounts the stairs slowly, cautiously, even hesitantly, like someone armed only with a lighted candle in a strange house. She remembers that the floor for male patients is the third. When she ascends to the third floor, she again feels that caving weakness in her loins and she begins to shiver. Bracing herself, she pushes open the stairwell door and lets it close softly behind her. She notes that the doors to most of the rooms are either completely or partially closed. To her far right, she spots a light from one of the nursing stations, but she sees no nurses there. Keeping close to the wall on her left, Denise passes door after door, pausing to read the posted names of the patients as she goes. When she reaches the end of the hall, she crosses and works her way back down the opposite side until she almost reaches the point at which she started. Dennis's full name on a slotted card on the last door diagonally across from the stairwell stops her. After glancing quickly down the hall to the nursing station where a single nurse is now seated at her desk and shuffling through charts, Denise seizes the door knob, turns it firmly, opens the door, enters the room, and holds on to the door knob so that the door does not pull shut with a click but closes as quietly as a curtain being drawn by hand. Then Denise stands with her back to the door. In the slanting glow of the bedlamp she sees Dennis in bed. There is a bandage over his eyes and he has apparently not heard her since he does not turn his head to one side or the other. She wonders if he is asleep. Just then, Dennis, as if sensing her presence, sensing even her thoughts, lifts himself up on one elbow and turns in her direction. He waits in that position for several minutes as if expecting her to break the silence, but she remains flush against the door like a thief. When he speaks, she holds her breath. At last Dennis lies back on the bed and crosses his hands on his chest. Then he says, "Denise?" He waits and leans up on his elbow again. "Denise," he says again, "is that you?" Denise takes a step toward the bed and stops. She wants to answer, but the words refuse to come to her. Dennis is saying, "I know someone is here. Answer me, please." Denise takes the last few steps to the bed and embraces Dennis before he realizes what is happening. For a moment he is shocked. "Denise, it's you. I knew it. I really knew it," he says and holds her next to him. When they separate, he swings his legs over the side of the bed and sits on the edge. He holds out his hand to her, and she takes it. Then, with a slowness born of disbelief, he draws her toward him. He puts both hands on her cheeks and then moves his fingers over the contours of her face. He can feel her tears on his fingertips, and he stops. He draws her toward himself and kisses her on the mouth . . .

Even as they kiss, she keeps her eyes open and looks at the bandages. They arouse a new fear. What really happened in Eze? Why are the bandages still on? It's been more than six weeks. She draws back, but he still keeps holding her hand as he says, "I can't believe it, Denise. Night after night I've waited for this to happen, and now it's happened. It's happening. How did you get here? Are you alone? Talk to me." "I came from Paris, Dennis. I came by myself. I had to see you." "From Paris? When did you go to Paris? Why didn't I hear from you?" Denise wonders how much she should tell him. Finally she says, "My father wouldn't let me come back or write to you, Dennis. He was afraid . . ." "Afraid of what?" "It had something to do with the police. He made it sound . . ." "It's all right, Denise. As far as the police are concerned, the whole business was an accident. I never told them a thing about you or your family. I don't know if they believed me or not, but that's the whole story." "But was it an accident, Dennis?" "I don't want to talk about that now, Denise. I really don't." After a long pause, Denise says, "I know the truth now, Dennis. I know it wasn't an accident." "Who told you that?" "I found out myself. I made Seth admit the truth to me. And I know why you never told the police the real facts. It was because you wanted to spare me." She waits for him to answer her, but he says nothing. "I couldn't go on living in Paris," continued Denise, "because I couldn't stay away from you just to protect my family. I tried as long as I could, but it was no use." "But how did you get here? Did you fly? Take the train?" "I came on Anubis." "On Anubis?" "Yes, on Anubis. And I came by myself." "But how did Anubis get to Paris?" "It's a long story, Dennis. I'll tell you later . . ." "Where did you park it?" "Outside." "You mean you came all the way from Paris to Cimiez on Anubis! I just can't believe it, Denise." He smiles and shakes his head slowly before his expression gradually changes. He continues to shake his head, but the smile vanishes. Denise asks, "Is anything wrong, Dennis?" He turns toward her and waits, then waits a bit longer before he says, "I won't be riding Anubis any more, Denise. No Anubis, no wirewalking, no clowning any more." He taps the bandage over his eyes and murmurs, "The right eye's dark and the left one's half dark. I have to wait for the world to come to me now, Denise. I can't shake it by the neck any more." Denise feels herself grow limp. Having never been told the nature of his injuries, she is now hearing of them for the first time and the news stuns her. She looks at him as if she expects him to erase what he has just told her, but the parallel furrows in his forehead just above the top of the bandage remain fixed. "I'm going to have to learn how to change, Denise. Before this happened, I thought the worst fate in the world would be to end up like Ramuz. Remember when I told you that? Now I won't have that to worry about."

Denise puts her head on his shoulder and lets him embrace her with his left hand. They remain that way like two friends who have just watched the ship of their salvation sail away without them, leaving them nothing but the sea and one another for company. She lifts her head from his shoulder and says, "I came here so we could leave, Dennis. Together." "When?" "Tonight." "Just walk out?" "Just walk out." "But why tonight? For a month and a half, nothing. Then, all of a sudden, tonight." "You have to trust me, Dennis. It's the only thing we can do." "Where can we go?" "To Italy. We can ride Anubis to Italy. I have friends near Savona. We can live there, work there."

Slowly he lets his arm go loose around her. He stands up. She is about to reach after him, but he moves by a yard out of her range. He steps tentatively toward the door, his hands held out in front of him like a man walking through a dark and unfamiliar house. When he reaches the door and touches it, he does an about-face and walks back to the bed where Denise is seated. He tells her, "Do you know how long it's taken me to do what you just saw? It's taken almost three weeks. From the time I first tried it until this minute, it's three weeks. And that's the best I can do, Denise. Now tell me the truth. What kind of a job can I find in Savona?" "But *I* can work. And we don't have to stay there. We can go to Milan. There are a lot of research laboratories there, and I'm good enough now to do research." "And what would I do? Wait in the dark for you to come back in the evenings?" "Just for a little while. You'll get better. I know you will. And then we can go wherever we want." Dennis reaches for her hand, locates it and, holding it firmly, says, "I'm almost glad I can't see you at this minute, Denise. You probably have that look that can see through anything and that can convince me faster than words." "Dennis, you have to listen to me. We have to leave here." Dennis releases her hand. After fidgeting for a moment with the bandages over his eyes, he finds the end of one of the gauze loops and begins to unwind it slowly, band by band. While she watches him, Denise has the impression that she is watching a mummy being unwrapped. The image is so bizarre that it frightens her, but she cannot dislodge it from her mind. The longer she watches Dennis at work with the unlayering gauze, the more she locks on the image of a man being unwrapped from the tomb because of her, because she, simply by being where she is, made it necessary. When Dennis finally finishes with the bandages, he looks at her. She notices that the skin around his eyes as well as the eyelids themselves have the pale and moist appearance of flesh that has been covered for long periods of time. But the eyes themselves *seem* normal to her. "This is the way I am now, Denise," says Dennis, "and it's the way I'll be. I can't see anything out of the right eye. It's gone for good. With my left eye I can make out forms. That's all. I can see you on the bed, but you're just a darker shadow against another shadow. The doctor told me that the left eye might get a little stronger, but not much. And that's it. That's the story of the future of Dennis Holt." Denise stands in front of him and embraces him around the neck while he remains at limp attention, his hands at his sides. They remain so for several minutes without speaking until Dennis says, "We've waited this long, Denise. We can wait a little longer. The left eye might get better here. At least I know that it can't get any worse. I keep hoping that it will get strong enough so that I can see the faces of people who are looking at me. That would let me go back to clowning. I know the business on the wire is over for me. You need to have depth perception to walk a wire and you have to have two good eyes for that." He pauses and then says, "I've come to terms with myself, Denise. If I have any luck at all, I won't have to give up too much. It could always be worse." "But it could always be better. It didn't have to happen at all." "It happened. We can't erase that." He embraces her, first loosely, then tightly, and says, "The only thing that was driving me crazy was not hearing from you, not knowing anything about you. I was starting to believe that you were gone forever. Now that you're here, the world makes sense again. I'll learn to live with what's happened. Just stay beside me. That's all." "I love you, Dennis." They continue embracing. There is no desperation in it, only a mutual calm. Still holding him, Denise says, "Believe me, Dennis. We have to leave here. Tonight." "Why?" "We just have to. I can't explain everything. You must trust me. I mean what I'm telling you." "But what aren't you telling me? What makes everything so urgent all at once?" "Please believe me, Dennis. We don't have much time." "Denise, you're going to have to tell me more than that. For a month and a half, silence. Then you make a trip all the way from Paris on Anubis. Now you want to go to Italy. That's going from the North Pole to the South Pole in one move." "But it would take too long to explain. We may be too late now." "Too late for what? Tell me. Tell me whether I understand it or not." Denise sits on the edge of the bed while Dennis waits for her to answer him. When she speaks, she almost whispers, "Dennis, the situation with my father hasn't changed. I know now that he is just waiting until you are released from the hospital here in Cimiez so that he can have you sent out of the country. He has friends who will do that for him and he is determined to do it. I'm positive of that." "Why? I can't believe it." "But it's true. He's been against us from the beginning, and he is still the same, despite what happened.

198

He is only concerned now with two things. One is that I forget all about you. If he has to deport you to make that possible, then he will do it. The other is that he does not want Seth to be charged with what happened in Eze." "Was he the one who sent your brother to Eze?" "I don't know, Dennis, but what difference does it make?" "It makes a difference to me. I've always thought that Seth just lost his head for a minute in Eze. If your father put him up to it . . ." "Dennis, you don't really understand how deep this is with my father. All my life I never spoke a word against him. I loved him. And I still love him now. But this has made him a different man. I'm afraid of him, afraid of what he might do." "And your mother? Does she feel the same way?" "No. She is with me. She is with both of us." "Then I'll have to meet with your father and see . . ." "Dennis, listen to me, for the love of God. Please stop trying to reason your way through this. My father is not what he used to be. He is not what you think. All that he wants is to see that you have a medical release, have the whole case closed, and then have you deported so that there will never be any more questions and so that I will come to my senses. Once you are gone he knows that we could not see one another for years, maybe never. You could not return to France and he would see to it that I would not be permitted to leave. I know that this is all that he has on his mind." Denise watches Dennis walk in a small circle as if digesting what he has just heard, sorting it out for himself, weighing the alternatives. "Is there more?" he asks her. "More of what?" "Is there anything more that you're not telling me?" After a pause she says quietly, "No." She wonders if something in her tone has suggested to him what she is determined not to tell him—the matter of her visit to Dr. Jacob. Was there some nuance she did not quite conceal that made Dennis suspicious? "There's something else, Denise. You sound as if there's something you're holding back." "No, Dennis. I've said every-thing. Isn't it enough?" Dennis walks in another circle before he says, "It's enough, but it's not everything." He stops and adds in a changed voice, "Dr. Russi is going to be slightly upset tomorrow when he comes here and finds that his prize patient is gone." "Who is Dr. Russi?" "One of your father's employees. He's a good doctor, but he's still an employee." He starts to remove the top of his blue pajamas. "Denise, there's a locker somewhere in this room where they put my clothes. Will you get them for me? If we're going to take Anubis to Italy, I can't go in my pajamas." Denise hurries to the locker and returns with trousers, shirts, underclothes, and socks in a laundered stack. She returns to the locker for his shoes while he steps out of his pajamas and, naked, feels the stack of clothing until he locates his undershorts and puts them on. Denise helps him with his shirt. While she fastens the buttons, it occurs to her that this is something she might be doing regularly for the rest of her life. After fastening the last button, she lets him hold her for support as he steps, left leg first, into his trousers. She asks him to sit on the bed while she puts on his socks and shoes. Everything she does seems doubly important to her now, but why? She ties the laces of each shoe with more than necessary care, making sure that the bow loops are equal on either side of the knot. Crouching, she suddenly feels again the stab of pain in her loins. She puts her hand on the floor to keep herself from falling. Then she waits for the pain to come again. Nothing. She stands with care and faces Dennis. Even though she knows he cannot see her, she masks her apprehension from him. "I can feel you in front of me, Denise, but I can't see you. It's remarkable, you know. I've learned a lot about seeing in the past month. When you lose your eyes, you find out that your body has other eyes you never knew about . . ." "I've just had a terrible thought, Dennis. What if the nurse walked in right now? What would we do?" "Don't worry about that. She made her last rounds more than an hour ago. The only problem we have is to leave the hospital without being seen. That way no one will discover I'm missing until tomorrow morning." "Are you ready?" "Ready. You do the leading." Denise takes him by the hand to the door and stops. Just as she did when she entered, she twists the doorknob slowly and opens the door wide enough to give herself a clear view of the nurse's station. The nurse is still leafing though a stack of charts. Denise closes the door softly and says, "The nurse is sitting at the desk. She was there when I came in. She's busy with some papers, but all she would have to do would be to lift up her head while we were crossing the hall, and she would see us." "Open the door a little, Denise. Just wide enough so that you can see her. She has to get up sooner or later and do something else." "The door to the stairwell is almost directly across from your room." "Let's wait then. All we need

200

is a second or two when she goes to one of the patient's rooms."
Denise, still holding his hand, stations herself at the door so that she
has an unobstructed view of the night nurse. Now and then Denise
looks at Dennis but says nothing. She is amazed at how unexcitedly
and methodically she is behaving. All she has in her mind is that she
is exactly where she wants to be and that the course she has charted
for Dennis and herself is the only one that promises life. All the other
alternatives have the stamp of death on them. What bothers her now
is her fatigue. Her insteps ache and she keeps blinking her eyelids to
keep her vision clear. The pain in her loins is not acute, but she knows
it is there. She wonders what she will do if she has an attack on the
stairs, while she is driving Anubis, while she stops at the border
checkpoint beyond Menton. Is she hemorrhaging again? She refuses
to look down to see. Just then the nurse rises from her seat. "Dennis,
the nurse is moving. She's moving away from the desk. There. She's
gone." "Now's the time then." Denise opens the door and leads Dennis by the hand to the stairwell door. Still holding his hand, she guides
him to the banister, and they descend the stairs to the first floor without difficulty. Then they walk down the white-tiled corridor to the
exit and out of the hospital. "Did we make it, Denise?" "We're outside now." "Did anyone see us?" "No." "How far is Anubis?" "It's
right over there. Fifteen meters. I'll lead you." They cross the parking
lot to Anubis where Dennis, standing beside the seat, pats it as he
might pat the head of an old and faithful dog. "Are you sure you're
up to this, Denise?" "I can do it." Denise watches Dennis mount the
secondary seat without her assistance. Then she helmets herself, goggles her eyes, straddles the seat in front of him, starts the motor and
steers slowly out of the yard toward Nice. "What time is it now,
Denise?" "Almost ten o'clock." "I think we should pull off the road
after you go a mile or so and wait until midnight. They always have
fewer guards at the border then." After Denise reaches the middle
corniche, she drives for several miles and then pulls off into a clearing.
She helps Dennis dismount. Then they sit together beside the motorcycle while an occasional car passes from the west or the east on the
corniche. "How do you know that someone isn't waiting for us at the
border, Denise?" "I didn't tell anyone I was coming. I thought it
would take at least a day for my father to realize where I'd gone."

"Do you have enough gas?" "Yes." "Any money?" "Enough for a while." "All you need now is wings, Denise?" "Wings?" "Don't you remember the story I told you about Isis when we were in Eze." "Yes." "Remember how she covered her husband with her wings until she brought him back to life? He was wrapped up like a mummy, but she stayed with him until he started to breathe again." "Don't talk like that now, Dennis." "I'm only kidding you." "All those stories end with death. None of them has a happy ending." "That's the way they thought about love then. You had to go through death to find it." "Well, we're not going to listen to them." Dennis puts his arm around her and they lean back against the motorcycle for support. "Dennis?" "Yes." "I'm afraid to wait here any longer. I think the sooner we reach the border, the better. If no one knows we are coming, it won't matter how many guards are at the border." "We don't even have our papers with us." "Sometimes they don't ask for them. Please, let's leave." "All right."

Once they are back on the road, Denise keeps to the right lane and lets other vehicles pass her with impunity. She concentrates on the single headlight of Anubis that shines ahead into the darkness like a probe. Dennis holds the sides of the seat in front of him and shouts to Denise, "You've improved. You don't even need wings now." "Don't stop talking to me, Dennis. All of a sudden I feel so tired, and I can't get tired now. Talk to me, chéri. Say anything." "Take in some deep gulps of air. That helps." She swallows the onrushing air, mouthful by mouthful, until the drowsiness leaves her. She resists the impulse to speed. Instead she slows down so that she travels no faster than a runner. To her right she sees the shore lights of Beaulieu and farther on the sparkling promontory that is Monte Carlo. She soon turns her full attention to the road again. The very fact of her continuing to watch what's approaching under the bright smear of the headlight assures her that she is advancing, that the distance between her and the Italian border is being reduced with every revolution of the wheels of Anubis, that she is winning the battle with her own deepening tiredness. "Where are we now, Denise?" "Near Monte Carlo." "Can you see Eze?" Denise looks up and ahead as the clear silhouette of Eze rises before her. "I can see it." She begins her descent to the bridge that leads to Eze when she sees the swirling blue light of a patrol car. "Dennis!" "Why are you slowing down? What's the matter?" "I see lights on this side of the bridge, car lights. One is blue and turning in a circle. It's a police car." "Keep going. Maybe there was an accident." Denise proceeds another hundred meters and says, "It's not an accident, Dennis." "Did they see us?" "I don't know." "Can you turn and reach the border by the lower road?" "I'll try." Denise brings Anubis to a slow halt on the side of the road. She is now only about forty meters from the bridge that spans the gorge to Eze. "Dennis, I don't know what to do." "Just sit still and tell me what's happening." "My God, we're so close! We're almost there! How can anything happen now?" "Don't talk that way, Denise. Just wait and see what happens." "There are two men walking toward us now." "Let them come. Don't move. Don't do anything suspicious." Denise keeps her eyes on both men. One of the men is walking slightly ahead of the other. When he is within ten meters of Denise, he stops. Denise continues to watch him. She notices that his right arm hangs limply at his side. She sees him cup his left hand like a megaphone to his lips and call to her, "Mademoiselle de Savigny!" She feels a shudder go through her, but she does not answer. "Mademoiselle de Savigny, I am Inspector Gagnon. One of our cars has been following you for the past three kilometers. We know who you are, and we know who is with you. I want you to drive your motorcycle to the car with the blue flashing light at the bridge. Your father is waiting for you there, and I have to ask you a few questions." Denise still says nothing. The man stands his ground, and the blue light swirls like a lighthouse beam in the distance. Dennis touches Denise on the shoulder and says, "It sounds hopeless, Denise. You better do what he says." "But we are so close, Dennis. It *can't* end this way." Again Inspector Gagnon cups his left hand around his lips and calls, "Mademoiselle de Savigny, you will please follow me now." Still straddling Anubis, Denise stands and screams, "No! No! I won't!" Dennis puts his hands on both of her shoulders and turns her slightly toward him and says, "It's really hopeless, Denise. There's no alternative." The inspector says, "Mademoiselle?" Denise faces Gagnon and shouts, "Why can't you leave us alone? Why is everything against us? Everything! All we want is to be together!" "Mademoiselle de Savigny, your father is waiting for you." "No, I'm not coming with you!" She turns to Dennis and says, "I can't go back, chéri. What is there to go back to? I can't die all over again. And that's what will happen. It will be like death for both of us." "Mademoiselle de Savigny, I am not going to wait any longer!" Gagnon puts his left hand down and watches as Denise starts to coast toward him. After she goes a few meters, she revs the motor all of a sudden and speeds past him toward the bridge. Gagnon starts to trot and then sprint, but Anubis is already outdistancing him. Without taking his eyes off the motorcycle, he sprints faster.

Wings

Gagnon watches Etienne hike up the trail from the gorge. He waits until he reaches him and asks, "Both dead?" Etienne shrugs and answers, "Both. The ambulance drivers are down there now with a pair of stretchers. The two of them landed side by side, but the motorcycle is in a thousand pieces at the bottom of the gorge." Gagnon turns away and faces the bridge. The blue light on the roof of the police car is still sweeping like a beacon across a small crowd that has gathered at the bridge railing. Gagnon nods to Etienne and says, "Have one of the men start to disperse that crowd and keep the traffic moving across the bridge. One accident is enough for one night. I don't want another one." As he watches Etienne stride off in the direction of the crowd, he recalls with even greater vividness than the fact itself how just a half hour earlier he sprinted after the motorcycle as Denise de Savigny sped past him, how he watched for a moment as the girl increased her speed when she neared the bridge and then suddenly veered off to her right and over the low retaining wall into the gorge. For a second the motorcycle seemed to Gagnon to become inexplicably airborne, hanging there in the dark space with its two doomed passengers as if the machine were driving itself, the motor still roaring, the headlight piercing the night like a lance. Then the flight ended and the motorcycle plunged down and out of his line of sight. By the time Gagnon reached the retaining wall, he could still hear the motorcycle falling and clanging and breaking on the rocky sides of the gorge . . .

He never imagined that the evening would end like this. It seemed so routine in the beginning, so ordinary and procedural. Trying to understand, trying to make some sense of what he has just witnessed, Gagnon keeps bringing his left hand to his forehead and scratching the spot where his eyebrows meet. Etienne returns from the bridge and tells him tersely that the crowd is thinning out and that traffic is moving normally again. "Very good, Etienne. And how is de Savigny?" "I'm sorry, Inspector, but I didn't hear you." "The girl's father. How is he?" Etienne shrugs and gestures toward the police car with the flashing blue light just as the light is turned off. Gagnon asks, "Is the doctor still with him?" "Yes, but what can a doctor do now? The man just saw his daughter kill herself." "I keep trying to understand this, Etienne, and I come up with nothing." "This is a different generation, Inspector. You have to be ready to expect anything." "But why would a girl from a good family—I've known her mother for years—do something as desperate as that? It doesn't make sense. All I said to her was that her father was here and that I wanted to ask her a few questions. And she answered me like a lioness, and the rest you know." "Here come the stretcher bearers with both bodies, Inspector." He pauses and adds, "After they put them in the ambulance, where do you want the driver to go?" "To Nice. That's the best place now." "Do you want me to ride with them?" "No. You and I will drive back together. De Savigny and the doctor can follow us, and the ambulance can come last." "You better tell the girl's father. After the doctor told him that the two of them were dead, he didn't say another word. All he's doing is sitting in the back seat and looking straight ahead at nothing." "Thanks, Etienne. I'm going over there now." As Etienne follows the stretcher bearers to the ambulance, Gagnon walks slowly to the police car. He can see Sanche de Savigny in the rear of the car, his head against the seat, his eyes closed. A doctor in a white service coat is sitting beside him. Gagnon opens the door of the car and leans toward de Savigny, who, having been alerted by the sound of the door being opened, is sitting up. His face is the color of gray putty. Gagnon has seen the same expression before on the faces of defeated soldiers during the war or of men who are dying of cancer and know it. "Monsieur de Savigny, you will have to return with us to Nice. It will be difficult, I know, but I am obliged to ask you to make an identification . . ." "No," says de Savigny tonelessly. "I regret having to ask you, but this is unavoidable," continues Gagnon. "The usual procedure is that the identification be made by a member of the family . . ." "No, Inspector, you can't expect me to do that. I'm not able to look at her." Gagnon gestures to the doctor to leave the car so that he can talk to de Savigny by himself, and the doctor hesitantly complies. When they are alone in the car, Gagnon says, "Monsieur de Savigny, I want you to know you have my sympathy. I mean that sincerely. But I have to tell you in all candor even at this time that I never expected what happened here to happen. There seemed no cause. At least there seemed no cause based on what you told me. Perhaps now there is something else that you would like to say to me." "No. There is nothing more to tell you. You know everything there is to know, everything that is necessary." "Do you mean that your daughter and this American were just as you described them after the incident in Eze six weeks ago?" "Yes, Inspector." "And there is nothing more?" "Nothing." "Then how do you explain what happened here? Why would she have gone to the hospital to take him with her?" "With all respect, Inspector, I've said everything I have to say. I don't want to discuss this any more. I can't." "Very well, but if there . . ." Gagnon stops in midsentence. His anger is beginning to get the better of him. He wants to tell de Savigny that what happened tonight might have been avoided if he had been frank with him in the first place. For years he has hated the pomposity of the man who is now sitting like a tired patient before him, but he has no heart to press whatever advantage of the moment he suspects is his. Instead he says, "For the sake of your wife and your family, I'm entering this as an accident in my report. And I'm doing this even though I think that what happened in Eze a month and a half ago and what happened here are tied together. I think I have grounds enough to open the investigation involving your son, but I see no point in it now. I'm dropping the entire matter. That is what I will tell the press as well." "Thank you, Inspector," says de Savigny quietly. "This will be painful enough for your wife, and it is Madame de Savigny that I'm thinking of. She does not deserve this." Gagnon gestures to the doctor to reenter the car as he closes the door and hurries back to his car where Etienne is already seated behind the wheel. After Gagnon seats himself on the passenger side of the car, he hears Etienne tell him, "The girl's mother called the station from the airport in Nice." "In Nice?" "She flew from Paris." "Does she know what happened?" "No. And I told the airport police to keep her there until we call them." "Good." "There's more. The police just called me back and said she's on her way here." "Here?" "She found out where we were from the station and took a taxi from the airport. She should be here in fifteen minutes or so." "Jesus Christ!" "I did the best I could do, Inspector. I'm just telling you what they told me." Gagnon rubs his eyebrows with his left hand and says to Etienne, "Get the ambulance out of here. Tell the driver to go to the hospital in Cimiez and report this as an accident. I'll follow with the details later." Etienne leaves the car, runs to the ambulance, and returns. In silence he and Gagnon watch the ambulance driver pull onto the corniche and head toward Nice. Most of the people who were on the bridge are now gone. Only the two police cars remain at the scene, Gagnon's and the one holding the doctor and de Savigny. Both have their headlights on and the combined light illuminates a swatch of ground adjacent to the berm. Etienne puts a match to a cigarette and says, "Why are you reporting it as an accident?" "I can't prove it wasn't." "You could call de Savigny in for questioning. He knows more than he's saying." "I know he does." "Then why are you holding back? You've been wanting to get that collaborationist bastard for years now." "This is different." Gagnon waits for a few moments as Etienne puffs on the cigarette. Then he says, "Do you believe in love, Etienne?" "It depends." "I have a feeling, just a feeling, that love can explain everything here. I think that the de Savigny girl loved this American and that something happened between the two of them and her family that somehow drove her to this. I suspected that something was being held back from us at Eze, and I'm sure of it now." "What convinced you?" "That girl. The facts. A trip by motorcycle all the way from Paris. A refusal to see her father or me when I confronted her near the bridge. And all for what? For an American clown who was almost blind from a fall in Eze that no one, not even the clown, would discuss with the police. Only love can explain that." "It's a big price to pay, Inspector." "It's the last price! My God, when I think of it, it's like a story out of a book." "I haven't read a book in twenty years." They sit in silence before Etienne throws his half-smoked cigarette out of the window and asks, "You know the girl's mother, don't you, from the war?" "Yes." "Are you going to tell her what happened? You yourself?" "No. De Savigny will have to do that. He will have to tell her and explain it as well as he can. I don't envy him that." "Does he know his wife is flying here from Paris?" "He didn't say so. Anyway, he doesn't know she's on her way here.

And I'm not going to tell him. That way he won't be thinking about it." Again there is silence, and Etienne, looking over at Gagnon and seeing him rub his eyebrows with his fingers, asks, "What are you thinking about?" "I can't get that girl off my mind. It takes a lot for a young girl to choose death as the only life left for her—that kind of death. The alternatives had to be a lot worse than driving a motorcycle off a cliff. Otherwise, why did she do it? Why did she have to do it?" Gagnon turns in his seat and looks out the back window. The high profile of Eze is still visible against the Mediterranean sky. The memory of his old associations with the village calm him for a moment: Eze of the seaward winds, Eze of the moon, Eze of the myth of Isis, Eze of the answers. It seems to explain something to him that he is only just beginning to understand. The still pulsing memory of his sprint after Anubis shatters whatever it is that is ripening to an answer in his mind. He remembers how he ran and watched the motorcycle hurtle with the two of them toward the bridge before Denise turned suddenly to the right and, with Dennis holding her tightly by the shoulders, raced toward the low rampart and over it. Gagnon's memory locks on the instant when the two of them catapulted into space over the killing gorge and seemed to ride the air for just a second or so—clear of the earth, beyond help, beyond gravity, free . . .

Etienne nudges Gagnon and says, "There's the taxi. It's pulling off the road and coming toward us. She's in it." Gagnon opens the door and walks back to the car behind him. He can see the doctor and de Savigny seated side by side but not talking in the rear seat. Both of them watch Gagnon as he opens the door of the car on de Savigny's side. "Monsieur de Savigny," says Gagnon, "the taxi that is parking over there is bringing your wife. She's come from the airport. She does not know what happened here." He pauses. "You will have to tell her."

Design by David Bullen
Typeset in Mergenthaler Granjon
by Wilsted & Taylor
with Centaur display
set by Custom Typography Service
Printed by Maple-Vail
on acid-free paper